BEACH BLANKET ZOMBIE

WEIRD TALES OF THE UNDEAD
& OTHER HUMANOID HORRORS

BEACH BLANKET ZOMBIE

WEIRD TALES OF THE UNDEAD & OTHER HUMANOID HORRORS

MARK McLAUGHLIN

WILDSIDE PRESS

Published by Wildside Press LLC.
www.wildsidebooks.com

Stories from this collection previously appeared in *Aberrations, At the Foothills of Frenzy, The Book of All Flesh, Chews Life, The Dream People, Fantasy Macabre, Freaks, Geeks & Sideshow Floozies, Heart Attack, Horrorfind, I Gave at the Orifice, Midnight Premiere, Midnight Zoo, Motivational Shrieker, Night Terrors, Not One of Us, OctoberLand, Once Upon a Slime, Palace Corbie, The Piano Player Has No Fingers, Pig Tales: Tales from the Trough, Rehearsals for Oblivion, Small Bites, Split, Strangewood Tales, Terror Tales* (website), *The Third Alternative, Twisted Tales for Sick Puppies,* and *ZOM BEE MOO VEE & Other Freaky Shows.* Cover art by Mark McLaughlin.

CONTENTS

HUMANOID HORRORS

HUMANOID AUTHORS

To
Michael S.
who can always reanimate me when I'm feeling down.

To
Pamela and Mike McC.
good friends, like the living dead, are a joy forever.

To
Kyra
the prettiest ghoul in town.

INTRODUCTION

STILL ZOMBIE AFTER ALL THESE YEARS

I get a kick out of zombies. I've been writing about them for years.

Oh, sure, they like to hurt people. And kill people. And ultimately, eat people.

But hey, we've all got to eat. We all consume other life-forms every day, plant or vegetable, whether we like it or not—and whether *they* like it or not. I have yet to meet the person who can live off of minerals, water, and/or air.

I enjoy writing about zombies because they are truly the baddest of the bad. They don't follow the rules. Vampires and werewolves obey very strict regulations. Vampires only come out at night and werewolves only do their dirty work during the full moon. Vampires can be repelled with garlic, crosses and holy water and werewolves can be sent scurrying with wolfbane.

On the other undead hand, zombies shamble about the countryside whenever they please. The only thing that will discourage them is a shotgun blast to the brain or, of course, decapitation.

Zombies and werewolves are created when a person is bitten by one of those toothy terrors. But zombies—! They can rise from the dead for lots of reasons. Any horror movie enthusiastic can tell you that.

Sure, a zombie's bite can turn its victim into one of the living dead. But that's not all. Corpses can be turned into hungry zombies through voodoo, nuclear power, viruses, parasites, ancient Egyptian curses (if you count mummies as zombies), toxic chemicals, the Black Mass, hypnosis, or even sonic radiation waves (whatever those are), like in the movie, *Let Sleeping Corpses Lie*, also known as *Don't Open the Window* and *The Living Dead at the Manchester Morgue*.

Zombies are delightfully flexible and versatile. And their insatiable hunger for the flesh of the living has given me a lot of food for thought.

In this volume, you will find a bumper crop of zombie stories—seventeen in all. Among them, you will find three stories about zombies created by Internet witches and four set on the isle of Zovemba, also known as Zombie Island, ruled by the very beautiful and very dead Necrilda Voltaire.

I've also added sixteen stories about other types of humanoid horrors for your amusement. So sit back, relax, and let all my hideous, undead darlings shamble into your brain and maybe, into your heart.

After all ... zombies need love, too.

ZOMBIES

BEACH BLANKET ZOMBIE

Lornetta fluttered her false eyelashes at her hunky boyfriend. "Golly, I can hardly wait for the big pig roast tonight, Turnpike." She shifted on her beach towel to give him a better view of her new bikini top.

Turnpike flashed her a big toothy grin. "Honeybee, it's gonna be a gas! Big Kuka-Lu-Lu and the Beachtones are even gonna make the scene."

"Big Kuka-Lu-Lu? He's the grooviest! Except for you, of course!" She gazed up into his sky-blue eyes and wondered: Would tonight be the night? Would Turnpike actually make all her dreams come true and let her wear his class ring?

A sea gull, flying in from the open waters, squawked wildly. "Man, that bird is loony tunes!" Turnpike said. He turned toward their friends, who were playing volleyball. "Moonray! Darlena! Sandburn! Foreign exchange student Yvetta! What's up with that wacky bird?"

Yvetta pursed her glossy pink lips. "Perhaps it has—how you say?—an emotional disorder."

Lornetta laughed. "You kooky foreigners with all your Freud and whatnot! I'd better not tell you about those doughnuts and sausages in my dream last night. Moonray, what do you think?"

Moonray turned his goofy patched hat sideways—he did that whenever he had to think really hard. "Hmmmm. I know that government island where they do those creepy, far-out DNA experiments is about three miles that way." He pointed out to sea.

Sandburn nodded. "That's right, dude. Big Kuka-Lu-Lu works out there when he's not singing and racing dune buggies."

"Golly!" Darlena moaned, dreamy-eyed. "I didn't know the Big K worked in a fancy lab. Yvetta's so lucky to have him for a boyfriend! So he's some kind of scientist, huh?"

"Yep!" Turnpike said, "and he's half-Swedish and half-Hawaiian, and a prince on both sides of the family. He's a best-selling novelist, too. Why, here he comes now!"

A muscular, bronzed man with thick blonde hair and startling green eyes swam to shore. "Hey, gang! I'm sure glad I found you crazy cats. We gotta get out of here, and pronto!"

Lornetta gasped. "Leave our favorite beach? Whyever for?"

Five other young bronzed men also swam to shore, with guitars strapped to their backs. Big Kuka-Lu-Lu grinned. "I'm sure glad the band is okay. They work out on the government island, too." He rushed up to Yvetta. "Sweetie, in case we don't get out of this scrape alive, I just want to say: I love you!"

Yvetta swooned into his meaty arms. "I—how you say?—love you, too. But why are you acting so funny? I bet it's because of those genetic experiments on the island. My uncle who works out there—Dr. Frankensvenson—has mentioned them from time to time."

"It was one crazy shindig out on that island last night, baby!" Big Kuka-Lu-Lu cried. "You see, we had a pig roast and I was the chef. We cooked up an old sow—the mother of all the pigs we've been experimenting on. I even made bacon sandwiches. I just loooooove bacon!" He licked his full but undeniably manly lips. "Unfortunately, an unwelcome guest crashed the party. You see, we'd mixed in some radiation-infused human chromosomes with the DNA of one of the sow's little piglets, and it grew into a mutant that looked like a human, except it had a curly tail."

Lornetta, who was eavesdropping from a polite distance, grinned as she said, "A curly tail? That sounds cute!"

Big Kuka-Lu-Lu shivered. "The tail may have been cute, but the rest of him was a freaked-out nightmare! He had crazy crooked teeth and one eye was way bigger than the other—and it glowed! The mutant tried to attack Dr. Frankensvenson last week, so the doc shot him dead. But the crazy thing came back as a zombie!"

Yvetta cocked her head to one side. "Why did he do a silly thing like that?"

"Because he's radioactive!" said Big Kuka-Lu-Lu. "We stuck him in a cage, but somewhere also the line he'd also developed psychic powers, so he read our minds and found out what we did to her mom. So he busted out of his cage, found a chainsaw and a surfboard, and crashed our party."

"So, he was the unwelcome guest, yes?" Yvetta asked.

Big Kuka-Lu-Lu nodded happily. "You catch on quick, dollface! I've written a song about what happened then. Hit it, boys!"

The Beachtones strummed their guitars—except for Slim, who blew on a conch shell—and Big Kuka-Lu-Lu began to sing:

"Dancing to the beat, eatin' lots of meat—bikini beach bacon tastes so sweet. But looky out to sea, whatever can it be—something on a surfboard, golly gee!"

The Beachtones sang the chorus: "He's a ... beach blanket zom-bieeeee! Beach blanket zombieeeee!"

Big Kuka-Lu-Lu sang on. "Genes got messed in a government test—one piggy acts different from the rest! He's an undead male with a cork-screw tail—if they throw him in a cell I ain't raisin' bail!"

"He's a ... beach blanket zombieeeee! Beach blanket zombieeeee!"

"Zombie lost his cool, stole a powertool—evil psycho-killer screa-min' PORKERS RULE. He's got a crazy plan, gonna find the man—who cooked up his mama in a fryin' pan."

"He's a ... beach blanket zombieeeee! Beach blanket zombieeeee!"

At this point, Slim performed a brief but stirring conch shell solo. Then Big Kuka-Lu-Lu continued: "Ravenous and rude, flatulent and crude—zombie's steamin' mad and I'm totally screwed. Gonna eat my nuts, tear out all my guts—no more sex with bikini sluts!"

"He's a ... beach blanket zombieeeee! Beach blanket zombieeeee!"

Big K and the band then dropped to their knees and sang together: "*Oh, yeaaaahhhh!*"

Yvetta put the back of her hand to her forehead. "I am—how you say?—terrified. Where is that awful zombie now?"

Big Kuka-Lu-Lu shrugged. "We don't know. That crazy zombie has been killing scientists all last night and today, too. He even scared a sea gull. That was when I decided to swim over here. I figured, since that zombie was psychic, it might have read my mind enough to know about the beach party here tonight!"

Suddenly an attractive blonde businesswoman in a pinstriped blazer, mini-skirt, and high-heels rushed up to Big Kuka-Lu-Lu. She put down the briefcase she was carrying and shook his hand. "How do you do? I just heard your song while I was buying a hot dog and frank-ly—it's terrific! I'm Marigold DeLaVanQuester, the big record producer, and I'm gonna make you a star! You'll be rich!"

"Marigold DeLaVanQuester? Wow!" cried Lornetta, who was still eavesdropping. "She's the lady who turns unknowns into stars! I read about her in all the Hollywood magazines!"

Big Kuka-Lu-Lu turned to Yvetta and hugged her to his manly chest. "Did you hear that? Now we can move away from this unholy, zom-bie-infested beach. We can bring the gang, too, since I'll be needing backup singers and roadies!"

The gang cheered, "Hurray! Hurray for Big Kuka-Lu-Lu!" The band began to play and they all danced. Lornetta and Turnpike slipped away to have their own private skinny-dipping party ... which actually worked out in their favor. Two minutes after they left the scene, Yvetta put a dainty finger to her temple.

"I just—how you say?—realized something," cried the enticing foreign exchange student. She looked at Marigold DeLaVanQuester. "There isn't a hot dog stand on this beach."

The producer smiled as she opened her briefcase. "A gold star for Lady Einstein here. No hot dog stand *yet!* But it'll be open for business in about ten minutes."

Marigold pulled off her—or rather, *his* rubber mask just before revving up the mini-chainsaw in the briefcase. A corkscrew tail, wagging briskly with happiness, popped up from under the mini-skirt. "*Human* hot dogs, and they're all for me! Because after all—" Foamy spittle flew from his leathery lips as he sang, "I'm a …. beach blanket zombieeeee! Beach blanket zombieeeee! *Oh, yeaaaahhhh!*"

VULTURE SOUP FOR THE SOULLESS

Driving home, Inga began crying again. Then she glanced in the rear-view mirror and wailed—she'd completely ruined the make-up she'd applied after her earlier crying jag.

She tried to wipe the tears out of her eyes, but that only rubbed in her eyeliner, turning her eye-sockets into blue-black pits around her sky-blue irises.

"Too skinny?" she had sobbed to her boss, Mrs. Blair, earlier that afternoon. "But I'm supposed to be skinny. I teach aerobics. I'm providing a good example! There isn't an ounce of fat on me."

Mrs. Blair, a fiftyish woman with mouse-brown hair, winced at her words. "I'm afraid that's the problem. There really *isn't* an ounce of fat on you. Frankly, you don't look healthy. You look ... emaciated. Anorexic."

"I eat plenty. I really do!" Inga folded her bony arms over her petite bosom. 'You can't discriminate against someone because of their weight."

"Oh please. That argument only works if you're too *fat*." Mrs. Blair brushed a mousy lock out of her face. "Besides, your class only has eight people in it. All the other instructors have at least twenty in their sessions."

That was when Inga had started to cry. She'd rushed into the women's locker room to fix her make-up—she'd also needed to touch-up her beige foundation, which helped to conceal her pallor.

Now her face was ruined again. Fortunately, she didn't have any stops to make on the way home.

She peeked at her reflection again. God, but she looked like a skull. But she couldn't help it. She'd always been bony and pale. She simply couldn't gain weight. Fatty or sugary foods just gave her diarrhea. As for a tan: any amount of sun only burned her. And when the lobster-red eventually peeled away, she'd be back to her usual chalk-white.

She felt like Hell—but at least the drive home was pretty, down a country road lined with trees. It was late October, and all the leaves had turned yellow, orange, brown and red. She rented the upper half of a married couple's house, outside of town. Trent Graves, a high school teacher, and his wife Claire needed the extra money because they had a lot of medical bills: he had diabetes and she had some sort of odd sleep disorder. The top floor didn't have a kitchen, so the Graves let her use theirs.

She liked the couple, but she knew she couldn't live with them forever. Claire watched TV and generally puttered around downstairs at odd hours, and sometimes the noise woke Inga. She didn't want to make Claire feel self-conscious by complaining about it.

What was she going to do for money now...? Well, she could always go back to the perfume counter at Hedley's department store. All the socialites who bought those prissy, pricey fragrances were just as trim as her. But still, it wouldn't be as much fun as aerobics. She simply loved making folks happy and being on the go.

Inga rolled down her window—the brisk autumn air felt good on her skin, and it dried her tears, too. A bright-red leaf blew into the car and landed right in her lap. It matched her hair exactly. When she was little, the other kids used to make fun of her hair, but she loved the color anyway. She picked up the leaf and tucked it over her ear. She took one more quick glance in the mirror. Now she looked like some kind of savage tree spirit, with her shadowed eyes and that bold leaf nestled in her flaming locks.

Suddenly she realized—she couldn't show up at the Graves house with her make-up all smeared. It would be obvious she'd been crying, and she didn't want to upset or worry Trent and Claire. Plus, the raccoon eyes would only remind Claire of how bad *her* eyes looked... She always had dark circles around her eyes from lack of sleep.

Inga couldn't fix her make-up in the car—she'd need to wash off the old stuff first. Where could she go...? She didn't want to drive all the way back to town. The Graves' only neighbors were a bestselling author and her husband—but nobody ever saw them. The writer, Rose Tremble, had churned out some fancy self-help book called *What Color Is Your Karma's Air-Bag?* Inga had looked at it in a bookstore once—pretty drippy stuff. It compared life to a car trip, and people had to decide if their life's car had a white air-bag or a black one. Apparently it all depended on how they reacted to stress.

Inga saw the lane to the Tremble house coming up on her left. Well, she couldn't stop there—or could she? A cardboard sign, duct-taped to a tree, declared BOOK SEMINAR in bold red letters. The lane was lined with orange balloons attached to slender black stakes.

Perfect! She'd go in, sneak into the bathroom and fix her make-up. If anybody saw her, she'd just laugh and say she'd heard a sad song on the radio. A dumb excuse, but believable. And then she'd finally get to meet the reclusive author. Heck, she'd even buy a book. Claire would love a nice perky self-help book.

She headed up the lane. The house was huge—about three times bigger than the Graves place. She noticed that all the vehicles parked around the place were luxury cars. Most were red or black and all had tinted windows. There were several hearses, too. Maybe they were part of some Halloween-oriented publicity stunt for whatever book Rose Tremble was promoting these days.

She parked, got out of the car and half-hid her face behind a handkerchief as she walked inside. She was no more than a few feet into the house when a tall, middle-aged woman stepped up to her.

"Welcome! Thank you for coming!" The woman was a vision of pink, yellow and lots of gold. Pink foundation and rose-pink lipstick, yellow hair, dark golden eyes, gold jewelry, a gold silk dress with thin yellow and pink stripes. She had a square-jawed face, a too-wide mouth, and practically reeked of rose-scented perfume.

She stared at Inga, her thick lips stretched into an enormous smile. "My word, look who we have here! Outstanding!"

Inga didn't know how to respond to that, so she said, "Oh, thanks. I try! I'm Inga. I stay with the Graves."

The golden woman laughed. "Of course you do! I'm Rose Tremble. You're just in time! Right this way."

Inga followed the golden woman down a hallway, past gilt-framed oil paintings and little statues on cherrywood tables. They were walking too fast for her to get a good look at any of the artwork, but she did notice that most seemed to depict creatures out of various mythologies. Nymphs, griffins, satyrs, centaurs, mermaids—and zombies. Were zombies part of some mythology? Maybe Haitian lore.

She wasn't sure what to do about her face. It was a complete mess. She'd only wanted to use the bathroom, buy a book, chat for a minute and leave. Now it seemed she was going to have to sit through a whole seminar. She followed Rose into a large room, took a quick glance at all the seated people and—

People?

Oh, no. These weren't *people*.

People were flesh-colored.

People were made of living tissue.

People were more or less *symmetrical*...

Inga wanted to run screaming, but the sight before her was so bizarre—so hideously *compelling*—that she simply couldn't move. She had to just stand there and absorb this grotesque vision.

The things seated in the chairs had humanoid bodies, shapewise—but their tissue, which could hardly be considered living, came in a variety of inhuman colors. Navy blue. Lime green. Magenta. Purple.

Most of them were clearly rotten. Bugs and all. The room stank like a combination of a busy outhouse and the dumpster behind a butcher shop. But even so, the audience members were moving, jostling in their seats, whispering gurgly little phrases to each other. As for symmetry... Based on what she was seeing, it was clear that decay was a terribly *uneven* process.

Rose walked up to a lectern at the front of the room and cleared her throat. The grotesque horde immediately fell silent. She then looked toward Inga, who was still standing.

Inga found an empty seat next to a noseless blue creature with a gap-toothed grin.

"First, I'd like to thank all of you for showing up," Rose said. "I know that for most of you, travel is something of an ordeal."

Amused murmurs and warbles sounded throughout the room. Strangely enough, the more Inga looked at the creatures around her, the less they frightened her. At least they were behaving. And for some reason, they seemed to accept her presence completely.

"I thought I was on top of the world after the publication of my first book," the golden woman stated. "It made me a ton of money. I got to be on a lot of talk-shows. I became an overnight celebrity. But you know what?" She leaned forward and cocked her head to one side. "I wasn't happy. I had my problems, but I was sugar-coating them. And worse of all, I was ignoring my inner monster."

Most of the audience members nodded what roughly corresponded to heads.

"Then," Rose said, "I found out that my husband, who was also my literary agent, had been having an affair—spending my money on a waitress whose bust-size was higher than her I.Q. That was about the time I started workshopping my rage ... addressing my own deep-down needs. My first book, with all its happy-crappy philosophy—what a waste of paper! I finally realized I'd been in complete denial when I'd written that. Eventually, my husband hired his sweetie's drug-addict brother to run me down with a rusted-out Camaro."

Low moans of pity echoed through the room.

The hideous blue creature next to Inga turned toward her. "My husband tossed the hair-dryer in my bath water," it whispered.

Before Inga could respond, Rose Tremble continued with her story. "Oh, sure, I could have just thrown in the towel after that Camaro hit me. But you know what? I've never been a quitter." The golden woman pounded the lectern with her fist. "I wasn't about to let some low-life just run over me and get away with it. He stopped the car to steal the jewelry off my corpse, and that's when I got back on my own two feet—and ripped out his throat with my teeth!"

The audience greeted this statement with wild clapping and bubbly cheers of approval. The clapping raised a small cloud of dust. One especially desiccated cadaver clapped so eagerly that a couple of its fingers flew off.

"I came straight home after that," Rose said. "And, my husband and his little sweetie were here. Up in the bedroom. Since they enjoyed each other's company so much, I took care of them both at the same time. After that, I put them in the freezer for a few months. This morning they were in the oven, and later, when we have our cocktails—and of course, the book signing!—you'll find what's left of them on the hors d'oeuvre trays."

Next to the lectern was a table covered with stacks of thick books bound in black leather. Rose picked up one of the books. "I'll be reading to you from my latest work, *Vulture Soup For The Soulless*, published by Abomination Press. Plenty of copies here for everyone! But before I start reading, I think we'd all like to hear a few words from a surprise guest we have in the audience."

She then pointed straight at Inga. Everyone turned to stare at the aerobics instructor.

"I've never met a vampire before," Rose enthused, "but I've read all the ancient texts—research for the book!—and so I know one when I see one!"

Everyone *oooohed* and *aaaaahed*.

When Inga stood to say something—she had no idea what—some of the creatures began to clap. Again their clapping raised soft billows of dust, and a swirl of it drifted across Inga's face.

And she sneezed.

And coughed.

"Oh, dear!" the golden woman said in a tone that was low to the point of ominous. "It would seem I was mistaken. Just listen to those lungs! Apparently we have a *breather* on our hands."

"A breather! I should have guessed!" cried a lumpy horror behind Inga. "She doesn't have any stink on her!"

The audience members began to snarl. A feral red glow sprang up in their eyes.

"We don't like being deceived!" Rose thundered. "Or—*spied upon!*"

"Now wait a minute!" Inga cried. "I just came in to buy your book. You're the one who led me in here."

The creatures turned toward Rose.

"Well, that's true..." the writer admitted.

"In a lot of ways, I'm in the same boat as you folks," Inga said. "Look at me. Ninety-one pounds. Pale as a sheet. Hair as red as an apple. People have made fun of me my whole life. They've called me Stringbean, Scrawny, Goth-Chick, Skeleton Girl, and lots of worse things, too. But I can't pick up weight. I just can't. And I can't tan. I don't go out much because..." She sighed. "I don't get that many offers. I'm scared of most guys anyway. They're so much bigger than me. I don't want to go out with somebody who might crush me if he sat on me by accident in a dark movie theatre."

"Do you have brittle bones?" said the cadaver who had lost the fingers.

"No, my bones are okay. In fact, I've always been pretty athletic. But my boss fired me today because I look too scary to teach aerobics."

"Nonsense!" bellowed a burly corpse across the room. "You're not scary at all. Actually, you're pretty cute!"

"Adorable!" another stiff squealed.

All of the audience members grunted or hooted in agreement.

"Oh! Thank you!" Inga said. "But I'm afraid my boss was right. Living people have a problem with me. My class isn't even big enough to pay my salary. It's a pity you folks don't need an aerobics instructor."

"Exercise doesn't agree with us," Rose said. "We try to avoid excessive movement. And sunlight."

"And animals," a one-legged green atrocity said. "A dog ran off with part of me last week."

Soon all the audience members were talking about their various inconveniences—the trials of trying to exist in secret, in a world of unsympathetic living beings.

"Flies!" one mushy heap exclaimed. "Do you know how hard it is to keep the flies off? And don't get me started about *maggots!*"

"I've got plenty of money," the burly corpse said, "but how am I supposed to go shopping? I can't go walking around the mall!"

"I can pass for living," Rose said, "but how long is that going to last? Make-up and perfume can only go so far! And I simply *can't* go out on hot days. It would be nice to have someone to help with the touch-up work ... and the *maintenance* ... but who can I trust?"

Then the noseless creature said," Yeah, it's not like there's some living person we could pay to help us out on a regular basis."

A thoughtful silence settled over the room.

Then heads slowly began to turn—all toward Inga.

"I'd pay cash!" the lumpy horror said.

"I've got gold coins! So many pretty gold coins!" creaked an especially withered she-thing.

"Would you like a new car?" one dapper cadaver offered. "I bought a lovely red sports car about two weeks before I died. Why, it even matches your hair!"

"You could move in here, if you like," Rose said. "I don't use most of the house, so you'd have the run of the place. Say, can you type? I'm thinking of writing another book, but I'm starting to get CDS—Carpal Decay Syndrome."

Inga wasn't even worried when new tears—of happiness—began to flow down her cheeks. Her make-up was already ruined, and her generous new friends didn't care how she looked anyway.

THE AGONY OF CLAUDE BAWLS

The Muzak played *Alley Cat* as Landford stepped off the elevator.

Instantly he knew something was up. Everybody in the office had that deer-in-the-headlights look—a look no one likes to see at work. He was a half-hour late, and for a frantic second he wondered if some crisis had taken place which had required his attention. But no: the fright-eyes weren't focused on him.

He dropped off his valise and coat at his office and headed for the staff lounge. If gossip was on the wing, that was where it would eventually go to roost.

He found Marla, the receptionist, and Peg, an intern from the community college, by a plate of jelly doughnuts, exchanging sotto voce comments. He tried to maintain his most serious, concerned expression as he snatched a raspberry doughnut. "Everything all right?" he said.

Peg turned to him with a grimace of a smile. "Oh, Isaac. You haven't heard? It's so—" She rolled her eyes, as if searching her brain for the right word. "—freaky. In a bad sort of way."

Marla stepped closer to him. "It's Zuzie's husband. Claude."

Zuzie Bawls was Landford's supervisor, a fiftyish, dark-haired woman who wore black blazers and loud, flowing scarves. "Claude? The piano teacher?" he said. He had a quick mental image of a keyboard lid slamming down on plump fingers. He pushed the thought out of his mind.

"It's just so freaky. *Really.*" Peg whispered.

"Yes, dear, we know." Marla gave the girl a withering glance, then turned to Landford. "He was walking down Caslon Street last night. You know that area? Hilly, with steep lawns?"

"Yeah..." He couldn't imagine what the terrain had to do with anything.

"Someone was cutting their lawn by lowering the mower down the hill with a rope. Claude was walking by at the base of the hill when..." She gulped—visibly, audibly. "When the rope came loose."

"My God." In his surprise, Landford squeezed his doughnut, slopping a bit of raspberry jelly on his silk tie.

"That'll never come out," Peg said, dabbing his tie with a napkin. "Claude's hurt real bad. Zuzie told us what happened and then shut herself in her office. She's still in there."

He exhaled slowly. He didn't know Zuzie very well, but as office relations went, he was her best friend in the company. "I guess I'd better go say something to her."

The two women nodded in synchronized sympathy.

As he walked to Zuzie's office, he heard the bee-buzz of employee whispers. Here and there he caught a few words: *terrible...what about his hands?...I heard...tried to push it off and...*

He knocked on Zuzie's door. "Zu? It's Zack." he smiled at that. Zu and Zack: sounded like a comedy team.

"Oh! Oh, Isaac." Her warm voice cracked. "Yes, come in, please."

He opened the door to what he called Cat Land: Zuzie had dozens of cat statuettes scattered on shelves on each wall. Cats of jade, glass, silver... wooden tabbies, chintzy plastic Siamese kittens...even a china collector's figurine of Felix the Cat.

Zuzie had mentioned that she had twenty-seven cats at home, and that she liked to read to them. And cook gourmet meals for them. And sew little costumes for their special kitty parties. As she put it, "Pets are good for you."

Zuzie stared up at him with puffy, reddened eyes. She was clutching a cat figurine he had never seen before. It was about eight inches tall and carved, very badly, out of dark red stone.

"You shouldn't have come to work," Landford said. "I mean, the bank would understand if..." His words trailed off. Zuzie wasn't paying attention. She simply moaned and ran her fingers over the stone cat.

He moved a little closer. "Do you want me to drive you home, Zuzie? I'd be happy to. Really, no problem. You should get some rest."

"Rest?" She glared up at him. "We have three pianos in the house. How can I rest, seeing those pianos, knowing he will never—"

"Claude's going to be okay, right?"

"He'll live. But it won't be much of a life." Zuzie set down the stone cat.

Landford got his first clear view of the red cat's face, and it was—*horrible*. Huge round eyes, topped with heavy brows. A mouthful of jagged teeth, surrounding a thick tongue that protruded in a viciously comic expression.

"What hospital is Claude at?"

Zuzie turned away from him to stare out the office window. "He's not in a hospital. He's with friends."

"Friends? Just how badly is he hurt?"

He waited for her to reply—to even turn back toward him—but after a minute, he decided that perhaps she needed to be alone. Alone with her cats.

But still... *Friends?* He hoped at least one of these friends knew something about medicine.

* * * *

Months passed, and Zuzie never mentioned Claude's condition again. When coworkers asked about him, she just walked away.

Zuzie already had been considered the office eccentric, and that title was shifting into 'office weirdo' territory. Even so, when Landford decided to throw a dinner party, he invited her, figuring she simply wouldn't show up.

On the day of the party, he returned home from work to find his wife Nicole drowning newborn kittens in a bucket of water. This was the third litter in the past two years she had finished off.

"I wish you wouldn't do that," he said. "We can just give them away. And besides, did you have to do that today?"

Nicole nodded toward Pickles, their tabby, who was watching from behind a rose bush. "I didn't want Pickles to get used to them. That would be just too sad, separating a mother from her babies." She prodded the kittens with a yellow pencil. Then she picked up the shovel by her side and began digging a hole by her favorite lilac bush.

Landford returned to the living room. There the caterer, Mrs. Green, was waiting for him.

"What your wife is doing is just awful." The plump, iron-haired woman brushed some sugar off of her sleeves. "She's a very nice lady, but she has some very disturbing ideas about God's good creatures. Poor blessed angels. I hope their tiny angel souls can forgive her."

"Nicole never had pets when she was little," Landford said, hoping a little white lie might smooth things over. "She doesn't really know much about animals. Not as much as you, Mrs. Green." That, at least, was probably true: the old woman had a menagerie of stray dogs and cats.

Mrs. Green smiled. "Dinner will be ready by seven. I'll start setting out the hors d'oeuvres."

Nicole entered the living room. Landford noticed she had a smear of mud under her right eye, and he wiped it off. Mrs. Green stared at Nicole.

The Hendersons from next door showed up shortly after six, followed by the Finlays and the Dietrichs. Nicole had put on her best green dress and she looked fabulous. Landford wondered for the millionth time how such a beautiful woman had fallen for him. He wasn't the handsomest guy in the world—he always thought he looked like Winnie the Pooh—but he knew that, unlikely as it seemed, some women actually liked teddy bear guys.

Marla and Peg showed up together. Landford didn't understand why they hung around together. Their conversation usually ended with Marla shooting down the younger woman's silly comments.

The guests were a standard middle-class mix, and that was fine with Landford. Middle class was just fine for a teddy bear guy. They had invited ten people: he had complained that might be too many, but Nicole reminded him that Zuzie and Claude would be definite no-shows. Every now and then, one of the guests sat down at their piano and pounded out a snippet of tune—usually *Chopsticks.*

"So. Is everybody here?" Marla asked Landford.

"Everyone except Zuzie and Claude."

"Do you think they'll show up?" Peg said, eyes wide. "God, has anyone seen Claude since the accident?"

"Of course not," Marla said. "I heard he was mangled. People like that don't walk around in broad daylight, let alone go to dinner parties. Really, Peg."

Landford sampled Mrs. Green's cheese puffs and eggrolls—commonplace but delicious. Good, solid teddy bear food.

At about six-fifty, the doorbell rang. Wine glass in hand, Landford answered the door.

The middle-aged man standing at the threshold was tall, pale and obese, and dressed in a filthy sweat-suit. His feet were bare, and his hands—

Weren't there.

His arms ended at the elbows. His face was covered with long, deep scars. His thin ginger hair was matted down with grease.

"Oh... Well. Hello, Claude." Landford didn't quite know what to say. But at last his sense of responsibility as a host kicked in. "Won't you come in?"

Claude grunted and shambled through the door, followed by Zuzie. She crept in timidly, staring at the floor.

"He insisted," she said hoarsely. "I told him to stay home but he insisted." She shuffled to the couch and plopped down into the cushions.

Claude's lips curved into a crooked, yellow-toothed smile. "What's tuh eat?" he said. His voice sounded stupid, Landford thought. Stupid in a mean sort of way—and oddly hollow. Like a cannibal in a cave, grunting for raw guts to gnaw on.

The guests simply stared. Nicole crossed to the liquor cabinet and poured herself a brandy, splashing a good portion of her drink on the counter. Mrs. Green made the sign of the cross repeatedly.

Landford checked his watch—six fifty-five—then cleared his throat. "Dinner was going to be at seven, but I think our new...guests...Zuzie and Claude Bawls, need a moment to..." He looked to Nicole for help, but she was busy refilling her glass. "...to socialize. And to try some of Mrs. Green's delicious cheese puffs."

Everyone watched as Claude marched up to the hors d'oeuvres and lowered his face into the nearest plate.

Nicole stumbled to Landford's side. "We've got to call the police," she hissed.

"Why? Because he's hogging the cheese puffs?" he whispered.

"Well, do *something*."

Landford moved closer to Claude. The fat man was voraciously working puff after puff into his mouth with his tongue.

"We were all really sorry to hear about your accident," Landford said. "Are you...feeling better...?"

Claude grinned up at him with cheese-smeared lips. "Oh, yeah. I used tuh hurt a lot, but they took care of me. They sure did."

Zuzie sat up on the couch. "Remember, Claude. Don't bore the nice people with all the details of your treatment."

Claude sucked up another cheese puff. "Can I tell them 'bout the House of the Ankh?"

Zuzie looked daggers. "No, you may not."

"How 'bout the Red Nurse?"

"Again, no."

Claude cocked his head to one side. "The leeches? The Moon Scarab? The Cat Man? How 'bout—"

"No, no, NO!" Zuzie flew across the room and began stuffing eggrolls into her husband's mouth. "Just eat, Claude. Please. Just. Eat."

A movement by the patio doors caught Landford's eye. Nicole had opened the doors for some night air, and now the cat, Pickles, was creeping into the living room. Her paws were covered with dirt, and in her mouth she carried one of her dead kittens.

Landford hoped no one would see Pickles. He hoped the cat would simply carry its horrible burden to its blanket in the shadows under the piano and go to sleep. But then Peg said—

"Oh my God. That cat just carried in a dead kitten."

Everyone's attention turned from Claude to the cat. Pickles carried the kitten to the piano. Instead of curling up in the blanket, Pickles jumped on top of the piano and began to lick the kitten clean.

"Enough!" Mrs. Green screamed. "I can't stand it! I've got to get out of this *devil house!*" As she ran out the door, she shouted, "I'll send you my bill, you—you *monsters!*"

Landford ran to the threshold. "But we hired you for the whole evening! You can't—"

That was when he heard it.

It would echo in his dreams for the rest of his life.

The medley.

The cheery strains of *Alley Cat*, intertwined with *Kitten on the Keys*, and *Memories* from that musical, the one he'd seen with Nicole a few months earlier. *CATS.*

Slowly Landford turned around. Claude was seated at the piano, his back to the party. His playing was—Inspired. Lively. Bubbling with enthusiasm.

Landford looked at the arm stumps, hanging down like deli salamis on each side of the fat man, and wondered: *What the hell is he PLAYING with?*

Zuzie began to sob. "I told him to stay home. I told him I told him I told him *I told him...*"

The guests stared at the raving woman. Then Mrs. Finlay poked an elbow into her husband's ribs and nodded toward the door.

Mr. Finlay walked up to Landford. "It's been an interesting evening, Isaac. But we've got to be going. You understand."

Mr. Dietrich and Mr. Henderson moved forward. "It's getting kind of late," Dietrich said. Henderson just nodded frantically.

In a moment, all the guests were rushing out the door. Marla and Peg grabbed hands and sped out by way of the patio.

By now Zuzie was sobbing so loudly that it echoed off the glassware with a slight *brrringggg*. "They said he'd be all right! And I believed them. Pets are good for you, you know. They said he'd be as right as rain..." She blew her nose on a corner of the couch cover.

Landford slowly walked up to the pianist. He looked over the fat man's shoulder. A moment later, he wondered why he was feeling so dizzy. It dawned on him: the sight before him had temporarily made him forget to breathe. He gasped for air and sucked in a whiff of Claude's putrid stench.

Claude's sweatshirt had been pulled up—or more probably, pushed back—over his protruding gut, to reveal a raw, gaping opening. Three orange cats had crawled out of the opening, but they hadn't gone far. They were attached to Claude by thickly veined umbilical cords. The cats were capering merrily on the piano keys, pounding out the feline hits. A couple of them wore slime-streaked miniature tuxedoes. The third wore a black velvet evening gown. All of them had bulging eyes, heavy brows, and jagged yellow teeth.

A loop of slithering tissue spooled out of the opening and wrapped around Pickle's dead kitten, pulling it into Claude's belly.

"Pets good. *Soooo* good," Claude whispered. "Come to Papa."

I'VE GOT THOSE SYNTHETIC-ZOMBIE-PENIS/ANDY-WARHOL-CAME-FROM-VENUS/CHA-CHA-DANCIN'-HEADLESS-MOVIE-MAMA BLUES

THE FATE OF HUMANKIND HANGS IN THE BALANCE

One two chopchopchop:

B-movies told us that Mars needed women, but in reality, it was the citizens of Venus who had a mighty fierce hankerin' for MEN: big sweaty stallion-butt hunky guys like the ones in old prison movies. The thing is, they didn't want the whole guy. Just the cock. Venusians liked to cook up Earth cocks for dinner. They liked to fry 'em up in a fiendish alien compound that tasted a lot like the substance known to Earthlings as garlic butter.

You could always tell Venusians because they were platinum-blonde, with a vacant stare and wispy little voices that sounded all stupid, like they were reading cue cards. Years ago, the man-hungry Venusians sent Special Agents M and W—a.k.a. Jayne Mansfield and Andy Warhol—to acquire human cocks for their trendy Venusian supper-clubs, where big clunky Cuban heels were all the rage.

The Venusians weren't really mean: they knew guys kinda liked having cocks. So after they cut off some fella's yogurt-gun, they replaced it with a fully functional synthetic boner made out of durable alien bio-plastic, capable of having seven orgasms in a row.

So Agents M and W travelled the world, luring hunky-boys to their evil lairs, plying them with pills and cigarettes laced with hog tranquilizers, then chopping off and teleporting the tasty tube-steaks to Chez Twilight Zone. The woozy hunky-boys then woke up with big plastic schlongs, complete with faux veins, waggling around between their legs. And first the hunky-boys would be all freaked out—but then they'd find out that these particular Thanksgiving turkey-necks were able to spurt home-style gravy 'til the cows came home. That made them feel a little better.

But: there was a side effect.

IT'S ALL UP TO ME. STORED IN A MISSILE SILO ON THE DARK SIDE OF THE MOON, I STAND READY TO PROTECT THE PEOPLE, THE FLOWERS, AND ALL THE LOVELY BOOKS.

You'd think a guy with that much money could afford a better haircut:
Death doesn't exist on Venus: them jet-trash space jackanapes used to just wear out...just erode away like living pencil erasers. And all the little chunks and bits that wore off kept on living. If something and someone cut up a Venusian with a machete or farm implement or something equally nasty, the pieces instantly became separate entities that could not be reattached. You could hardly walk down the street on Venus without stepping on somebody's pinky or spleen or something. But then, if you were wearing big clunky Cuban heels, you probably wouldn't notice. If a Venusian was badly injured, or got really sick, he or she would just take a nice refreshing decades-long nap. The sort of nap any Earthling might easily mistake for death.

That whole 'ain't-gonna-die' quality is inherent in all things Venusian—even their bio-plastic. So, when those radically-altered hunkyboys passed away, their undying synthetic boners would begin sending polymeric pseudo-nerves through their rotting flesh. It would take about fifty years, but finally, revivified zombie-boys would come a-scratchin' and a-squirmin' and a-creepin' out of their graves—and oh, surely each was a slave to the rampant Venusian trouser-boa between its legs.

Fast forward:

One fine day, John Q. Spaceman and Little Miss Meteor were flying around on Buck Rogers jetpacks, happily blabbing about all the test-tube babies they'd have after they were connubially interfaced. They had just landed in Neutron Park, right next to the statue of Rex Reed, America's most beloved President, when suddenly! from out of nowhere! Andy Warhol and headless Jayne Mansfield came strolling along. Despite a touch of worm-nibbling around the edges, Jayne looked pretty good for a women whose head had been snicked off in a car crash. She carried a sequined pink bowling bag, swinging it back and forth in time to the swaying of her hips.

As for Andy Warhol: well, he'd always looked a little zombied-out anyway, so his groovy dirtnap (in his top-secret vault beneath the employee lounge of a Campbell Soup factory in Idaho) had actually improved his appearance by fifteen percent.

And THEN! John Q. Spaceman and Miss Meteor were felled by simultaneous heart attacks when they saw the unspeakable horde that followed Agents M and W. Those wacky plastic-penised hunky-boys had risen from their graves, and now they were on the loose. The crusty, lusty zombies bumbled forth like erotic rumba dancers on acid, sticking their insatiable pseudo-salamis into every available hole: knotholes, beehives, even the sundry orifices of two young lovers who'd dropped dead of fright directly in their path.

A ROBOTIC SENTINEL (DESIGNED BY THE RENOWNED NEP-TUNIAN SCIENTIST ERNEST HEMINGWAY) BIO-ENERGIZES ME TO OUTLANDISH PROPORTIONS, MUTATES MY HIDE INTO A METALLIC CARAPACE, AND SLAPS A FEW HEAT SHIELDS HERE AND THERE FOR GOOD MEASURE.

Sassy neck-stump lookin' fine/gonna make it mine all mine:
Cha-cha-dancin' Jayne Mansfield and an undead battalion broke into the jetpack factory, and soon the skies were filled with happy-pronged zombie flyboys. Andy Warhol led his troops into the studios of government-regulated PTV (all propaganda, all the time) and began producing and directing art film/pseudo-documentaries about zombie junkies having sex with zombie boywhores. Somewhere along the line, Andy Warhol took a moment to broadcast a message to Venus: "Fire up the frying pans. OPERATION: EARTH-SAUSAGE back in action."

But what Andy Warhol didn't know is that, while he had been asleep:
The body of Theda Bara, megalomaniacal Plutonian empress-in-exile, had been stolen from its mausoleum by a league of intergalactic vampire performance artists, led by their trans-dimensional high priest, Aleister Crowley. The vampires melded Theda Bara's genes with those of a prehistoric praying mantis and a Mercurian rock-crab, creating a gigantic chain-smoking transvestite BugBitch in blue velvet pumps. Aleister Crowley then unleashed this glamorous creation on the penis-eaters of Venus. In no time at all, Theda Bara used her granite claws to crush the undying bimbos into a really delicious pâté.

The vampires then turned the Planet of Love into an enormous coffee shop. (After drying the pâté in huge ovens, they ground it up to make their espresso. And there you have it: How To Exterminate A Seemingly Immortal Alien Race.) They had just run out of powdered Venusians when they received Andy Warhol's message. The insouciant vampires reviewed all of Earth's TV and radio broadcasts (the sort of thing B-movie aliens loved to do), assessed the situation, packed the giant Theda

Bara monster into their biggest battle cruiser and headed her toward Earth. For Aleister Crowley had a plan:

Them jumbo-baloney zombies were already screwing the Earth up, down and all around. Once Theda Bara began her attack, civilization soon would be reduced to a fleshy frappe. At that point, Aleister Crowley would send down his vampire legions to set up the building-sized coffee roasters and grinders.

The smirking high priest put an eye to his most powerful telescope and watched with glee as Theda Bara spouted bright orange poop onto the faces of Mt. Rushmore. He threw back his head to cackle with triumph—and so, didn't notice the bright flash of silver that zipped, quick as a cork popping out of a champagne bottle, from the moon to the Earth.

THE ROBOT SENTINEL FIRES ME TOWARD THE GREENS AND BLUES, HIGHS AND LOWS, SWEETS AND SOURS OF EARTH. A MOMENT LATER, I STRIDE FORTH TO DEFEND CULTURE, KITTENS AND PUPPIES, AND PARIS, MY BELOVED PARIS. ALONE AGAINST IMPOSSIBLE ODDS (IF ONLY ALICE WERE HERE!), STILL I PERSIST: FOR I, POSTMODERN-WARRIOR-CYBER-GODDESS GERTRUDE STEIN, HAVE A JOB TO DO—A WAR IS A WAR IS A WAR—AND DAMN ALL THESE ALIEN FUCKS! IF THEY SO MUCH AS LAY A FINGER ON THE EIFFEL TOWER, I'LL RIP OFF THEIR BUTTOCKS AND FLOSS MY TEETH WITH THEIR LOWER INTESTINES.

PRETTY-BOY

Edgar Blanchard handed a glass of champagne to the young woman on the couch. "Can't you stay just a little longer?"

Claudia glanced at the cobbled-together clock on the wall. One hand was a dagger; the other, a pink baby spoon. The gears were housed in a human skull painted bright green. According to Blanchard, the timepiece had been made in 1927 by a Brazilian serial killer with a genius IQ. "Maybe another twenty minutes," she said, "but then I have to go. I'm looking at a two-hour drive. I'll only be able to squeeze in six hours of sleep before I have to start getting ready for Jason."

"Getting ready?" Blanchard sat next to her. "For what?"

"Good God, Edgar. I'm just meeting him for breakfast. I take a long time getting ready for you, too."

"How old is Jason anyway? Does he know about me?"

"Twenty-three. And no, he doesn't." She smiled as she ran a hand through Blanchard's salt-and-pepper hair. "I don't tell people I'm sleeping with my dotty old professor." She then noticed a reddish-black wooden figurine on the coffee table. It looked like a bat, or a cat with wings. "What's this?"

"I don't know. I got it from an Englishman—a modern-day Oscar Wilde with huge buckteeth. He didn't even know what it was. His friends call him 'Lamby.' He has major tax problems and he's selling off family antiques. I bought a lot of things so he tossed in that little statue. He had an old steamer trunk full of them."

As Claudia studied the bat/cat's cruel face, she caught a glimpse of a thin crack under its chin. "So what else did you get?"

"A chandelier, about a dozen books, three hatchets with ivory handles, some very nice lockets..." Blanchard leaned closer to her. "And Lamby's grandfather, the cannibal."

* * * *

Claudia clapped a hand over her nose as Blanchard raised the coffin lid. The box rested on a gurney in Edgar's workshop, a basement room lined with shelves of tools and chemicals.

"I'd like you to meet Lord Paxton," he said. "Lamby filled me in on the family history. Rumor has it the old rascal ate the hearts of six of his servants. And he was a sorcerer. And what am I forgetting—? Oh, yeah.

Every now and then he grew wings and carried off small children. Busy guy."

His Lordship had not aged well. His flesh was brownish-green, and his wispy hair was matted with blue fungus. Dead spiders nested in his eye sockets. The fingernails were yellow, crooked and caked with dirt.

"A colorful character. I'll have to swab him down with formaldehyde." Blanchard slipped on rubber gloves and lifted Lord Paxton out of the coffin. "The old rotter's got some meat on his bones," he said as he moved the corpse to a worktable.

Claudia couldn't help but smile. Blanchard saw this and smiled back. "Who's the grin for: me or my handsome friend?"

The young woman shrugged. "I was just wondering why such a nice man collects such awful things. Not that I mind. It's interesting in a Halloweeny sort of way."

"Well, I guess that's why. It's *interesting*. Mysterious. Baffling. Take Pretty-Boy here, for example." He lightly tweaked Lord Paxton's mildewed nose. "Why did this vicious old creep go around eating chunks of other people? It's easy enough to say he was crazy, or evil—or incredibly hungry!—but still, I can't help but wonder. Maybe he knew something the rest of us don't."

"Sure: like, what a human heart tastes like." Claudia pointed to a small black envelope taped to the coffin lid. "Look, he came with a warranty."

Blanchard opened the envelope. "It's a note: *Grampums cannot sleep in a strange bed.—Lamby.*"

The young woman leaned over Lord Paxton. "Would Grampums like a pillow? You need all the beauty sleep you can get."

Blanchard sighed. "You'd better be going. I wouldn't want you to miss breakfast with your fellow toddler."

"Now you're being difficult," she said. "Try to see things my way."

His Lordship's hand fell over the edge of the worktable; the lovers gasped, then laughed nervously.

"I think Pretty-Boy is eavesdropping," Claudia said. "I'll call you tomorrow." She kissed Edgar's cheek and left him to his work.

In the living room, she checked her purse for her car keys. Then she remembered she'd laid them on the coffee table. There she saw the figurine and picked it up. She noticed that the crack she'd spotted earlier completely encircled the neck. A thought occurred to her, and on an impulse she twisted the head.

It began to unscrew.

Once the head was off, a thin pink mist swirled out of the neck, clouding her vision for a moment. She caught a whiff of perfume: an odd combination of roses, chocolate, and old leather. She tipped the figurine over her palm, but nothing came out. Her eyes began to water furiously. A dull pain crept into her neck and shoulders.

A loud clatter rose from the basement. There were sharp, crunching sounds, like wood being broken to bits, followed by the crash of breaking glass.

Claudia raced to the basement door and listened for a moment. Someone was shuffling around, grinding the glass underfoot. "Edgar! Are you okay?" she shouted. "What's going on down there?"

Something held Claudia back as she tried to descend the basement stairs. She screamed as she found herself surrounded by enormous black-bristled wings—

Then she noticed that the horrid, hairy things had sprouted from her shoulder blades.

Amazed, she stared up at her new appendages. They had caught in the doorway, and seemed to be wedged in tight. When at last she remembered the commotion below, she looked down into the basement.

She found herself in the presence of royalty.

Lord Paxton was crouched on the stairs at her feet, eating a red object shaped much like an apple, except larger and not as firm. Dried spiders rained from his eye sockets as he stood up. He ran a bloodied claw gently over her face. She struggled as the creature sought to embrace her.

"Now you're being difficult," Lord Paxton whispered in a hoarse falsetto—a throaty, vicious parody of Claudia's voice. His blood-stained lips twisted into a savage smile. "Try to see things my way."

So saying, His Lordship raked out her eyes with a single swipe of his talons.

MINTY BELASCO'S TOP TEN MOST HIDEOUS AND/OR SPLENDID MOVIES OF ALL TIME

Translated From The Original Croatian

Introductory note from the translator: Last year, while vacationing in Europe, I visited film critic, fashion designer, and international trend-setter Minty Belasco, who was living in an apartment above a Goth nightclub in Munich. Minty is tall, thin, pale, and extensively tattooed. His age is anyone's guess. He is the author of seventeen books on a variety of subjects, including menswear, ancient Egyptian mummification rituals, bonsai trees, and his favorite topic of all, movies—the cheaper and trashier, the better.

His books have been published in Russia, Poland, France, India and Japan. But not one has been published in the United States, because as Minty said, "Most Americans don't want to know what I think. Besides, that's where Momsy and Daddy live, and I'm not talking to them."

Minty's parents, Momsy and Daddy, are in fact multimillionaires Regina and Cuthbert Belasco, owners of Belasco Beer, Belasco Premium Cigarettes, Belasco Fried Chicken, and Belasco Funeral Homes.

Minty can write and speak in thirty-five different languages, but these days he only writes in Croatian. He told me, "My new massage therapist speaks Croatian and I'm just mad about that tongue—that language, I mean."

The article below, written by Minty, appeared in a Croatian film magazine with a name that translates to *Eye Feces*. Fortunately, I know several languages myself, so Minty said that if I wanted to go to the bother of translating the article, he would give me his permission to sell it to an American editor, making it his first publication in this country.

On behalf of America, I thank you, Minty. Some of us really do care what you think.

* * * *

MINTY BELASCO'S TOP TEN MOST HIDEOUS AND/OR SPLENDID MOVIES OF ALL TIME

No. 10 and Stinkingly Hideous:
I Took Piano Lessons from a Zombie (1939)

Lots of folks consider this a horror classic, but I think it's a steaming bucket of goat dung. Glubb the undead piano teacher strikes the keys at random while staring off into space. Are we to assume that only a mindless zombie would play the piano that way? That's just how avant-garde pianist Feng Pao Goldstein, a visionary, a genius, used to tickle the ivories. I once went to one of his concerts, and I loved listening to Feng as he played the baby grand in the middle of that cattle-yard. You see, even the locations of his concerts had to be avant-garde. He was on life support for five months after the stampede.

* * * *

No. 9 and Hideously Vile:
The Amnestyville Horridness Part XVII: Better Latte Than Never **(1997)**

The movie that started this series, *The Amnestyville Horridness* (1979), was pretty much a supernatural kitchen-sink drama about a family trying to adjust to a new house and all its nutty little quirks: creaky floorboards, drafty hallways, faucets squirting pus and tentacles flailing out of the refrigerator. It wasn't great, but it had interesting main characters and some nice creepy moments, with a satisfying ending that still left the door open for a sequel. Well, so far no one's been able to shut that damned door.

In the first five sequels, the house changed ownership time and time again, before the local priest wised up and burned it down in No. 6. But that didn't end the Amnestyville curse. In this one, No. 17, a haunted coffee-maker from the evil house is given to a perky, innocent family in a suburb of Chicago. Soon their happy home is crawling with undead spirits, all hopped up on caffeine. The machine is never shown making latte, so the title is just a cutesy witticism. Actually, that's the only clever thing about this plodding exercise in plot recycling. Elements from the previous sixteen movies are tossed in like wild greens in a salad from

Hell. To be fair, the coffee-maker angle does deliver one nice chill—like when we find out that the couple's breakfast coffee was brewed from the cremated remains of another couple that died in sequel No. 16.

There's one thing I can't understand about haunted house movies. Why don't the people just buy another house? Houses can't cost that much—Daddy had dozens of them. He even had one he never told Momsy about—that was where he kept his lover Pasha. I can't remember if Pasha was male or female ... probably a he/she. Daddy always had trouble making up his mind.

* * * *

No. 8 and Ridiculously Hideous:
The Legend of Flaming Arrow (1993)

This big-screen, mainstream release was about five-thousand times worse than most of the cult films and shoestring-budget drive-in oldies I usually watch. Classically trained actors think they can play anything from baby chicks to Siamese twins. Fine-boned blond British actor Basil Cheltenham has played Hamlet and Romeo, but sorry, he is simply out of his league as Indian warrior Flaming Arrow.

This was supposed to be a very intense film, and a bit of a dark fantasy, with Flaming Arrow going on spirit quests in his own head and talking with bear gods and eagle ghosts and other celestial Nature types, but the whole effect is ruined by Cheltenham's presence. They dyed his hair black and gave him brown contacts and slathered him with shoe polish to darken him up, but under all that one can tell he's still just a snooty pretty-boy. My nanny Helga raised me right: I simply will not tolerate pretense.

* * * *

No. 7, Hideous Corporate Propaganda:
Let's Learn More About Soybeans! (1993)

This wasn't ever a theatrical release. It's a trade-show videotape I watched while spending the weekend at my friend Roger's beach house. Roger's family is even richer than mine, if that's possible. His brother sells soybeans and soybean-related products, whatever those are. The brother had left the tape behind so Roger could learn more about the world of soybeans and perhaps want to get involved in it, but Roger is doing quite well as a butt model. That's his rear in all those Calvin Klein underwear ads.

This wretched little trade-show video is narrated by some fat, awkward soybean executive with a triple chin and sideburns. It seems that soybeans can be made into anything—cattle feed, protein shakes, plastic, medicine, cars, buildings, you name it. Roger and I got drunk on rum-and-cokes and made fun of the tape from beginning to end.

It's funny, though. I look around at things now and think: Is this made out of soybeans? Is that made out of soybeans? Exactly how much of my world is made out of soybeans? Ten percent? Fifteen? Fifty? More? The mind boggles. For all I know, I might be surrounded by the damned things. So hurray for soybeans, I guess.

* * * *

No. 6 and Hideously Nauseating:
Sidewinder Sally (1954)

Usually I hate big, lush Hollywood musicals, especially ones set in the Old West—crusty geriatric campfire cooks and square-jawed ranch-hands bursting into song over sunsets, sycamore trees and newborn calves staggering toward their loving moo-cow mommies. Yes, usually I hate them, but there's something I hate even more: big, lush Old West Hollywood musicals starring Marla Malone.

Saccharine-sweet girl-next-door leading lady Marla stars as Side-winder Sally, a scruffy Nebraska tomgirl who cleans up right purty. In fact, she's gosh-darned glamorous, with straight white teeth, shining golden hair and perfect skin in a wild-and-wooly frontier without tooth-paste, shampoo or astringent.

I know what you're thinking. You're thinking, "Minty, don't you usually critique movies with monsters and killers and aliens in them? Sidewinder Sally is just some corn-fed cowboy chick." To which I reply: "Whole generations of women grew up feeling woefully inadequate because they weren't as perfect, as winsome, as talented, as zit-free as Marla Malone. Men loved her, but they all knew they she was too good for them. Why would the flawless Marla want some loser with a potbelly, a bald spot, halitosis and a dead-end job? So doesn't all that make Marla a bit of a monster, making male and female victims alike feel like crap, spreading a loathsome epidemic of low self-esteem?" If that ain't a monster, I don't know what is.

It is amusing, though, to see Marla strutting around in buckskin pants, shooting rifles and punching varmints. Sidewinder Sally's more of a man than my weak-chinned, drunken Daddy ever was.

* * * *

No. 5 and Directed by a Hideous Moron:
Baby Schnookums of Arabia **(1998)**

I wasn't sure what to make of this one... I'm not much of a history buff, but I'm vaguely aware of the existence of some soldier or diplomat or whatnot named Lawrence of Arabia, who used to have real-life intrigues somewhere in the Middle East. Arabia, I imagine. But why make a kid's movie—a feature-length cartoon with an orchestral score and everything—about his baby brother? And by baby, we're talking diaper, pacifier, the works. Baby Schnookums toddles off into the desert to have hee-haw-larious adventures with asps and mummies and guys with swords. He eventually joins up with a talking flying carpet named Ruggles and a baby camel named Humphrey. Momsy used to ride camels on her safaris. Elephants, too. Momsy was quite the hunter. I once went with her on one of her hunting trips and she bagged three lions and some kind of enormous pig. She'd hunted in that part of Africa before—the local guides call her 'Insane Death Goddess.'

But back to the movie. All the symbols on the walls in the pyramid scenes were wrong. I know a bit about hieroglyphics, and the curse above the entrance of the tomb in the movie was supposed to say: HE WHO ENTERS THIS TOMB MUST PAY THE TERRIBLE PRICE. But actually it said: BEETLE BIRD BEETLE, GUY-POINTING-LEFT, BIRD BIRD, BEWARE OF CROCODILES, BEETLE BEETLE BIRD, PHARAOH STINKS.

* * * *

No. 4, Hideous and Slightly Splendid:
Don't Look in the Crawlspace **(1972)**

Why do some houses even have crawlspaces? Like any normal kid, I grew up in a lovely big mansion, with occasional trips to the summer house, and neither of those places had any dark old smelly crawlspaces, as far as I know. People were meant to live in airy, palatial surroundings, not stuffy burrows. To my notion, a house without pillars just isn't a house. It's a shack. I have no idea why some people live in trailers. A house on wheels? That's just wrong. I refuse to set foot in a house on wheels. It could roll off a cliff or something. The house in this movie doesn't have wheels, but it does have cannibals living in its dark, wet hidey-holes. And they cook their victims in a cave below the house—they don't just eat them raw. So they do have some class, though they don't bother with a recipe. Ideally, human flesh should be served dotted with cloves, slow-roasted and generously brushed with either a ginger glaze or plum sauce. Or so I hear.

* * * *

No. 3, Equally Hideous and Splendid:
Living Dead in the Horror Museum of Wax (1988)

I found this Franco-Italian horror opus altogether intriguing. True, they set it in a fictional town—Hellwich, which sounds like a terrible sandwich—in Massachusetts, and it was painfully clear that the writers and director had never been to America, let alone New England. Nights in Massachusetts don't echo with the chatter of monkeys and the snarls of lions. Men in bars don't cry out, "More ale, serving wench!" But still, the movie makes up for those weensy flubs by being wonderfully energetic and creepy. The zombies prowl the town by night, then just before dawn, they go back into the museum, dip themselves in a vat of molten wax, and then stumble to their displays and harden into encased figures to be on show during the day. Then at the end of the day, they break out of their wax and the hunchbacked museum janitor cleans up all the broken wax and throws the chunks back into the vat.

One thing I don't understand is this: molten wax is pretty hot, right? And the zombies immerse themselves in it. Wouldn't the zombies be cooked by now? But then, maybe evil supernatural creatures are more heat-resistant. They're built to endure the flames of Hell—so what's a little molten wax?

* * * *

No. 2, Hideous With Lots of Prehistoric Splendor:
Dracula, 10,000 B.C. (1964)

A vampire caveman! It sounds like a stupid idea, but I loved it. Plus, the part of Drah-Ku-Lah is played by Tony Carpelli, a very handsome Italian actor with just a touch of a lazy eye, and I've always thought there was something really sexy about a lazy eye. Years and years ago, my sister Taffy had a boyfriend with a lazy eye. He was German, a foreign exchange student named Klaus, and he and I used to spend entire afternoons taking nature walks in the timber behind the summer house. Well, we told people they were nature walks. Last I heard, Klaus became a spy, but not a very good one, because he was caught and he's in a Siberian prison now.

Cave-vampire Drah-Ku-Lah terrorizes a bunch of Neanderthals and it's up to Von-Hel-Sing, the really smart caveman who's a little higher on the evolutionary scale, to save the day. The dinosaurs look pretty fake, and I really don't think dinosaurs and cavemen lived at the same time, but still, you really can't have a caveman movie without a few dinosaurs. I mean, the prehistoric world without dinosaurs would be pretty boring. Just a bunch of cavemen fighting pigs and monkeys and big rats. Who wants to see that? My favorite part is when Drah-Ku-Lah bites the pterodactyl and then the pterodactyl turns into a vampire. A few minutes later, it flies into a big tree and a branch spears it through the heart, so it doesn't have time to turn any of the other dinosaurs into vampires. I wonder how Klaus is doing in Siberia? I'd send him a sweater, but that would just make the other prisoners jealous.

* * * *

No. 1, Tremendously Hideous and Deliciously Splendid: *Horror in der Haus* (2003)

This direct-to-video horror movie is a complete mish-mash. A sixty-ish voodoo queen living in a ghetto befriends an extremely old German guy living by himself in a big spooky house surrounded by an electrified fence. In the house is a locked door with the metal letters K.K. nailed to it, and the doorknob always has an icicle hanging from it. That may seem like an especially odd detail, but trust me, it works into the plot eventually. The old guy turns out to be a mad Nazi scientist doing experiments in longevity, and he's about a hundred and twenty years old. He has a lock of Hitler's hair in a little jar, and he keeps trying to clone it into a full-grown Adolf, but the hair-guck that Hitler used had corrupted the DNA. So he tricks the voodoo queen into turning the hair into the person it used to be, telling her that it was a precious lock from his dear departed wife. The voodoo queen takes pity, whips out her big book of spells and works some magic on that evil snip of hair.

So, Adolf Hitler is born again, and not just as a baby—he's all grown up, moustache and all, and speaking English with a thick German accent, so I guess the voodoo queen must have thrown in a linguistic spell. From this point on, the movie just gets more and more ridiculous. Eventually Hitler becomes a rapper, Big H, who sets his rants to a hip-hop beat. Did Hitler have any sort of musical talent? I guess the voodoo queen threw in a music spell, too. Big H makes everybody in the hood think he's their friend, but needless to say, that's all one big lie. He steals the voodoo queen's book of spells and raises all his old Nazi buddies from Hell, and soon they're goose-stepping through the streets, up to all their old nastiness again.

Then the director tries to play a tune on our heart-strings. By this time, the elderly Nazi has fallen in love with the voodoo queen. He sees the error of his ways, so he decides to become a good guy and stop reborn Hitler. In a movie this stupid, anything can happen, and while I don't want to give away the ending, I will tell you that the K.K. on that door stands for Kris Kringle—yes, even jolly old Santa Claus gets caught up in the whole confusing, catastrophic brouhaha. This movie is like a massive ten-car accident: it's not pretty, but you really do need to have a peek, just to see how sickening it was.

The world is full of great movies, good movies, mediocre movies and poorly made movies. But truly bad movies are like two-headed calves: rare, strange, loathsome and miraculous. So visit your local video store, rent some of these tapes and feast your eyes upon their hideous splendor. If you are like me, I am sure they will make you vomit with rapture.

GREEN

A pale creature with infected green fingernails he was, and yet there was something utterly genteel about the way he nibbled at the dead rat. I was determined to save him from himself.

"Good Mr. Social Worker," he whispered, "your services are not required here. I pray you leave me be. I am expecting old acquaintances... very old! I asked them to visit many years ago—a terrible mistake—and they do insist on returning every now and then."

"You need help, my friend." I smiled and patted his bald head. "The department will take care of you. We'll put the color back in your cheeks."

"Yes...but which color?" The old man wrapped what remained of his dinner in a sheet of green waxed paper. "You must have other appointments to keep. My guests shall be arriving at any moment. I cannot imagine that time has mellowed their dispositions." He shuffled over to a cupboard and placed the tidbit in a stack with several other small green bundles.

A single faint knock sounded at the door. Can a sound have a chromatic quality? A tint? Certainly that soft, soft knock was coated with a sickly green patina.

"Hellfire!" the old man whispered. "Under the bed with you, young fellow. It would not do for my guests to find you here." So saying, he pushed me to the floor—his strength was inhuman!—and rolled me into the suggested hiding place. Then he threw open the door and in they swarmed.

Green was the color of their desiccated flesh and glowing eyes. Green was the mold that grew in huge swirls and splotches on their tattered garments. Their throats, clotted with green dust, coughed forth a mad litany of vicious truths and delicious lies for hours on end. Listening, I learned that these singular individuals had discovered a magical means of turning death back into life...

A greenish sort of life.

In time, one of the dusty guests (his name was Mr. Crowley) brought forth a piece of green chalk and etched the outline of a door on the wall. He made a series of gestures and a portal of green fire appeared, through which the guests passed, dragging the old man. Then the portal vanished and I was alone.

I left the old man's ramshackle house, my eyes brimming with tears—green tears, because of all that dust. My hands and clothes were streaked with the hideous stuff.

Churning green clouds rolled across the sky as I drove through the city. A growing stench filled the air—a nauseating green reek. I had stopped at the store before visiting the old man, and so sacks of produce and packaged meat rested on the seat next to me. The contents of these bags had decomposed into a thick green slime. I rolled down the window and flung the sacks from the car.

Green concrete towers loomed before me like lichen-shrouded monoliths. The flesh of the people on the sidewalks putrefied before my eyes, taking on a horrid green cast. The other drivers I glimpsed bared their decayed green teeth at me.

Suddenly, there was a furious crash of metal. My head snapped forward and back—bones cracked in my neck. I had collided with a dark green car driven by a smiling green thing in a dusty shroud.

Green mist clouded my vision. Needles of green pain danced in my brain. I stumbled from the car and my legs gave way beneath me.

In a moment, Mr. Crowley began to trace around my body with a stub of green chalk.

THREE CHEERS FOR THE DEAD, BITE AND CHEW

Brytni was sipping her low-fat, sugar-free, cherry-mocha-flavored latte, chatting about boys and clothes and shoes with Ashlee, who had ordered a chai tea sweetened with organic honey, when the commercial came on.

"Bring out your dead and get out the vote!" bellowed a phlegmy male voice.

The patrons of the Hallowed Grounds Coffee House looked up, and most performed simultaneous spit-takes of surprise in response to what they saw on the TV screen above and to the left of the cash register.

The pus-yellow eyes of the man on TV competed with his bruise-purple skin and feces-brown teeth for the title of Most Disgusting Color Ever Found On A Supposedly Human Face. They all lost out to the slime-green streams trickling down from his flared nostrils.

"Like, is that a zombie or what?" Ashlee cried.

"Good evening, fellow Americans!" intoned the grinning cadaver. "My name is Telemachus Vuurmek, and I am running for president of the United States."

"Can a zombie even run for president?" Brytni wondered aloud.

"A lot of you are probably wondering if a zombie can even run for president," Telemachus gurgled. "The answer is: Yes. I was born in America and I am certainly old enough. The laws do not require any candidate to have a heartbeat. I sincerely hope none of you will discriminate against me, just because I am pulse-impaired."

"He has a point," Ashlee said. "We can't hate him because he's, like, different."

"But what does he stand for?" Brytni asked.

"You're no doubt asking, 'Where does a zombie stand for?'" rumbled the campaigning corpse. "I am the only candidate willing to speak out about equal rights for the dead. Zombies are up-and-coming members of the community, as many of you will learn before this night is through."

"What do you suppose that means?" Ashlee said.

"It probably means he's not the only zombie in the world," Brytni surmised.

"I'm sure many of you have surmised that I am not the only zombie on Earth," Telemachus croaked. "My living campaign planners ... the Resurrectionist Party ... summoned me from beyond the grave to run for office, and they've been traveling the highways and byways, raising supporters in every major city. Once my newly risen supporters put the bite on you, you'll be joining the party, too!"

"Like, I don't get what he's saying!" Ashlee whined. Outside the coffee house, prolonged screams echoed in the distance.

Brytni's eyes brimmed with tears as she said, "It sounds like our country is filling with the shambling bodies of the hungry dead, rampaging for living flesh upon which to feast, and once we are bitten, we too shall become ravenous zombies, prowling the blood-spattered streets, creating more and more zombies with our infectious bites, until at last the Earth has become a spinning, planet-wide graveyard of agony and doom."

Up on the screen, Telemachus Vuurmek smiled and nodded. "Yeah. What she said."

TEARS OF THE EXPRESSIONIST APHRODITE

(SELECTED PASSAGES FROM A TRANSCRIPT OF THE DOCUMENTARY)

The Poet

I hate being called a poet. I've met too many people who think all a poet is good for is coming up with clever rhymes. I prefer to think of myself as a text-orchestrator. And as for rhyme: it's only useful when you are trying to replicate the brain-wave patterns of deceased idiots. And there are other psionic applications. Orgasmic waves, for example, break down roughly into sestinas. But a poem that could drum the rhythm of life into the dead: or better yet, that could inspire the dead to fuck! *That* would be something.

The Painter

I've been criticized for going on and on about pain and suffering. And having said that, I shall proceed to talk about pain and suffering anyway, since I know whereof I speak. They put my father behind bars for what he did, but really, he should have received an arts grant. Slamming that car door on my hands—first one, then other—was a genius thing to do. Really. I was pissed off at the time, but now: the pain, it's all right there on the canvas. The color theory of pain, the geometry of pain... My hands may not be the prettiest things in the world, but they get the job done.

The Boywhore

Yes, I used to fuck for money, but I'm beyond that now. I once thought that being hypersensitive was a curse, but with life experience, I've gained confidence. If only *everyone* were hypersensitive! That would be nice. A world of considerate lovers... A boy can dream.

I've been working on the development of the perfect virtual reality fuck program: layering the levels. Simultaneous auto-, homo-, hetero-experience. And everything else I've ever done, or anyone else for that matter. Dildoes. Pumps. Dogs. Every possible fetish, every sex toy, every—But you get the idea.

The Priest

It all started when I baptized a dead man and he became a zombie. A lot of people had a problem with that. But then, a lot of people had problems with electricity, flying machines, the car... Some people still think that radio waves can filter into their brains and drive them crazy. The baptism was simply an experiment. The process—I hate the word 'ritual'—centered around a supplication to the true Aphrodite. Eventually I loaded the zombie in the car and hit the road.

This documentary surprises me: most people don't want to hear about anything that could actually bring about *change*. But I do have faith that in time, everyone will embrace the new way.

The Historian

Society is all screwed up. It's disgusting. I've read textbook after textbook and they're all wrong. I can't stand reading lies, knowing that the next person to read them just might be stupid enough to believe them. Truth can be such a burden. The bigger the truth, the bigger the burden. I wish that I could be stupid, but still able to discern the truth instinctually. Like animals in the woods: they know which plants are poisonous, don't they? I'm fairly sure they do. I'll have to ask the Scientist.

The Scientist

Consciousness. It's grounded in every cell. The dead ones, too: even *rot* has a sort of intellect. Biology craves a purpose.

Each cell says to itself: *I have to do something.* The stupid ones just say it slower.

That's my little joke. I shouldn't say silly things. People think less of me when I do. Like I'm not supposed to have a sense of humor. But if I didn't laugh every now and then, well, I'd probably die from ulcers and high blood pressure. My cells want me to speak my mind, and vice versa.

The Director

At first, I had trouble finding funds for this documentary. But when word got out—through the grapevine, articles here and there, radio interviews at ridiculously small college stations—money started trickling, then spurting, then pouring in. There are businesses and committees out there that want to see me succeed. They probably don't even *know* about the Expressionist Aphrodite, per se. That makes me laugh: people who don't know why they do what they do. Sure, they're probably just following their instincts, but aren't we all more than just flowers turning our petals toward the sun?

The Poet

At my most recent readings, I've performed my poem, *Tears of Ecstasy, Iridescent Eyes.* Each time, the entire audience was transfixed. That particular poem, that sestina, can turn the listener into a melancholy idiot. I'm not sure why it doesn't fuck *me* up. I suppose I'm just a... Tool? Doorway? Organ? Maybe I'm a reptile: rattlesnakes manage to carry around their venom without dying. Isn't that a vile image: little old me, the text-viper, stunning the brains of my mousy listeners. Making them stare and drool and sigh with sad wonder. Some of the folks from my audiences have been fetched and detained by family members, but eventually, most have wandered back to me. For a while, I was giving some of them crackers and setting them in abandoned buildings. Posing them in amusing tableaus.

The Painter

Aphrodite is the inspiration for all Expressionism. At my last exhibit, everyone kept staring at *Pain Flowers,* staring and soaking in my pain. It's odd that they didn't want to leave, since they weren't having much fun. Oh no. They were all gently crying. That mindless weeping gave me a few anxiety attacks, but eventually I got used to it. Really, though, crying isn't a bad thing. Deep down, I think, we all need to shed a few tears. Sure we do. Isn't an orgasm a sort of bodily crying jag?

The Boywhore

I tried out the first draft of the fuck program on some old friends—clients, actually. It reduced them to a gritty, quivering paste. And let me tell you—it's a crazy thing, to have eyes staring at you out of pink slime, staring in an accusing sort of way. Not that it made me feel bad. I don't believe in guilt: it just holds you back, and really, who needs that? And besides, nobody died. That slime was—*is* alive, and I've saved every ounce. If there's *any*thing anyone should feel guilty for, it's waste.

The Priest

I've set up my own church in a little ghost town in the Midwest. Toad City. It's near a huge, swampy lake, full of critters, so that's probably where they got the 'toad' part of the name. As for 'city': probably just wishful thinking. Or, who knows? Maybe prophecy. I happened to pass through the town during my travels with zombie No. 1. The place consisted of twenty broken-down buildings and a cemetery. No one was around to stop us, so the zombie and I dug up the dead people and baptized them. At the time, I didn't know what they were going to *do*. They had a complete lack of focus.

All in all, things have a way of fitting together. For me, that's an unusually optimistic statement, but what the hell. Technically, I *am* in the optimism business.

The Historian

Aphrodite—the real Aphrodite—was never the goddess of love. But various cultures copied her. Distorted her. *Softened* her.

In ancient times, the people of Babel worshipped the true Aphrodite. The tower legends, as the world knows them today, are all wrong: the language thing, for example. A very sloppy metaphor. Religious texts won't tell you this, but the bricks of the tower contained bits of flesh and shit and cum and other goo. But back then, they didn't have the guidance. Or the manpower. Or enough goo. So the whole project fell apart.

I tried to set the academic community straight on these points, but they never listened. Oh no. They always wanted *proof*. Information gleaned from visions simply wasn't good enough for them. I did eventually met some sympathetic souls, and their support meant everything to me. For a while there, I was actually beginning to doubt my sanity.

The Scientist

I HAVE TO DO SOMETHING. I can hear my own cells crying out. Perhaps that voice is the tiny—what *would* one call the reverse of amplified?—voice of Aphrodite, goddess of Expressionism. She is not Life: she is the shadow that Life casts. And once that shadow falls on you... A gorgeous feeling of pain and sadness that goes on forever. A feeling so strong, it warps the reality around it. A study needs to be done on the effects of warped reality on various plants and animals. I've got that on my 'Things to Do' list.

The Director

After I found my funds—or rather, they found me—the whole project came together quickly. Phone numbers were sent my way anonymously. Volunteers would stop by my house, asking if I needed anything done. I had stumbled upon something, and it began to engulf me. You wouldn't believe how much help I've received... How many *gifts*. And all the people who've wanted to sleep with me.

Regarding the six main players in this undertaking: I contacted some by correspondence, others by phone. Eventually I met them all in person. They were of different ages, social backgrounds, even countries of birth. But they all talked the same: meaning, they sounded the same, and even chose their words in the same sort of hyper way, like—Me. And they all had that long, pale face with deep-set eyes. Like mine.

For that, I don't have an answer. But I do have some thoughts on the matter. Have you ever seen a jigsaw puzzle where all the pieces were shaped exactly alike? They may be the hardest to put together, but when you're finished, there's such a sense of satisfaction.

The Poet

I received a letter from the Priest in the Midwest. It took me a while to figure everything out—we exchanged letters for about three months—but finally, we arranged for all of my permanently dazed audience members to be spirited onto buses and out to Toad City. We had to pay off a few people, but our project had some extremely generous sponsors.

These days, I'm sharing a house here in Toad City with the Painter. We're working on some truly breathtaking collaborative projects.

The Painter

The Priest's letter came at a good time. I was getting quite a bit of negative publicity. Isn't it always the way? A person can work for years at their craft and no one gives a rounded fuck. But the minute people start going crazy *en masse*—! The priest and I found a way to have my addled art lovers corralled into vans and shipped to that little town in the Midwest.

The Poet and I have so much in common. Sometimes we start talking and before we know it, a couple days have passed and we haven't had a bite to eat or a minute of sleep.

The Boywhore

The priest invited me to move the production company out to Toad City. The fuck program operates off of an intricate headset: we had dozens manufactured, and then we hitched them to those sad cretins that the Poet and the Painter trucked in. We stood the poor things in a tank to catch the goop.

The Priest's zombies follow directions fairly well, so we taught them to mix the paste with powdered plastic to make salmon-colored bricks. Lovely. They give slightly when you squeeze them. And they hum, too. I used to carry one of the bricks around with me, just to hear it hum. But then my hands started hurting, so I had to leave the brick in my quarters, under my pillow. My hands finally stopped hurting after these little flaps opened up on my fingertips. Now my hands can taste textures.

The Priest

For a while, I was writing to dozens of people: business folks and culture vultures with checkbooks and of course, the Historian—we'd met back in college, and we saw eye to eye on so many points. He shared his thoughts on the Babel Tower with me and I thought: this was the missing piece in my fantastic puzzle. And so I wrote to the Poet, the Boywhore and the Painter. I'd heard about them on the TV news, and for that, I must thank this country's marvelous electronic media.

The reborn dead have been a joy to work with. They are so good at taking orders. Some of them are beginning to show signs of actual personality, and that's good: I want them to enjoy their work, and embrace the new way with glad hearts.

The Historian

Well, let's see. I had been corresponding with the Priest and the Scientist: the Priest wrote to me about his little town in the Midwest, and the Scientist told me all about his friend, the Boywhore. So, first thing, I went to Toad City and shared my ideas with the Priest. The perfect combination: I had the plans, he had the manpower—or rather, corpsepower. The Priest wrote a few letters, made a few connections, and soon, we were on our way. This time, the Tower of Babel would be done right.

Society is an organism: it has to change and grow. *Evolve.* Old cells die. New senses emerge. Extraordinary.

The Scientist

I'd been in touch with the Historian (a brilliant man) and the Boywhore—I was one of his technical consultants. According to the Historian, the problem with the original Tower of Babel was that it was phallic. To embody the Expressionist Aphrodite, it should have been an architectural womb. A holy place.

The zombies built a magnificent temple out of the salmon-colored bricks. The Expressionist Aphrodite is the queen bee of intellect. Upon completion, the living womb began the process of parthenogenesis. And it's still going strong.

Still, that doesn't mean we can rest on our laurels. I've always been what you'd call results-oriented. Like I said, I have some studies lined up. I'm going to begin a whole new line of research in a few weeks. By then, this lump on the side of my head will have become... Something. Maybe another brain. I've got my fingers crossed.

The Director

The Babel-womb continuously sprouts monsters-in-pain: the living tears of the glorious Expressionist Aphrodite. Fantastic creatures with... with just everything: hundreds of knowing eyes...swollen sex organs blossoming like giddy flowers...wagging tongues and bell-like ears and dripping, snuffling noses...sensuous hands with dozens of soft fingers. Experience nourishes them, and reality twists to accommodate their passage. I doubt that civilization as we know it can withstand such an onslaught of *change.*

And speaking of change: I can't help but wonder what will become of me. I suppose I've been in Toad City too long. This must be how a tadpole feels. New bits keep popping out here and there, and I'm not at all sure what they're for. The Priest keeps talking about embracing the new way...

The Boywhore told me I looked sad this morning and gave me a chaste hug. It took us the better part of an hour to separate. Our flesh had grown together as he held me in his arms.

ARLENE SCHABOWSKI
OF THE UNDEAD

(WITH KYRA M. SCHON)

Really? Right now?

Okay.

Let me tell you about a nice lady, who lives not too far from here. She was in the movie. And still is, in a way.

Her name is Lorraine Tyler—and also Arlene Schabowski. Lorraine is in her early forties, though you couldn't tell by looking at her. She has long, wavy blonde hair. Arlene is nine years old, and she has long, wavy blonde hair, too. Most people would agree that she looks quite dead.

Lorraine played Arlene, all those years ago. Lorraine stopped, but Arlene kept right on playing.

After the zombies swarmed the building, Arlene devoured most of her parents—they were hers, so she certainly deserved the best parts—and then simply wandered off into the night. And the night was filled with shambling, ravenous corpses, feasting upon the flesh of the living. But the undead knew she was one of them, so she was safe from their hunger. Her body held no warmth, no nourishing spark of life to entice the other zombies. That was the last the viewers ever saw of her.

But she needed food, for she was—and still is—always hungry. Deliriously hungry. For there is a deep black coldness within her that constantly needs filling. Sometimes, right after she has eaten, she actually feels alive again. Perhaps even better than alive. She felt that way after she ate her parents, and she wanted to feel it again. So she wandered through the woods, through the darkness, until she came to another farmhouse.

Now at this point, one might ask, "They never showed what happened to the little girl after she wandered off. Didn't the police get her when they came and shot all the zombies' brains out?"

Obviously not.

One might also wonder, "'Fear-Farm of the Undead' was only a movie, wasn't it?"

Well, yes and no.

Lorraine Tyler's father was one of the producers and stars of the movie, which was made on a shoe-string budget. The money her family put into that movie back then wouldn't even buy a decent new car these days. Her father, mother and some of their friends wanted to make a movie, so they pooled their resources, found a few more investors and did it. And Lorraine got to play a little girl who gets bitten, turns into a zombie and eats her parents.

Lorraine went on to become a school teacher with a cool website selling "Fear-Farm" memorabilia. Teachers get time off during the summer, so she started going to conventions, meeting fans, doing a lot more to promote her memorabilia sideline. She did that for years. Made good money, too. Last year she made enough to buy a nice little vacation in Mexico.

People still watch that movie all the time. Still think about it. "Fear-Farm of the Undead" has spawned hundreds of knock-off versions, most of them released direct-to-video. And Lorraine has watched every one of them. Because she is also Arlene Schabowski, and wants to know what other zombies are doing.

Somewhere out there, it is always night, and a little dead girl who is also a living school teacher is always hungry.

Anyway. Back to that other farmhouse.

Arlene could hear cows mooing in the distance. The sound made her hungry. She crept up to the house and looked in the window, into a quaint, tidy living room, with knick-knacks on little cherrywood tables and furniture draped with lace doilies. An old woman was sitting at her desk, reading some papers. She had long white hair and wore a dark-gray housecoat. Of course, everything in that world is black and white or shades of gray, just like in the movie. The old woman must not have turned on the radio or the TV that day or night—she looked so peaceful, it was clear she had no idea what was going on.

The little dead girl went to the front door and knocked. The old woman called out, as cheery as can be, "Who is it?"

Now, none of the other zombies in that movie were able to talk. All they ever did was grunt and roar and squeal. But Arlene was able to think really hard and call upon the abilities of her other self, Lorraine. And she managed to rasp out the three-word phrase from the movie for which she is best known. She also says a four-word phrase early in the movie, but most folks don't remember that. No, they only remember what she says just before she turns into a zombie: "Help me, Mommy."

"Mommy? I'm nobody's Mommy!" the old woman cried. "Who's out there? Is this some kind of a joke?" So saying, she threw open the door. "My God! Little girl, are you hurt? There's blood all over you!"

Arlene held out her arms, just like she did before she killed her movie-Mommy, who was played by her real-life mother. Again, she said, "Help me, Mommy."

"Of course I'll help you, you poor thing." The old woman knelt before her. She must have had something wrong with her knees, because she winced with pain. "So tell me, who did this to you? Who—"

Her next few words were lost in a thick gurgle of black blood, because by then Arlene had her little teeth embedded in the old woman's throat. And even though the dear old thing was past her prime, she was still full of warm, delicious, intoxicating life.

Arlene ate her fill and by the time she was done, that sweet old woman looked like a car-wreck victim, sans safety belt. Arlene turned and strayed into the night. She didn't wait around to watch the old woman's gnawed carcass scramble back to hungry life.

Mind you, while all that was going on, poor, confused Lorraine was hiding in some bushes in the school playground, screaming and wondering why all these bad things were going on in her head. The other kids thought she had gone nuts. Her parents and the teachers talked about it later, and based on what she'd told them, they decided she had an over-active imagination. They told her not to let the bad images scare her—they were make-believe, so they couldn't hurt her. It was all in her head, they said, and in a way it was. Hers was a sort of Reality Surplus Disorder. It's hard to concentrate when you've got another personality playing in your mind.

My best guess is all the movie's fans created that personality, that black-and-white world of death—all those watchers in the dark, thinking about that movie, those zombies, and of course, poor little Arlene Schabowski. All that feverish brain energy. What is reality, anyway? A mental collective, that's all. The result of multiple minds, mulling over enthralling stories. I'm sure that somewhere, out there, Moby Dick is still swimming and the House of Usher is still falling. I'm sure Dorothy is still wandering down the Yellow Brick Road, having new adventures, fighting more witches and flying monkeys. And I'm sure she's still a tiny young thing, just as Arlene Schabowski is still a tiny dead thing.

But let us return to Arlene. She walked down a gravel lane until she came to the highway. Car lights were heading toward her. She held out her bloodstained, skinny arms and waited. The driver would stop. Of course they would. She was just a little girl.

So she waited. And the driver stopped—a fat, middle-aged man with a bulbous nose and horn-rimmed glasses.

"Was there an accident?" He ran up to her, crouched and thrust his fat face near hers.

"Help me, Mommy," she said.

"You poor thing," he said in a low, sad voice. "What the Hell happened to you?"

Another one who thought she was simply a poor thing. She smiled, leaned forward and bit off his nose—it was too large and juicy a target to resist.

He screamed, so she bit off his lower lip, which made him scream that much louder.

She gnawed and gnawed until he was too cold for her to stomach. Then she began shambling down the road. And because that entire movie took place at night, the daylight never came. She wandered an eternal night of fields and rural back roads and farmhouses, feasting on innocent country folks who only wanted to help her.

And Lorraine ... She endured Arlene's adventures in her head, and finally even got used to them. A person can get used to anything, really. Folks who live near airports soon learn to ignore the roar of planes coming and going. Lorraine grew into a tall, willowy lady. Always slender. Having a zombie in your head is enough to spoil anyone's appetite. There were plenty of times when she would sit down to dinner, and Arlene would suddenly go on a rampage in her mind. Little zombie-girl would rip apart a couple farmers, tear out their guts and gobble them down, and suddenly that plate of lasagna would seem like a hideous, visceral thing. But Lorraine wouldn't scream over it—wouldn't even bat an eyelash. She'd just push the plate away.

As I mentioned, Lorraine eventually became a school teacher. Because a part of her was still a little girl, she liked being around children. She lived in a big nice apartment building, surrounded by families—all the kids her thought she was great. Some of the people in her building had seen her movie, and they were always telling their friends that their neighbor was a movie star. Sometimes folks who had seen the movie would call her Arlene. She'd smiled to be polite, but she didn't like it. "Hey, Arlene—'Help me, Mommy!'" was the favorite greeting of the fat guy who lived six doors down. She'd always try to take a different route to avoid him if she saw him coming.

Eventually she started dating the school's janitor, and all of her friends made fun of her for that, joking that the lovers were probably always sneaking off to the boiler room or some such place. The janitor, whose name was Kurt, was a good-looking man, only in his mid-thirties and in fine physical shape. And truth to tell, the two did sneak off together sometimes. To Kurt's office. His door had a fancy title—environmental control specialist—but it still meant janitor.

Once while she was in his office, Lorraine saw a key hanging from a little nail on the wall behind his desk. The key had a scrap of paper taped to it. The word ATTIC was written on that scrap in blue ballpoint ink. She waited until Kurt's back was turned, and she took that key.

Even while she was reaching for it, she wasn't sure why she was taking it. She just knew she had to have it. After school, she stayed behind, waited until everyone was gone and then went up to the attic. It was all storage up there, and the things that had been packed away up there so long ago were now all but forgotten.

Remember where little Arlene ate her parents? In the attic. That's where the movie-family went to hide from the zombies. The movie-attic had a bed in it, where Arlene used to sleep. She says her four-word line while she's in that bed. The school attic had a broken cot among its various odds and ends. Obsolete schoolbooks, tennis shoes, sacks of that pinkish, pulpy stuff to sprinkle on barf to soak it up and make the smell go away. Lorraine strolled among rows of dusty boxes and stayed up there for about an hour, looking at spiderwebs and old papers and outdated globes. She realized then that this was the first time she'd been in an attic—any attic at all—since the filming of that movie. Her parents had always lived in apartments. Her dorm room in college had been on the ground floor. A life without attics. She now felt oddly at home—but was it a good home?

When she came down from the attic, left the building and went to her car, the world around her seemed different somehow.

A little less—colorful.

A moment later, Arlene Schabowski saw red in her night-world for the first time. Usually the blood of her victims was shiny black. But she looked down at the hitchhiker she had just torn to bits and saw red, red everywhere. Then she saw that her dress was stained not merely with various splotches of gray, but horrible gouts of rotted filth and gore—red, yellow, brown, green, a veritable rainbow of decay. It made her smile.

A few days later, Kurt was completely confused by Lorraine's birthday gift to him. "Rainy," he said, for that is what he called her, "this tie—don't get me wrong, I think it's great. And silk, it must have cost plenty. But purple? I don't know if I'm the purple type,.."

"Oh," she said quite softly. "Is it purple? I thought it was some kind of dark silver. Are you sure it's purple?"

Lorraine sometimes would bring a book to school to read in the attic, after hours. In the days to come, her students became more and more confused by some of the things she said—especially during art class. Whenever one of them did a drawing, she would ask things like, "What color is that horse?" Or, "That's a very pretty mermaid—which crayon did you use for the hair?"

Arlene began to notice green leaves among the gray, when car headlights hit them just right, and some of the towns she meandered through were bigger than the little country burgs she usually came across. One even had a supermarket. She would hide in the bushes bordering the parking lot and watch the front of the supermarket. Watch all the people rushing in and out. It made her hungry. Sometimes one of the shoppers would hear something rustling in the bushes and go see what it was, worrying that it might be a lost child. They were right to worry.

Lorraine found that the drive back to her house seemed a little shorter every week. And there were fewer cars on the road. Not as many buildings behind the sidewalks. Less kids in the school, but more birds in the light-blue sky. There was still a bit of color in her world, but not much. The changes were all huge yet gradual. Kurt usually wore a nice polo shirt and some jeans to work. It didn't even surprise her when he started wearing coveralls, or when his voice started to take on a rural twang. He even took to calling her 'Honey.'

Arlene just kept on wandering—she was so good at it. Wandering and eating, eating and wandering, always keeping to the shadows, which was getting harder, since there were so many streetlights around. But she was finding more homeless people, so at least she had been eating more regularly. No more fields—she was in the suburbs now, and the skies were starting to lighten. Night was slowly giving way to a light-blue morning.

You see what was happening, don't you? They were starting to meet in the middle. Why do you suppose that was happening? Maybe it was because Lorraine was spending so much time up in that attic. I suspect attics have strange powers. They come to points at the top, like pyramids. They're rather intriguing, aren't they? And bear in mind, zombie movies were becoming more modern—perhaps the imaginations that had pulled Arlene into existence were pulling her into the present day.

Lorraine was getting pulled, too, but in a different way. Into something—but what? One morning she thought she saw a tractor drive past the school. Later that day, she knew she heard cows mooing in the distance. She broke off her relationship with Kurt. He was becoming more and more rural, like some of the extras in 'Fear-Farm of the Undead.' He was growing too much hair and losing too many teeth. That wasn't the kind of boyfriend she wanted and this certainly wasn't the life she wanted to lead. She didn't like it. No, not one little bit.

Especially when she found herself chewing on what was left of the Algebra teacher, late at night up in the school attic. She couldn't even remember what she had done to get him up there. Not that it mattered. There were shreds of flesh under her nails, and her belly was swollen with food.

She wasn't sure if what she had done would turn the skinny old teacher into a zombie, but better safe than sorry. She went down to Kurt's supply closet, grabbed a hammer, and used it to cave in the old man's gnawed head.

And then she waited.

Pretty soon she heard the tappity-tap, tappity-tap, tappity-tap of little-girl heels coming up the stairs to the attic. And then—

That's when you walked in, Arlene.

You walked in and said the four-word phrase that you said in the first half of that movie, in the scene when your mother was putting you to bed: "Tell me a story." Most people don't remember that you said that. But you did, in that sweet, soft, cheery voice. Though that's not what your voice sounds like now. You sound like a record that's slowly melting as it plays.

So. Did you like my story, Arlene? It was all about you—and me, too. But I said "Lorraine" instead of "I" because... Well, I don't really feel like me any more. But I'm not you.

I don't know who I am, where I am or even what I am.

Hmmm...?

No, I'm not your Mommy, and I'm afraid I can't help you.

But who knows. Maybe pounding your head open with this hammer will help me.

TALES
OF THE
INTERNET
WITCHES

THE FIVE MOST LOATHSOME SECRETS OF THE INTERNET WITCHES

Prepare your mind for horror, for you are about to learn the five most loathsome secrets of the Internet Witches.

But first, let us cover the basics:

- The Internet Witches are all pale with dark red hair.
- They laugh like dogs barking, even the baby witches.
- Their unholy websites feature recipes, always for desserts.
- Their favorite treats are vulture's egg cupcakes, hell muffins, and cheesecake made from the milk of black goats.
- They live among mortals and always work at jobs that involve computers.
- You must never click on the green glowing eye in the bottom left corner of every Internet Witch webpage. Nothing will happen if there are others around. But if you are alone, green lightning will spring forth from the screen, split in mid-air, and strike you in both eyes.
- If you are hit by the green lightning of the Internet Witches, you will fall to the floor dead. Then a crow will appear (even if there's no window), pluck out one of your eyes and fly off, the same way it arrived. A moment later, your glowing, one-eyed corpse will walk the earth as a radioactive zombie as that crow carries your eye far, far away, to the main computer of the internet witches. It will stick your eye on a wire and upload everything you have ever seen.
- The information acquired via the eyeball upload will be used by the Internet Witches to shame and destroy all of your loved ones, and maybe a few of your coworkers, too, if there's time. They are very busy, these Internet Witches.

Now the lesson shall begin. Do not forget a single detail—for if you do, you shall surely die screaming, the victim of an Internet Witch.

* * * *

Secret No. 1: Viruses

The Internet Witches are responsible for all computer viruses, which look like tiny electric-blue monkeys with orange teeth, corkscrew tails and eyes as black as death.

The viruses evolve on a daily basis, constantly learning innovative ways to ruin the computers and lives of mortals. They cannot leave their sizzling electronic world, so whenever they are hungry, they upload a human victim, right through the computer screen.

The Internet is their madcap jungle and if you are not careful, my friend, you will become their next banana.

Secret No. 2: Spam

If you are a spammer and dare to spam an Internet Witch, she will visit you in your bed, tear off your head and sew it on backwards.

She will then reanimate you and upload you into the rocky wastelands of the Website of the Living Dead, where you will wander forever as a clumsy Backwards Zombie, constantly stumbling over jagged chunks of cyber-basalt. Believe me when I tell you, it will feel just as hard as real basalt.

Secret No. 3: JPG Files

If you slight an Internet Witch, she will eventually kill you, but first, she will shame you.

She will transform all the JPG files on your personal or business website into freaky S&M pictures involving whips and manacles and rusty needles and clamps and two or three corpses, maybe four.

Then she'll e-mail all your relatives and coworkers with a link to your altered website which reads, "Now you know."

Secret No. 4: Online Transactions

Beware of online transactions, for the Internet Witches can and will steal your identity and bank accounts and spend all your money on sex-toys, candy and daggers.

When the Witches have had their fun, they'll zap all the candy wrappers, sticky used sextoys and bloody daggers onto your front porch. One of the daggers will be sheathed in the back of a dead department store Santa, even if it's summer.

Try explaining that to the neighbors. And the police.

If you manage to talk your way out of that, the Internet Witches will send you a PDF file.

Secret No. 5: PDF Files

Usually PDF files are harmless and very convenient for sending documents filled with words and graphics. But when an Internet Witch sends you one, PDF stands for Pile of Dog Flop.

That is what the repairman will find inside your computer.

Perhaps you are thinking, "Oh, that does not sound too bad. At least I won't be killed." But you will, and so will the repairman, for that Pile of Dog Flop will be teeming with incurable tropical diseases. It takes three weeks to die from these diseases. In the meantime, your nose and ears and genitals will wither and fall off.

* * * *

So ends your lesson.

No doubt you are wondering who I am, and why this message has appeared on your computer screen.

I am one of those Backwards Zombies mentioned in Secret No. 2. But I wasn't a spammer. I was an Internet Witch myself, and had angered the leader of my coven by daring to love a mortal. She'd found a love letter I'd written but had not yet delivered, and so she decided I had to be punished. I now find the Internet Witches loathsome and needlessly cruel. Is it so wrong to want love?

I managed to escape the Website of the Living Dead by adding a link to the website's HTML code and following it out to a friendlier domain. The Internet Witches did not realize I knew how to do that.

I am telling you all this because I wrote that love letter to you. I used to be a coworker of yours. You probably do not remember me, since we never talked. I didn't even work in the same area as you. But I used to watch you, fantasize about you.

Now the Internet Witches will no doubt try to destroy you, even though your only crime was being attractive. That is why I have sent you this information. Try to stay alive long enough for me to figure out how to upload humans into the Internet. It's something I've never done before, but the viruses can do it—surely I can do anything a silly little virus can do. You can live with me here in my online hidey-hole.

I am also trying to figure out how to download myself back into the human world. That might even be easier than trying to pull you into the Internet. We can then find some little love nest where we will be safe. Now that I am a Backwards Zombie, I may not the prettiest girl in the world—but rest assured, my amorous enthusiasm will more than compensate for the questionable aesthetics of my appearance.

Do not worry, my angel. All will be well.

One way or another, we shall be together.

CYBER-VENGEANCE OF THE INTERNET WITCHES

A CAUTIONARY TALE

You are about to learn the shocking fate of those who do harm to an Internet Witch. Let the lesson begin.

* * * *

Clifford and Irving told folks they shared a super-sweet bachelors' pad, but really, that just meant they lived in the basement of Clifton's grandmother's one-story house. The scrawny old woman's name was Opal and she walked around her home wearing only a fluffy pink robe, which always just happened to fall open whenever she alone in any room with Irving. And Irving always gagged a little whenever he saw the flaccid, heavily freckled fleshbags dangling down her ribcage, the tips of her disturbingly long nipples swinging at the same level as her belly-button.

The two men, both in their late twenties, burned incense whenever they were home, but not because they were trying to cover the smell of pot-smoking. They did it to mask the stench generated by the litter-boxes of Tiger and Mr. Boom-Boom, Opal's flabby house-cats. The litter-boxes were located in the kitchen near the door to the basement stairs, and their stink drifted with eerie precision down into the living quarters of Clifford and Irving.

They toiled at the same fast-food emporium, Happy Klown's Burger Karnival, and because they stood over greasy cookers during their workdays, both presented oily, zit-splotched faces to an unsympathetic world. They were quite bright and knew much about computers, but they were also slobs, and even businesses that regularly hired slovenly nerds wouldn't give either of them a courtesy interview, since the resumes they submitted were always coffee-stained and reeking of cat-pee.

Dark-haired, chubby Clifford and thin, blond Irving were not happy lads, and so they took out their anger on civilization by creating computer viruses and unleashing them upon the businesses that had rejected them.

"Dude! This is totally super-sweet!" Clifford said one Saturday morning, turning from his huge computer monitor—it had cost two paychecks—to address his roommate, who was working at his own machine at the other end of the basement. "I sent my Guess-Who-Loves-You Virus to everyone at Channel 13 a few minutes ago, and now their website is down! Go check the TV upstairs, maybe they're off the air!"

"I'm not going up there!" Irving replied. "Your skinny-assed granny will just flash me with those floppy tube-socks she calls tits!" He tapped his computer screen. "The IT department at Turtledale Medical Center will go nuts about thirty seconds after one of their employees opens the STD Virus I just sent them!"

"Refresh my memory..." the chubby cyber-vandal said. He took a wad of tissues out of his breast pocket and blew his nose, filling the flimsy paper with tarry greenish-yellow sinus-infection goo. "What'll this new virus of yours do?"

"In every e-mail and medical record in their system," Irving said, "the word 'pneumonia' will be replaced with 'rectal warts,' 'vaginal discharge,' or 'scrotal rash.' And, all patient bills will be reduced by a random amount exceeding fifty percent—so the hospital will be totally screwed!"

"Super-sweet!" Clifford said, turning back to his huge monitor. "Hey, what's up with this?"

Irving crossed the basement and stood by his friend's side, where he gazed in complete bewilderment at a black screen covered with bright lime-green words, which read:

**Welcome to the Cyber-Vengeance of the Internet Witches.
SOON YOU SHALL BE REBORN.**

Suddenly the O in YOU turned into a little mouth with bright-red lips. "You have tampered with the computer of an Internet Witch," said the mouth in a low, angry, yet very feminine voice with a slightly metallic tone. "For that, you shall feel the lash of our vengeance."

"Dude!" Irving said. "What's an Internet Witch?"

"I don't know," Clifford said, "but one of them must work at Channel 13."

The blond burger-flipper thought for a moment. "They've got a really pale anchorwoman with red hair..."

"Nurla Yormik," the lips said. "Yes, that is the one you have offended. Now prepare for our vengeance!"

"How can that webpage hear us?" Clifford said. "I don't have a microphone hooked up—"

At that moment, the two Os in SOON blinked and became glowing bright-red eyes with green irises. Twin green lightning-bolts shot out of the eyes on the screen—one hit Clifford in the left eye, and the other hit Irving in the right. The basement buddies fell to the floor, both completely paralyzed.

"We, too, create computer viruses. But ours are quite different from yours," said the lips. The O in REBORN flexed, twitched, and became a glowing blood-red anus, which opened wide and gushed a torrent of slightly chunky, pudding-thick, guacamole-green feces upon Clifford and Irving.

Some of the chunks began to move.

These crawling shapes—the viruses of the Internet Witches—resembled tiny monkeys with blue hair and shining green eyes. Six wee creatures tore through the clothes of the paralyzed pals to chew on their skin and meat, and the creatures grew as they ate, until they were as large as actual monkeys.

One of the viruses opened up Clifford's pants, pulled out his surprisingly large cock, and gripped it tightly around the base until it became hard. Then the virus opened its thick-lipped mouth, revealing jagged orange teeth and a flicking hot-pink tongue. The creature bit the bulbous head off the cock and then used its free paw to tear the skin in strips down the length of the male organ, peeling it like a banana. In a series of seven gnashing bites, the virus reduced the cock to a bloody stump, one fleshy inch at a time.

Another virus opened Irving's pants and wrangled out his heavy testicles, each as big as a good-sized walnut. The thing used a razor-sharp claw to slice through the wrinkled scrotum. It pulled one lump out of its sac, placed the prize between its teeth, and slowly brought its jaws together, popping the sperm-filled meatball like a juicy grape.

Then, after the virus-monkey did the same with the second testicle, it reached into the pants again, grabbed the cock and yanked it out by the roots. It hopped over to the computer monitor and thrust the blood-smeared cylinder completely into the glowing, chewing mouth of the word YOU.

The first virus-monkey then ripped Clifford's testicles off his body, hairy scrotum and all, and stuffed these nuggets into the mouth as well.

"Delicious," the lips crooned after swallowing the fresh man-meat. "Now the rebirth shall begin."

Three virus-monkeys began to twist on Clifford's head, while the other three did the same with Irving's. At last they had the heads twisted all the way around, and then they propped up the bodies so the faces were aimed toward the computer screen. Again, green lightning-bolts shot out of the eyes in the word SOON and struck the basement boys—one hit Clifford in the right eye, while the other hit Irving in the left. These bolts, however, did not finish in a split-second, like the first ones. The new bolts continued for more than a minute, charging the bodies with evil energy until they glowed lime-green.

Slowly, the pimply duo rose to their feet. Both were missing huge chunks of flesh from their arms and legs. Clifford no longer had a nose and thick, bubbling mucus poured down his face, dripping from his chin in gluey ropes.

"You have been turned into PDF files," said the lips. "In this case, 'PDF' stands for Pathetic Dead Freaks. Surely there is nothing more pathetic than a backwards zombie cyber-eunuch. Agony shall be your eternal destiny, without even the hope of sexual release to ease your torment. Now you shall be uploaded into the Website of the Living Dead—"

"Hey, what's going on down there?" cried Opal from the top of the stairs. "I hear a woman's voice. Did you two idiots pool your puny paychecks and buy yourself a hooker?"

The arthritic old woman clambered down the steps. When she reached the bottom, the virus-monkeys jumped on her and dragged her in front of the monitor. Her robe fell open, but Opal didn't move a muscle to close it. The shock of being attacked by such outlandish monstrosities had induced a fatal heart attack.

"A ridiculous old hag," the lips mused. "But perhaps she can be of some use..."

And so, my friend, you have learned most of what happens to those who do harm to an Internet Witch. There is still a bit more to learn, and that knowledge shall be imparted momentarily. Hopefully you now realize that one must play nicely when one is online—for if you cause harm to an Internet Witch, you may share the vile fate of Clifford and Irving. Here is the end of your lesson and their tale:

Forevermore, two pathetic backwards zombie cyber-eunuchs must roam the rocky wastelands of the Website of the Living Dead. Occasionally they stumble on the long, fleshy burdens that hang down below their bellies. Opal's slack, heavily freckled left tit droops down from Clifford's undead crotch, while her right one swings limp and forlorn between Irving's legs.

SCENES FROM A FOREIGN HORROR VIDEO, WITH ZOMBIES AND TASTEFUL NUDITY

Grainy, sweeping shots of skyscrapers, crowded metro sidewalks, hectic traffic, and a pale young woman entering an office building. The Daughter. Her thick black hair is piled high, and held in place with several large silver clasps.

Suddenly the camera sweeps up, up to a blazing sun, and shimmering blood-red letters appear: NIGHTMARE OF THE WATCHING DEAD. The words fade away, and then names, names and more names appear, shimmer and disappear. Then the camera sweeps down, down to a crow picking at a glowing eyeball on the hood of a black limousine.

The Reporter gasps as the bird flies away with its juicy prize. "Did you see that?" he whispers. "A terrible omen." He has deep, sullen eyes and grey streaks at the temples.

A passerby—a fortyish woman with maroon lipstick—laughs, though it sounds more like a bark. She is The Nurse. "I have seen worse," she says, matter-of-factly.

* * * *

The Heavyset Man cruises the internet, clicking here, clicking there. He is wearing a stained bathrobe and is sitting at his desk in the middle of his cluttered apartment. A crow watches him from the sill of an open window.

"What is this?" the man says to no one. "A website about witches?" The screen is filled with images of pale women with long, straight red hair. "They are pretty, these witches."

The image of an eyeball pops up in the corner of the screen. The eyeball begins to pulse with a greenish light. Intrigued, The Heavyset Man clicks on this link.

Instantly, a beam of green energy shoots out of the monitor. It splits in mid-air and hits the man in both eyes. He leans to one side, then falls out of his chair and hits the floor, dead.

The crow flutters into the room, settling on the man's neck. The bird leans forward, gently slides its beak around one of his eyeballs, then gives the orb a sharp tug, pulling it free.

The crow flies out the window, and the camera watches it disappear, up into the roiling clouds. When the camera turns to view the room again, the body is gone.

* * * *

A tropical island at night. Too many animal cries—growls, hoots, monkey-shrieks and crow-caws—echo at the same time.

In a pavilion swathed in mosquito netting, The Fat Witch hands a goblet to The Young Witch. Both are pale with red hair.

"Soon," says the fat one, "everyone will be screaming. No one can withstand the dead when they are instilled with the nuclear life-force." Occasionally, the movements of her lips match her words.

"Yes, it is a perfect plan." The young one drinks deep from the goblet, leaving a smear of red, too thick and shiny for wine, on her top lip. "But how shall we begin?" She wipes at the stain with the back of her hand, but only succeeds in spreading it along her cheek.

"The answer is easy. I have already begun the process. How the fools love their internet computers." The fat one turns suddenly, pointing, and the camera zooms in the direction of her finger. A computer monitor sits on a makeshift altar of bloody bones and broken keyboards. The screen of the monitor is broken, and a decayed hand is pinned on some of the larger shards of glass. The hand softly glows with green energy.

"The internet, yes." The Young Witch nods. "They do not know it is controlled by witches and nuclear power."

"We set sail in the morning," hisses The Fat Witch.

The hand twitches, fingers churning like the legs of an eager spider.

* * * *

The morning sun shines down on The Businessman's patio.

Here, practically everything is white—the metal furniture, the tiles, the marble rim of the pool. The water is blue, but it is a pale, oddly milky sky-blue.

The Daughter has finished swimming and is drying herself with a fluffy white towel. She is the pale woman who had entered the office building earlier. She looks up at the sky, lost in thought.

(I've done this before. I know it. A hundred, a thousand times before.)

She walks to a table where The Businessman, her father, is having breakfast with The Scientist, her boyfriend.

"Father," she says, "I saw a news program last night. They were saying terrible things about the internet."

"Ridiculous. An outrage." The Businessman spears a sausage with his fork. "The internet is good. My best investment yet. What lies were they saying on the television?"

"Pay them no mind—they are jealous," The Scientist says. He is very handsome, with boyish good looks.

The Daughter picks up and eats a sausage from The Scientist's plate. "They say the internet has too many websites about witches on it, and that people are disappearing. And, there have been many terrible omens. In fact, last night I had a dream." She takes another sausage. "I dreamed that mother was not dead. I dreamed that she was a witch on an island, and that she was very fat and evil."

The Businessman turns to The Scientist. "These liars on the television are upsetting Miracula. Take her into the house and look at the internet with her. See all the good things it has to show."

"I will do so immediately," says The Scientist.

"I do not like it when you two gang up on me," The girl says, pouting. "And I do not like it that you will not tell me about mother. You say she is dead, but even if that is so, I still have a right to know more about her."

The Businessman takes her hand. "Someday I will tell you everything." He then nods to The Scientist, and the young man leads her into the house.

* * * *

Scenes of the young couple looking at the internet, taking turns clicking on this and that.

Scenes of The Nurse, examining ancient, leather-bound books in cobwebbed chambers.

Scenes of zombies stumbling through dark, filthy alleys, tipping over trash cans.

Scenes of birds and bats flying out of shadowed church entrances.

Scenes of crows, always crows, carrying eyeballs in their beaks.

A close-up of one of the glowing eyeballs. The voice of The Fat Witch is heard: "How much they see, my pretty pets."

* * * *

Midnight. An enormous room filled with computers, monitors, cables. The very walls are lined with computers. Tiny lights of blue and white twinkle like stars.

This room is the mighty heart of the internet. Over the door is a framed portrait of The Businessman.

A fly lands on the portrait. The camera zooms in tight on the insect, cherishing the repulsive details of its filthy, squirming mouth. The fly zips off and the camera follows it, up and down, all over the room.

The fly darts through a disk slot in one of the computers. The camera continues to follow it on and on, through a mad eternity of flashing lights, shifting geometric patterns, clouds of blue lightning, and everywhere, eyeballs attached to sparking cables. The eyeballs glow green with radioactivity. Crows fly in to add new eyeballs, popping them onto free cables, or to take away old ones that have lost their glow.

* * * *

A cemetery under a full moon. Tombstones, dead trees, statues of angels with broken wings.

A young couple embrace, sitting on top of a large granite tombstone. A twig-snap echoes.

"What was that sound?" the woman says, startled.

"A stray dog. A cat. Nothing at all. Kiss me." The man has a gentle face and full lips.

"I tell you, I heard something." The woman looks around, then sees a faintly glowing figure, partially hidden by a tree, about thirty feet away. "My God. What is that?"

"You," the young man shouts to the intruder. "We see you. What are you doing there?"

Slowly the shape moves forward. It is The Heavyset Man, still in his robe, which is now even filthier. His body glows a faint, sickly green. He stares at them with his single eye as he advances. A thin line of green slime drips from the empty eye socket.

"Hideous," the man whispers.

"We must get out of here," the woman cries, tugging at her lover's arm.

"No. I want to see this. I have heard of these zombies." He moves a few feet toward the creature. "He is very slow. I can escape him easily."

"You are insane," the woman says.

"They say on the television that the internet is responsible." The young man moves closer, even as the zombie inches toward him. "There may be a reward for finding one."

"Madness," the woman hisses.

The man turns to his sweetheart. "If I had a rope, then I—" While he is looking away, the zombie rushes forward and leaps upon him, digging its meaty hands into the man's belly.

The zombie then looks up to stare at the screaming woman. A green bolt of energy blazes forth from his eye, and splits to strike both of her eyes.

She falls to the ground.

A crow lands on her neck.

* * * *

The press conference.

The Businessman and his associates are seated behind a long table. Each has his own microphone and glass of water.

Facing them, in rows of metal chairs sit The Reporter and his colleagues from various television stations and newspapers.

"More and more witch websites are appearing," The Reporter suddenly shouts, standing up. "Plus, more zombies are being spotted. They have attacked many innocent people. You cannot deny there is a connection."

"That is not a question," The Businessman says smugly. "Are you deciding the news for yourself? Is that how it works? And you call yourselves reporters."

This enrages the media people, and many begin angrily shouting questions. "What about the crows of death?" "Do you realize that radioactivity is involved?" "Can you explain the missing eyes?"

Suddenly The Fat Witch enters the room through a door behind the reporters, and The Businessman stands up. "What are you doing here?" he says. "Are you again trying to destroy my life?"

She smiles and nods, and steps aside as glowing zombies shamble into the room. They dig their strong hands into the throats and bellies of the media people. Green bolts fire from their eyes. Crows flutter gracefully into the room.

In the confusion, The Businessman slips away through a door behind some large potted ferns. The Fat Witch sees this and follows him.

Once she is through the door, she find herself at the top of a metal framework staircase. She sees The Businessman on the landing below. The two regard each other.

"So you are behind all of this. I suspected as much. You and your witches, making my life into an insane delusion." The Businessman's face is beaded with sweat. "Why can't you leave me alone?"

"Fool," she cries. "Can you not see that together, we are unstoppable?"

"I once loved you," he says, "but I cannot live in a world of misery and death. You want to control everything."

"Admit it. My power excites you." The fat one moves a step closer to him. "I love you. I am your destiny. Together, we can rule the planet. Without me, you will be dead. Your corpse will provide food for my zombies and the crows. You will be nothing. Do you hear me? Nothing."

"You talk of love. What do you know of such a thing? To you, it is just another word." He turns and scrambles down the stairs.

The Fat Witch does not follow. "There is no escape," she whispers. "No escape." A tear glides down the powdered roundness of her cheek.

At the base of the stairs, The Businessman opens the door to the parking garage. Glowing hands seize his arms, his shoulders, his throat.

* * * *

Scenes of The Nurse, rushing through busy offices, smashing computers with a hammer.

Scenes of zombies staggering down busy streets, into department stores and restaurants and hospitals.

Scenes of merciless hands tearing into soft flesh.

Scenes of glowing teeth ripping into gleaming innards.

A close-up of a beak, lovingly ripping an eye from its socket.

* * * *

Twilight. A parking lot, outside of a church.

"It is all so impossible," The Daughter says, wrapping her arms around The Scientist, crying on his shoulder.

(Why am I doing this? I do not love him. He is boring. He babbles like a fool.)

"I have learned the truth, Miracula," the handsome man says. "Witches have seized control of the internet through the power of nuclear reactions. They are using radioactivity to reconfigure the brainwaves of crows, and to re-energize deceased human tissue. They can even download images through the eyes of the living dead. Their power is horrifying."

The Daughter points to the church. "Then why doesn't God help us?"

He shakes his head. "I am afraid even God cannot defeat the science of the witches."

The Nurse walks up to the couple. She is tired and breathing heavily. In the fading light, her maroon lipstick looks black. "Excuse me. We have not met, but I know much about you from an old acquaintance. I used to be a friend of your mother."

"My mother? Tell me about her." The Daughter grabs The Nurse by the wrist. "I have waited so long to learn her identity."

"You will wish you did not know," the older woman says. "The truth will break your heart."

"And what is the truth?" The Scientist asks. "Tell us now."

"Very well." The Nurse takes a deep breath and stares into the girl's eyes. "Your mother is The Queen of the Witches. She is the most evil creature to ever walk the earth. I was once her handmaiden, but then I learned I was going to have a baby, so I escaped and hid myself from her. I did not want my child exposed to her vileness." She strokes the girl's cheek. "A few years later, when you were born, your father had the same thought. He stole you away from your mother while she was asleep. I helped him to hide from her. Your mother has been waiting for the day when she can at least reclaim you. Our only hope now is to destroy all the internet computers."

"I want to meet my mother," The Daughter says. "My love will make her good."

(I do not believe that. Why did I even say it? Why am I inviting doom into my life?)

"Impossible. You must hide," the older woman says. "I have looked in all the old books. You cannot win." Suddenly she sees The Young Witch at the far end of the parking lot. "There. That woman is spying on us. She is your half-sister. He father was one of the living dead."

"The living dead? Then she is a demon." The Daughter looks with fright—and curiosity, too—at the slender red-haired woman. "But running away cannot solve the problem." She turns and walks toward her half-sister.

"We must stop her," says The Nurse.

"Let her go. She has goodness in her heart," The Scientist replies. "She will speak to the witches on behalf of humanity, and God." He looks from the older woman to the church.

A moment later, The Daughter and The Young Witch enter a black limousine, which drives off into the gloom.

* * * *

Scenes of zombies ripping the clothes off of attractive men and women.

In some scenes, they simply devour the living. But in others, they drag their prey into the shadows, subjecting them to horrible pleasures of the flesh.

Close-up of a television screen.

"The situation is a catastrophe without end," says The Reporter. He is badly bruised, with scratches on his forehead and jaw. "The hungry dead continue to infect the world with their horror and radioactivity. The streets are filled with the torn bodies of the innocent. Plus, it has been revealed that the zombies are now forcing their victims to succumb to foul carnal acts. Authorities fear that these acts of abomination will result in grotesque cross-breed births. It is rumored that some of the resultant infants may grow to become internet witches. Stay tuned to this television channel for further developments."

* * * *

An enormous cave lit by blazing torches.

The Daughter's clothes are torn, and she is wrapped in chains. She has been placed on a blood-stained stone altar.

"So," The Fat Witch says. "We meet again, Miracula. I am your mother, The Queen of the Witches. Does that make you happy, my child? That means you are a Witch Princess."

"That does not matter," The Daughter says. All I have ever wanted is your love. Forget your evil and be a good and kind mother to be."

(This old whore is repulsive. I wish that she was dead. But I am trapped.)

"I could not do so even if I tried," the fat one says. "I could never forget the thrill of my great and terrible vices. A simple life means nothing to me. You are the one in the chains, but mine is the greater prison. Join me in the exquisite hell of ultimate power."

The Fat Witch touches a finger to The Daughter's forehead. Her black hair slowly begins to turn red.

"I do not want your madness," The Daughter cries.

The Young Witch enters the cave, followed by a male zombie. It is The Scientist. Both of them are naked except for loose strips of cloth wrapped around their hips. The Young Witch fondles his face and well-muscled shoulders, and then leads him into the shadows.

The fat one touches the chest of The Daughter. Her plump finger is just a few inches from the captive's heart. A red glow begins to spread through the girl's body, and she begins to scream.

"There is no escape, my sweet," The Fat Witch says. "Soon the world will be a radioactive wasteland inhabited by witches and the living dead."

The Young Witch, satisfied, emerges from the shadows. She takes the knife from beside the altar and, laughing wildly, thrusts it repeatedly into the chest of The Scientist. Then she jabs it into his empty eye socket.

The fat one smirks as the zombie falls to the cave floor. Then she turns back to The Daughter. "Waves of my energy are surging through you. Soon you will feel the power of my vast knowledge. And knowledge is simply another word for evil."

The Daughter begins to look around, and see—

(Now I see. Why I cannot remember my childhood. Why sometimes words appear in the sky. Why there is a toilet in the bathroom, but I never need to use it. This is not life—it is a twisted fantasy, a nightmare born in some diseased brain. No matter what I want, what I wish—it will never change. Why doesn't my God help me? Why—)

"Why does God allow this to happen?" the girl screams.

The fat one throws back her head and laughs. "Perhaps your God find this all very amusing. Yes, no doubt He is watching right now, enjoying this quaint little drama: the end of the world."

The Young Witch laughs as well. "Dear Miracula's hair is now red and her eyes—see how they glow with fire," she cries.

"But I do not want to be a monster," The Daughter screams.

(But I do. I want to destroy this filthy world of lies.)

She begins to cry. "I want to go back to my old life. I was happy then."

(Inside, I have always been miserable. I want to die.)

Suddenly a figure looms before them all. It is the zombie who had once been The Scientist. He pulls the knife out of his eye socket. With a roar of triumph, he lashes out, cutting through the pale throat of The Young Witch. He plunges the knife into the heart of The Fat Witch, releasing a torrent of black blood. He then begins to unwrap the chains that bind The Daughter.

"I—I love you," he croaks through his dead, dry lips.

"And I love you," she says, her smile suddenly hard and twisted.

(You disgust me. But that is a small matter. I am just a puppet hanging from unseen strings, dancing for a God who does not care.)

She takes the hand of the creature and leads him out of the cave, through winding passageways, into a world that they now rule. An endless domain of chaos, agony and tears.

Names, names and more names. Darkness. Static.

Rewind.

TALES FROM ZOMBIE ISLAND

ZOM BEE MOO VEE

The meaty old woman looked straight through me as she took my money. She shuffled through cards illustrated with lizards and drag queens, and said, in a voice like rusty hinges:

It is clear to me that in a previous life, you were the luscious and insouciant Necrilda Voltaire, princess of Zovemba Island. You may be saying to yourself, 'How can this be? I am a man,' but gender is not a quality that one carries from life to life. And at any rate, Necrilda was a man, too. Only a man would dare to be that beautiful.

Purple-black eyes and hair! Star-white skin and teeth! Silver finger-nails long enough to open envelopes! Her voice was shrill like some sort of insane insect, but what did it matter? At night she would reach her nails toward the skies and the love-smitten daemons who dwell in the clouds would surrender their secrets. And Necrilda would gather those secrets to her problematic bosom and become one with them. Secrets are power. Power is success. And success is beauty.

Too beautiful for words, and too beautiful to live! A waist that thin has no business holding working organs. Necrilda strolled into the garden with a green bottle, and poisoned herself in the name of fashion. As she fell into the flowers, the bottle flew from her hand, right into a bubbling stream.

Very soon the air above the stream was filled with swirling rainbow fumes, and all the wispy dragonflies fell down dead. Of course the fish died, and the plants, too. Soon the banks of the stream were littered with the bodies of cows and dogs and farmhands. And still the waters flowed on—into the town.

Very soon, Zovemba was an island of death.

* * * *

I grabbed the old woman by the elbow and said, You must be talking nonsense—you can't even look me in the eye! But she only pointed meek-ly, secretively over my shoulder, into the heavy shadows of her cluttered rat's-nest of a living room. I peered in that direction, but all I saw was a goldfish bowl on a cherrywood table. She continued with her ravings.

Dead bodies are funny things. They twist and turn: the foul gases of decomposition seep around, under the skin, making parts twitch and jump. Sometimes muscles tighten up in a most expected manner.

Well, Necrilda's extreme beauty prevented her dead body from doing anything too awful, rotwise. But in time, the muscles in her shoulders and arms began to tighten, until her hands shot straight up into the air. A few tiny facial muscles tightened, too, so that her eyes flew wide open. So there she was, regarding the heavens with open eyes and arms. Of course the cloud daemons, not knowing that she was dead, sent down their secrets, as was their way.

Secrets, you know, are simply the answers to hard questions. This time, the secrets sent down by the cloud daemons answered the question: how does one raise the dead? Necrilda embraced this secret to her bosom and slowly stood up, with a light shining in her eyes that wasn't life, but something just as good. Or bad.

Necrilda wandered about the island, touching the dead bodies of her people, sharing her knowledge with them. And they rose to follow her. Thusly did Zovemba become Zombie Island.

Necrilda still had silver fingernails, but now her eyes and hair were white, and her skin and teeth were purple-black.

* * * *

The old woman glanced at the clock, and then hurried into another room. She returned momentarily holding a bowl of raw meat. She wrapped a crimson lace scarf around her throat and gestured for me to follow her out the back door, into the night.

Her yard was a weed-choked jumble of old cars and broken washers and dryers. But soon I saw that these useless vehicles and machines had been made into shrines, decorated with fish skeletons and broken toy robots and candles shaped like children. In the back seats of some of the cars I saw the glow of yellow, green and bright pink eyes. The old woman threw shreds of meat toward every pair of eyes.

You were once Necrilda Voltaire! Deep inside you, in a place you cannot—yet—reach, you remember the facts I am telling you. The facts cannot die. And if I didn't know better, I would swear that the stars are slowly, slowly rearranging themselves to spell out NECRILDA.

* * * *

The story felt strangely familiar. Could it be true? I looked up, and indeed saw some sort of movement in the skies. I also saw the old woman's

goldfish bowl, floating serenely just beyond my reach. But was it a gold-
fish bowl? It was round and shiny and made of glass, and little shapes
seemed to shifting inside of it. The old woman sat on the hood of one of
the cars.

Many, many years later, a boatful of rich young thrill-seekers came to Zombie Island on a sunny, lovely day. Oh, they thought they owned the world! They'd been through many bottles of champagne, and so they strutted drunkenly about the island, saying stupid things like "Did we remember to tie up the boat?" and "Look at the claw marks on this tree!" and "What's that smell?"

There were five of them. Chad and Thad, the twins, young and handsome millionaire playboys. Clarisse and Mia, willowy fashion models with pretty pink smiles. And finally, Desdemona: so lovely, yet hard as steel, with eyes like black marbles and a hyena's laugh. She has seen it all, this one. Or so she thinks.

Thad wandered away from the others. This foolish boy, he'd had too much champagne, and he had to—drain his lizard? Is that what they say? Anyway, he danced off into the woods, singing a little song softly to himself. He found a tree, a big one, and unzipped his pants and stared up into the branches.

And there—!

Up there! Hanging down from the big shady branches like beautiful, horrible bats! Thad found he could not cry out: fear had stolen away his breath. White eyes regarded him: with admiration, then lust, and finally, hunger. They poured down the side of the tree like man-sized dollops of honey. They licked him and played with him and ran their long nails lightly over his soft flesh. Then they began to take huge bites out of him. And from nowhere and everywhere came a voice of booming doom that cried out, over and over, ZOM BEE MOO VEE, ZOM BEE MOO VEE, ZOM BEE MOO VEE.

* * * *

Now wait a minute, I cried. This story—I remember now! I've seen
it on the late show! I thought this was supposed to be my previous life. I
want my money back!

The old woman threw her arms open wide. She had quite a bosom on
her. I have it here somewhere, she said, find it if you can! I hadn't seen
what she'd done with my cash, but even so, I grabbed her and slid my
hand down the front of her dress. I've seen enough movies to know: that's
where ladies hide their goodies.

I was very close to her, and when her dark, striking eyes met mine, it occurred to me that she was not nearly as old as I had thought. Before I knew it I was in her bed. At one point I noticed that the thing, the not-a-goldfish-bowl, was sitting on a bric-a-brac shelf, half-hidden in shadow.

As we smoked thin black cigarettes, she began to talk. I was pleasantly tired, so I listened.

Mia went off by herself because she was very upset. She'd had a huge fight with Desdemona—over Thad, the poor little pisser! She found a fine, tidy cottage and thought, maybe there's a liquor cabinet, or even just a nice bottle of chardonnay. So she went inside, into the cozy twilight. By the fireplace she saw a cabinet with ornate carvings on its doors. She couldn't make out the pattern of the woodwork, but when she ran over hands over it, it bought to mind what it might feel like to stick one's fingers into someone else's mouth. She pulled her hands away, but only for a moment. How silly to be afraid! She grabbed the knobs of the doors and pulled. And—

A thin yet shapely figure unfolded itself from out of the interior. The most beautiful face in the world stared at Mia. Then, the most beautiful hand in the world raised a thin metal tube. Necrilda was not one to take big sloppy bites. The princess plunged the straw here and there, sucking and sucking until poor Mia was as dry as a slice of bread. And all the while, that doom voice, that tomb voice, bellowed, ZOM BEE MOO VEE, ZOM BEE MOO VEE, ZOM BEE MOO VEE. Then the princess brought out a knife and fork and made a polite little meal out of the meat. The bones she threw into the shadowy bushes outside the window. Her friends gratefully cracked them and sucked out the marrow.

Meanwhile, Clarisse and Chad were looking about for a place where they could make love.

* * * *

Chad's in for it now! I said. Womanizers don't stand a chance in these adventures. Thinking back, that was such a funny thing to say. My darling fortune teller, who now looked quite young, went on with her story.

Well, of course they picked the worst place possible—inside the Great Cave. The zombies watched from the shadows, and allowed the pretty little hors d'oeuvres to have a bit of fun. Soon the two were lost in passion, and they didn't even notice that they were a few too many hands grabbing and squeezing. Then the love bites started: little nibbles at first, but little nibbles have a way of growing. And before you know it, those awful zombies had those two spinning on a skewer, and they were taking bites out of them, just like happy children eating cobs of corn. ZOM BEE—bite, bite!—MOO VEE—bite, bite! On and on, the voice bellowed, on and on, the zombies ate, until it was night.

All this time, Desdemona had been exploring the old church in the middle of the village. She had discovered some ancient books that told of the cloud daemons. From a high window, she had glimpsed some of the zombies stirring in the shadows below. The zombies feared the church, so for a time, she was safe.

But she knew she couldn't stay in the church forever. She feared that the darkness and hunger would combine to make the zombies bolder. She realized she had to do something.

* * * *

I know I've seen this movie, I said, but I can't remember what she does next.

The zombies gathered around the church, smacking their uncouth lips. They broke all the windows with rocks and then threw diseased rats and poisonous snakes inside, hoping to drive the girl out—out of the church, or at least out of her mind. But our Desdemona: so resourceful— a real smart cookie! She climbed up onto the roof and struck a bargain with the cloud daemons.

Green lightning flashed and great birds like flaming peacocks soared across the sky. She held out her hand, but her new allies were not known for their manners. A giant claw of swirling grey mist reached down from the clouds and flung her into a completely different motion picture.

Look over your shoulder, my sweet.

* * * *

I did as I was told. The not-a-goldfish-bowl was just a few inches away, studying me. I could see now that it was, in fact, a large lens. Through it, I could see into a crowded movie theatre. The image was dim and distorted, but I could see that all the weensy theatre patrons were jostling about, tense with anticipation. They were watching me—I was simply a character in their monster matinee. And something ugly was going to happen. Something ugly and foul and splashed with great gouts of blood, blood, blood.

Very far yet all too near, the voice began to cry out, ZOM BEE MOO VEE, ZOM BEE MOO VEE, ZOM BEE MOO VEE.

I looked back at—Desdemona? Of course!—and she flashed a smiling mouthful of purple-black teeth at me. She said:

Don't you love a surprise ending?

* * * *

The transformation came over me in the blink of star-white eye.

Two can play at this game, I said, raising my shrill voice, my beauti-ful hand, my silver straw.

ZOM BEE TEE VEE

Transcript 3574b.677.a29:

Nice Old Lady: Hello, my friend. It is me, the Nice Old Lady. You had a good rest, yes?

Boy: Jiajia, who are you talking to?
Nice Old Lady: Ah, you startled me. You should not sneak up on people.
Boy: You were talking to what's under that sheet.
Nice Old Lady: You shouldn't even be in this room, you know. This is your Jiajia's special room.
Boy: You left the door open.
Nice Old Lady: Did I? Well, that doesn't mean you can just come strutting in without asking. Now what are you doing? Don't look at that.
Boy: I want to see what you were talking to. What is this thing? Some kind of computer monitor?
Nice Old Lady: If you must know, it is a machine known as a television, or TV. Now put the cloth back over it. Do not bother the nice TV.
Boy: I've heard of these things. I thought there weren't any left. Should you have one in your house? I heard they were all destroyed a long time ago because they were dangerous.
Nice Old Lady: 'Dangerous' is not quite the right word—'secretive,' perhaps. The government used to use them to spy on people. The TVs listened in on people and recorded everything they said, and then transmitted the conversations to a secret government agency. When people found out, the TVs were destroyed and the agency was disbanded.
Boy: So why do you still have this one?
Nice Old Lady: The agency is gone. If this machine is listening in on me: good. I like having an audience. Someone to talk to. I even think it likes me.
Boy: It isn't plugged in.
Nice Old Lady: That doesn't matter. The part that listens runs off of cosmic energy. Strange rays from the stars. Somewhere, some other machine is receiving its transmissions and writing down what I tell it. Again I say: good! No one else wants to listen to me.
Boy: That's not true, Jiajia. I like to listen to you.

Nice Old Lady: Yes, Marcos, you do pay attention to me. You are a good boy. Tell your mommy I want you to stay with me this summer.

Boy: You know she won't let me. She needs me at home. To wash the dishes and do the laundry. And cook. And—

Nice Old Lady: Your mommy is too lazy. I did not raise her that way.

Boy: She drinks.

Nice Old Lady: She takes after her father. That's too bad. Her daddy—your grandfather—was my first husband. Nothing but trouble. Necrilda took advantage of that. The whore! Oh, I am sorry. I should not use a word like that in front of you. Even though it is the truth. Necrilda was a true whore.

Boy: Necrilda?

Nice Old Lady: A character from his favorite movie. Necrilda Voltaire, the Zombie Princess of the island of Zovemba. The most beautiful women who ever lived. Or died. Though between you and me and the TV, she wasn't really a woman. A whore? Yes. A woman? No.

Boy: So what was she?

Nice Old Lady: Let us just say, some men aren't happy just being men. They like to play dress-up. Necrilda played dress-up so much, she had everyone fooled. Including herself.

Boy: Was she—I mean, he—being bad?

Nice Old Lady: It made him—but let's say her—happy, and that's all that matters, I suppose. It was a lie, but since it was how she felt inside, it was more true than the truth. When you are older, that will make more sense.

But that, my boy, was actually the least of Necrilda's deceptions. She wasn't even a real human being. Like I said, she was a character in a movie—and a dead character at that.

Her movie was called ZOM BEE MOO VEE, and it had daemons in it—cloud daemons, the wickedest kind! She used to ask them for magic secrets on a regular basis. After she died, she still looked so alive that the daemons gave her yet another secret: the secret of bringing corpses to life. And so she became alive again. Or at least, as alive as someone who has been dead can get. She also had a book of great power—but I will tell you about that later.

Boy: So where does my grandfather fit into all that? What was his name again?

Nice Old Lady: I haven't told you his name yet. It was Mr. River. He was younger than me, but he had a perfect face, and his beauty made me blind to his faults. It made me respect him, even though he did nothing to deserve it. In fact, I respected him so much that I always called him by his last name. I loved him like one loves the moon: so pretty, so alluring, but distant, too. He used to watch Necrilda's movie all the time. In those days we had things called videotapes—recordings of films contained in black boxes. He had a videotape of ZOM BEE MOO VEE. He would get drunk on orange juice and vodka and watch the movie, drink some more, rewind the videotape and watch it again. "It's no business of yours how much I drink!" he would say. Not his wife's business? Pah!

Sometimes I would watch ZOM BEE MOO VEE with him, trying to figure out why he liked it so much. It was all about a yacht filled with rich young thrillseekers and their trip to the island of Zovemba. Mr. River watched the tape far too much, and somewhere along the line he fell in love with Necrilda.

Boy: But she wasn't even real. And he had you.

Nice Old Lady: He fell in love with a lie, Marcos. It is very easy to fall in love with a lie. I was too real. He saw me when I was sick, he heard my burps and boom-booms, he could even smell my poopies after I went to the bathroom. Reality cannot compete with lies.

Boy: Oh no.

Nice Old Lady: Oh yes. He fell in love with all the lies that were Necrilda Voltaire. And his love served as a bridge, across which she could come and go as she pleased.

Boy: To where?

Nice Old Lady: To here. To the real world.

Boy: I think I hear a car in the driveway.

Nice Old Lady: Oh, your mommy is here to get you. Let me just cover up this old TV.

Boy: Tell me more of the story the next time I see you.

Nice Old Lady: I might as well. You've heard the beginning, you might as well hear the rest.

Boy: Okay, Jiajia. I love you.

Nice Old Lady: I love you, too, Marcos.

* * * *

Transcript 3574b.677.a47:

Nice Old Lady: Hello, my friend. It is me, the Nice Old Lady. You had a good rest, yes?

Boy: Do you always say that to the TV?

Nice Old Lady: Of course. I want it to know who I am. I want it to know I am nice. I am old. I am a lady. And, we are friends. I have talked to it several time since your last visit.

Let me look at your arm. Where did you get those bruises?

Boy: Mom hit me.

Nice Old Lady: Mr. River used to hit me, too. But not before Necrilda sank her claws into him. Before that, he was more like a normal man. Not too good, but not so very bad. Though he did drink too much and watch too much TV.

Boy: Tell me about those claws.

Nice Old Lady: After Necrilda died and came back to life, she had white eyes and hair, purple skin and teeth, and silver claws. And those claws were loaded with a sort of wicked love-poison. Mr. River was her slave, and oh, how he fawned over her. He used to wait until he thought I was asleep, and then he would sneak back into the living room and watch that movie, adoring her. In fact, this is the very TV on which he'd watch it. This TV has seen all the things I am telling you. It used to be my enemy. But really, it had no choice. And now it is my friend, because it has stayed with me. I am a forgiving woman. Where was I in my story...?

Boy: Something about a bridge. Necrilda could come and go.

Nice Old Lady: Oh yes. People in our city, in our neighborhood, started dying left and right. Right and left. Their bodies would be found all dried out, with neat little holes all over them. Necrilda was not a sloppy eater, like most of the living dead. She liked to suck the juices out of her victims through a silver straw.

Boy: Disgusting!

Nice Old Lady: Perhaps, but very efficient. Tidy. Not a drop was wasted.

Boy: Wow. Your husband's name was Mr. River, and he fell in love with a lady who liked to drink blood, and blood is a river. I saw that on a poster for giving blood. Blood is the river of life. That's weird, isn't it?

Nice Old Lady: Necrilda didn't just drink the blood. After she'd sucked out the juices, she would get out her silverware and eat all the nice meat. But yes, what you mentioned was weird. All of life is weird. Why, in my head, I still think I am twenty-four years old. I feel no different than I did way back then. And yet, when I look in the mirror, I see an old woman looking back.

Boy: Do you worry about being dead someday?

Nice Old Lady: Of course. Being dead would be very boring. No wonder Necrilda came back. And no wonder she wanted to get out of her movie. An island full of zombies—not much fun in that. I once said something about that to Mr. River. I said, "Zombies are boring—they just eat and kill. That's not interesting. That's just being an animal." He got so mad he gave me a black eye.

Boy: Why didn't Necrilda eat Mr. River? Or you?

Nice Old Lady: Necrilda wasn't about to feast on her bridge, so Mr. River was safe. As for me—Necrilda was out to steal my body.

Boy: Oh no!

Nice Old Lady: Oh yes. You see, I was very beautiful back then—

Boy: You're still beautiful, Jiajia.

Nice Old Lady: Thank you, Marcos. But not as beautiful as I was then. Men used to flirt with me all the time when I was out shopping or running errands. I really was foolish to stay with Mr. River for as long as I did—but I was young, and young people do foolish things. Except you. You are a very serious boy. Because of your mommy, I think.

I should have left, but my feelings for Mr. River were very strong. I thought I could win back his love against horrible odds. I know now that if you have to fight too much to win someone's love, it may not really be worth winning.

There was also another problem. Mr. River had brought me to this country—like Necrilda, I am from an island. Not Zovemba, of course! I knew very few people in the city. I had nowhere else to go. If I started telling people about zombies, they would just think I was a crazy foreign woman who needed to be locked me up.

Anyway.

As I said, Necrilda wanted to steal my body. One night while I was in my bed, I heard some noises, so I pretended to be asleep—but my eyes were open just the teeniest bit. I saw Necrilda enter the room. She ran over nails lightly, soooo lightly, over my head. Then she stood at the foot of the bed, tapping her purple chin with a long silver nail, and I heard her whisper to herself, "Just the right size. She will do...she will do..."

Boy: But why would she want to steal your body? And how could she do it?

Nice Old Lady: Necrilda was beautiful, in her own hideous way, but after all, zombies cannot go out in broad daylight. The sun would do them harm, as would all the frightened citizens. She needed a new body to travel freely in the real world.

As for 'how'... When characters in horror movies want different bodies, they always do the same thing. They switch brains. My skull was just the right size to hold her evil zombie brain.

Boy: Switch brains? How does that work?

Nice Old Lady: A mad scientist has to perform the operation. He opens up both heads and then, well—switches the brains around.

Boy: Did Necrilda know any mad scientists?

Nice Old Lady: Before I answer that, I do want to tell you this... I figured out all of these things, and I did it by keeping my eyes open. Observing. I did not ask Mr. River a single question. A woman cannot ask her husband, "Darling, are you in love with a dead woman from a movie?" I read the articles in the paper about all the mysterious deaths. I spied on Mr. River—usually late at night, when he thought I was in bed asleep. A few times I saw him talking in the living room with that horrible creature, talking in the dark by the pale blue light of the TV screen. I could not hear what they were saying, so I took to hiding tape recorders. When he was out of the house, I would search for the videotape of ZOM BEE MOO VEE so I could destroy it, but I could never find it. Either he hid it well or he had it with him at all times.

It is a horrible thing, to live in a home with someone you cannot trust. Someone who means you harm.

Boy: I know.

Nice Old Lady: Ah, I hear your mommy's car. I will tell you about the brain-switching next time.

Boy: I love you, Jiajia.

Nice Old Lady: I love you, too, Marcos.

* * * *

Transcript 3574b.677.a72:

Nice Old Lady: Hello, my friend. It is me, the Nice Old Lady. You had a good rest, yes?

Boy: So how come you'll only tell me about Necrilda in front of the TV? I thought you didn't like me to be in this room.

Nice Old Lady: Well, the only reason I didn't want you in here was because of the TV. But you've seen it now, and you are keeping my secret, dear boy that you are. People are still scared of these things, you know. They think of them as the living dead, for even when TVs are unplugged, they still function to some strange degree.

I'm telling you the story in front of the TV because the machine hears everything I say, and I believe my words are being recorded or transcribed. And I would like there to be a record somewhere, telling the world about Necrilda and her zombie ways. Now where did I leave off?

Boy: Necrilda wanted to switch brains with you.

Nice Old Lady: Ah. That was when Mr. River started watching lots of old movies with mad scientists in them. Mad scientists doing all sorts of horrible, bloody things. Bringing dead people back to life, or else stitching together parts from different people and bringing the patchwork people back, to walk and scream and kill. Switching people brains with monkey brains, or robot brains, or alien brains. One of the scientists even put big sharp cleaver-hands on crazy people, so they could go out and chop up everybody. I figured out that Mr. River was looking for just for right mad scientist to do the job.

Boy: But how would they get the doctor out of his movie to do the surgery?

Nice Old Lady: That puzzled me, too... For a while. That was when I started hiding tape recorders so that I could hear what Mr. River and his dead whore had to say to each other. Oh, I said that bad word again. Sorry.

Boy: That's okay. Go on with the story.

Nice Old Lady: Necrilda had a horrible voice. It sounded like how a cat's voice might sound, if a cat could talk. All syrupy mews and scratchy growls and dry hissing. An animal voice. She told Mr. River that in the church on zombie island was a book of spells. Spells using the magic of the cloud daemons. In the past, she'd used this magic to bring victims—fresh meat—to the island. Some spells helped her to leave the island for short periods of time. Once she used the book to turn into a real person for a short while. The cloud daemons are fickle. There is no telling how long a spell might work. That was the biggest reason for her to want to steal my real human body. She was afraid the cloud daemons might decide to make her dead again.

Boy: A zombie can be scared?

Nice Old Lady: Don't be so surprised. The future is always uncertain—full of hurtful, sometimes deadly puzzles—so is it any surprise that even the living dead might know fear? Necrilda was a victim, too. A victim of capricious fate. Like me. Like you.

Around that time, I learned I was going to have a baby. Your mommy. I think she has her troubles in the head now because I was so scared back then.

Boy: I don't understand.

Nice Old Lady: My own mommy used to say my brother was hairy because she was scared by a spider when she was carrying him. Maybe it is like that. Maybe your mommy is so crazy now because back then, when she was inside me, I was out of my mind with fright.

Boy: I don't think so. I bet she got all her craziness from Mr. River. You're nice. I wish I could live with you.

Nice Old Lady: I wish you could, too. I get very lonely, and a TV is no substitute for my Marcos.

I remember one night, I was walking home late from the store—I'd gone to buy toilet paper. Mr. River was using the car, so I had to walk. Toilet paper is one thing you cannot wait until the next day for, and I was too embarrassed to go to a neighbor and ask for some. While I was at the store, I saw some newspapers on sale, and the headlines: BLOODLESS BODIES BAFFLE POLICE. I suppose they would! I knew what was happening, and I knew what the newspapers, or maybe the police, didn't dare to mention.

They didn't mention that Necrilda had a great appetite, and that those bloodless bodies were missing big chunks here and there. Here is something I learned from the movie: if Necrilda does not want one of her victims to come back from the dead—for being a zombie is a disease, and a contagious one, too, transmitted by bites—she will eat both the brain and the heart. And that she did. I suppose she did not want zombies wandering around in the real world, because it would soon be her home—or so she hoped.

I remember well that night and my walk home. I'd bought a few food items, too, so it wouldn't look like I'd only needed toilet paper. Walking past an alley, a dark, stinking alley, I heard a horrible echoing moan, like someone dying. I did not want to go down the alley, with broken glass and garbage everywhere, and danger, too—but someone was hurt. So I called out, "Are you okay? Do you need an ambulance? The police?" I took a few steps, just a few, into the alley to see if I could spot the trouble. I was so scared, I thought I was going to soil myself. I felt breathless—I wanted to gasp for air, but that would have made too much noise. I had to hear what was going on.

I waited for a minute, listening. Perhaps I had just imagined those sounds.

Then, with a great Bang!, the lid of a dumpster flew open. Out of that filthy metal box flew the shredded and bruised remains of some poor old bum. The ruined body hit a building with a soggy thud, then slid into the piles of trash below. My throat felt as dry as sandpaper—there was a scream in me, but it came out as a ragged gasp.

Standing in the dumpster, with a dripping heart in one hand, was Necrilda Voltaire.

Boy: Oh no!

Nice Old Lady: Oh yes. She simply looked at me, taking bites out of that heart as though it were an apple. For the moment, she had abandoned the knife and fork she used in her movies.

"I know you are spying on me," she said in her vicious cat's-voice, "for I am spying on you, too. David will be mine, you little fool, and so will your body and your baby."

How that enraged me! Not that she was spying on me ... not that she had designs on my life and my baby's, too ... but that she dared to call my husband by his first name when talking to me.

What a trivial thing! And yet it was infuriating. The anger sent all the fear flying out of my mind, and I suddenly realized that I had the upper hand. She wanted to possess my beautiful face and body, so she wouldn't dare to injure me. I dropped my groceries and picked up a broken chunk of brick.

Boy: Did you hurt her?

Nice Old Lady: You will find out the next time you visit—I just heard your mommy slam her car door. Would you like to take home some of the cookies we made? That was very sweet of you to help your old Jiajia with her cooking this morning.

Boy: No problem. That was fun. I love you, Jiajia.

Nice Old Lady: I love you, too, Marcos. Run along, I'll be with you in a minute.

Boy: Okay.

Nice Old Lady: My friend, I hope you like Marcos. I feel so sad for him—he doesn't have a daddy, and his mommy is too drunk and crazy. He's really all I've got, besides you. I love him with all my heart. But I don't want you to be jealous. I love you, too, you know. Now I will put your cloth back over you, so you can sleep.

* * * *

Transcript 3574b.677.a98:

Nice Old Lady: Hello, my friend. It is me, the Nice Old Lady. You had a good rest, yes?

Boy: Hello, TV. I'm your friend Marcos. Jiajia's the only one who ever calls me that, but you can, too, if you want.

Nice Old Lady: Now where was I in my story?

Marcos: First we should talk about what Mom said to me on the way here. She doesn't want to bring me over here any more. She says it's too much work.

Nice Old Lady: Your mommy is too lazy for words. I will figure out something, don't let it worry you. Now, the story, let me think...

Marcos: You were going to hit Necrilda with a brick.

Nice Old Lady: And so I did! I leaned over the edge of that dumpster and hit her on the shoulder, the arm, and finally right in the face. Her bright silver blood was spurting everywhere, and I backed away so it didn't splash on me.

She screamed and screamed like the very devil in Hell, but she didn't lay a single claw on me. She climbed out of that dumpster, quick as a spider, and slipped off into the night.

It was then I finally decided that I should not go home. My anger had restored my senses. I realized what a fool I had been all that time. Why, if I'd have smashed the VCR while Mr. River had been watching that horrible movie, destroying the tape, I could have avoided that whole nightmare. Ah, but wisdom always comes too late. I decided I would find a shelter for ladies—that's where I would spend the night. In the morning, I would figure out what to do with the rest of my life.

Marcos: Well, I guess you didn't die, since you're telling me the story now.

Nice Old Lady: Good point. My Marcos is as bright as a penny—or a dime, those are even brighter. I looked in the phonebook, found the address of a shelter, and took a taxi cab there. The shelter was part of a church program, and the nun who talked with me was very kind. I did not mention zombies, of course—I said my bad husband had a girlfriend who was even worse. And that was the truth, no lie in that.

So I went to bed in a nice little room in the shelter. When I woke up, I was on Zovemba.

Marcos: What! How did that happen?

Nice Old Lady: Mr. River must have decided upon the mad scientist for the brain switch that very night. With the choice made, Necrilda went back to Zovemba and performed her ritual for spiriting people into ZOM BEE MOO VEE. When I opened my eyes, I was in the old church on the island. Necrilda was there, all bruised and bloody, and Mr. River, and a tall, distinguished man in a stained lab coat. He had yellow eyes and a scar on his face that ran from his chin in a thin zigzag up to his forehead.

Marcos: What movie was he from?

Nice Old Lady: I can't remember. But the name of his character was Dr. DeMonstra. Not only was he a mad scientist, but he was also part demon and part monster.

They tied me up and carried me to a chamber at the top of the church. My ears were filled with a loud, low humming, like the sound of some great machine. As they carried me up the stairs, I could see glimpses here and there out of some of the windows—glimpses of dark trees under a full moon. Glimpses of needle-mouthed purple zombies crouched in the branches. Zovemba is a terrible place, Marcos.

When we reached the chamber, I saw that the room was lined along the walls—not with lab equipment—but rather, TV sets, all with purple zombies capering on their screens. I think now that the humming sound must have been some sort of generator powering those TVs, since Zovemba surely has never had electricity.

Marcos: What were all the TVs for?

Nice Old Lady: To give power to Necrilda's vile spells. To create fields of wild energy. And perhaps, to amuse the capricious cloud daemons. They strapped me down to a lab table—Mr. River was drunk as a dog, and very rough with me. Always drunk wherever he went, even that strange island Hell.

Necrilda climbed up onto the table and rested next to me. She grinned at me with her purple teeth—many of them were broken. Her nose was broken, too, and caked with blood. They strapped her down very lightly—just enough to keep her in place during the operation. And they began to shave her head. The brain switch was about to begin.

Marcos: Oh no!

Nice Old Lady: Oh yes! Then suddenly, on top of one of the TVs, I saw it.

Marcos: What was that?

Nice Old Lady: The book! The book of spells that was the key to Necrilda's power.

Marcos: But you were strapped down. You couldn't get to it.

Nice Old Lady: I did not need to. You forget, I was very beautiful back then. Necrilda had her powers and I had mine. I said to the mad scientist, "Darling, that book over there is the secret to this zombie whore's power. Take it, my dear, and you and I can be rid of these two idiots."

Dr. DeMonstra might have been part demon and part monster, but he was still a man. A lonely, misunderstood man who surely had never known a woman's touch. A bright fire sprang up in his yellow eyes. "My beauty," he cried, "I like the way you think!" And quick as a flash, he tightened Necrilda's straps. Then he punched drunken Mr. River right in the middle of his pretty face.

Marcos: Serves the two of them right! What happened then?

Nice Old Lady: Oh, there was a brain switch, but not between your dear Jiajia and that purple bitch. Oh, I said another bad word! Sorry, my boy. I should not say such things. I wouldn't want you using such awful language in polite company.

Marcos: I won't. So whose brains got switched?

Nice Old Lady: Necrilda Voltaire and Mr. River. To this day they are both still on the island of Zovemba. They can never leave, for Mr. River was the bridge—but only when he was in the real world. Plus, before I left, I took the book with me, so they could not do any more magic.

Marcos: But what about Dr. Demonstra?

Nice Old Lady: Ah, the dear doctor! He turned out to be a very pleasant, attentive companion. We returned to the real world, where I bought him some nice clothes and some sunglasses to cover those eyes. He really looked rather dashing—I suggested that he should tell folks the scar was from a sword fight. I did not want another man with a pretty face—not after Mr. River. All Dr. DeMonstra needed was someone to love him and think the world of him. We paid an old priest to marry us in secret—it was not a marriage the government knew about, since the doctor had no identity in the real world.

Marcos: Where is he now?

Nice Old Lady: In a grave. He was hit by a taxi cab. It turned out the driver was drunk. I thought I, too, would die. I thought all my tears would make my body dry out until it was a pile of sand. Our love had been an impossibility come true. And then some fool with a bottle had to spoil it all.

Marcos: Mom is a fool with a bottle.

Nice Old Lady: Yes, I know. Plug in the TV, my boy.

Marcos: Oh! Okay—but why?

Nice Old Lady: We shall be using its power. Look what I have here— the book. Necrilda's book of spells. I have been studying its mysteries all these years, and I'm finally ready to use it. Your mommy will be here very soon. When she arrives, we'll send her into some movie, so she can never keep us apart. Once she is gone you can stay with me.

Marcos: Jiajia, what a wonderful idea! But where should we send her?

Nice Old Lady: A children's movie. Maybe a cartoon. A place without pain. A place where all the bottles contain soda pop.

Marcos: She probably won't like it there.

Nice Old Lady: Or maybe it will be perfect for her. Sometimes a change—any kind of change—can only be for the best. Ah, I hear her car! Let me just find the right page, and then... Magic time.

Marcos: I love you, Jiajia.

Nice Old Lady: I love you, too, Marcos.

ZOM BEE CEE DEE

(with Michael McCarty)

Necrilda Voltaire, Zombie Princess of the island of Zovemba, had grown weary of starring in the horror movie of her life. She was even tired of the soundtrack, which bellowed ZOM BEE MOO VEE, ZOM BEE MOO VEE every time a hapless victim was about to get eaten—usually by her.

"But you have every reason to be happy," said Red Eye, the hunch-backed dwarf-cyclops who served as her henchman. He had washed up on the island with the ruins of a storm-wrecked ship a year earlier. She employed him only because he was far too ugly to eat. "You rule the living dead. You have your own island. You are the star of your own movie. You have the cloud daemons at your beck and call. Yes, you should be happy."

Necrilda stared at him with her star-white eyes and gnashed her purple teeth. "Do I look like I care about happiness?" She tapped her purple chin with a silver finger. "I am bored. Horribly bored."

"I'd have thought that brain transplant would have been enough excitement for you," her servant said.

At one point in her adventures, shortly before Red Eye had appeared, a mad scientist had switched Necrilda's brain with that of a living man. But her undead body had rejected the foreign living organ—and without a brain, her body had died. Meanwhile, the aggressive DNA from her real undead brain had worked itself into her new living body, killing it and then refashioning it into an undead facsimile of her old body. So now she was right back where she had started—except that she no longer had her magic book. A human had stolen her book while she was being detained by the transplant. And while she was still able to ask the cloud daemons for favors, the loss of the book severely limited the scope of her powers.

The Zombie Princess sighed heavily. "Red Eye, I am so very tired of horror movies. And not just my own. All horror movies. Yapping were-wolves. Mummies and their filthy bandages. Ancient vampires with false fangs and bumbling Frankenstein monsters with loose stitches. They're all so predictable."

"But Princess," Red Eye moaned. "Where else would you go? What else would you do?"

"Why not a private eye thriller?" she mused. "Picture me in a trench-coat trying to solve a mystery..."

Her henchman thought about that concept for a moment. "I hate to say it, Princess ... but it is not you."

"Then perhaps something else," Necrilda said. "But right now, I'm going for a walk. Your naysaying has grown tiresome, just like this movie."

In truth, Necrilda was pleased with many aspects of dwelling in the dimension of movies. She never grew old, and she had power and prestige. If only she could find a way to change her own storyline—yes, that would be marvelous. That would provide her with more, more, so many more stylish adventures. For existence was nothing without style.

She was walking on the moonlit beach, pondering her sad yet curiously hectic afterlife, when she heard it. Happy music. The steady beat of tin drums, maracas and bongos. Music that made her hips start to sway.

A yacht, docked near the shore of Zovemba, was having a late-night party. She saw the captain and his vivacious blonde passenger sharing champagne on deck, listening to tapes of a reggae band.

She swam toward the yacht. When she reached the vessel, she climbed up onto the deck and hid in the shadows.

She listened as the captain explained to his companion about his career: he wrote scripts for movies. He then went on to state that the young lady would be perfect for his next feature film, Satan's School for Manicurists.

As she killed the humans and sucked out their juices with a silver straw, Necrilda pondered her own career options. This fat human male was a writer—perhaps she should try her hand at writing, too. She was quick-minded and creative—it might be fun. And she did need more fun in her life. After sucking out the juices, Necrilda used her silver knife and fork to eat the best bits. Eating these key parts—especially the brain and heart—prevented her victims from returning to life. And that was just as well: without those two organs, a body would only be fit for politics anyway.

Later that night, she raised her hands and eyes to the skies and asked the cloud daemons to give her the script to ZOM BEE MOO VEE. The daemons gazed into her eyes—those perfect, savage eyes—and found they could not resist. Her steamroller beauty flattened their will, and within seconds, the script floated into her slender hands.

Necrilda now had a new magic book—and it was ten-thousand times more powerful than her old one.

* * * *

As her first edit, Necrilda changed her movie's setting from the island of Zovemba to Los Angeles in the year 2050. She made Red Eye her agent instead of her slave—though the roles were really about the same. There were plenty of bands in L.A.: heavy-metal bands, Goth bands, industrial bands, Latin bands, oldie cover bands, swing bands, country bands, punk bands. But not even the most extreme of those genres could be led by a zombie singer with purple skin and teeth, star-white eyes and hair, and razor-sharp silver fingernails. It was clear that a new type of pop music was needed.

Undead Rock.

She added more characters to the script and formed her own band—Abra Cadaver.

She then brought back some of the greatest musicians of all time. In life, some had been black, some had been white—but in death, they were all purple. Louie Armstrong on trumpet. Liberace on keyboards. Jimi Hendrix on guitar. Keith Moon on drums. And vocals by Necrilda herself.

The voice of the zombie princess had an astonishing range. One of Necrilda's high notes shattered all the window panes within a block of the boarded-up warehouse where the band practiced. That same note also caused the steel strings of Hendrix's guitar to snap, and it popped all of Moon's drum membranes.

Clearly the band needed more durable instruments. So Necrilda scribbled a few notes in the margins of the script, listing what they needed—and the fresh gear appeared. The guitar was made from a Tyrannosaurus' spine, laced with barb-wire strings. The drums were fashioned out of huge toxic waste canisters. The piano was a marble sarcophagus with dried, twisted intestines as strings. The trumpet was a souped-up tornado warning siren. Their sturdy new instruments were so powerful, the band could easily have drowned out the bomb explosions of World War III.

Next, Necrilda began writing new material. Her Undead Rock decompositions included such numbers as "I Chews You Tonight," "You Spin Me Round (On A Rotisserie)" and "Even Purple Chicks Get The Blues."

Every now and then she would listen to the radio, to see what sort of songs were popular at the time. It seemed like every station was playing a singer named Hagdallah. All the music magazines Red Eye brought to her featured this pop diva. Hagdallah was a tall, thin, huge-breasted albino woman, with drawn-on black eyebrows, startling pink eyes and collagen-fattened lips. Hagdallah's first CD, a worldwide hit, was entitled *Papa, Don't Let Your Baby Grow Up To Be A Crack-Whore*.

One evening, after Necrilda and the band had put in several hours of practice, Red Eye showed up with some good news. "Necrilda baby!" The troll now wore a black-velvet suit, smoked Cuban cigars, and sported a silver-tinted monocle. "I've been shopping the demo tapes around. Ongan Records wants to sign you."

"That's marvelous, Red Eye," Necrilda said. "I knew I had a good reason for not feeding you to my undead island followers. That reminds me... I'll need to write them into the script as roadies. They're probably sick of that island, too." She picked up her pen, dashed off a few more notes in the margins, and the islanders appeared—dozens of sinewy purple creatures with bandannas tied around their heads, all wearing silver sunglasses and black t-shirts emblazoned with ABRA CADAVER in jagged silver letters.

"To kick off the release of the CD, they want you to perform a huge debut concert," Red Eye said.

"Excellent," the Zombie Princess replied. "But let's not hold it in the city. I want a setting with a little more drama..." She scribbled a few more notes in the script.

Suddenly an army officer with five rows of medals entered the warehouse. "Hello, I'm Commander Swenson, and—well, I'm not quite sure why I'm here."

"You'd like me to put on a concert on one of your big old battleships," Necrilda purred, writing down a few more notes.

"Oh!" His eyes lit up with understanding. "Yes, that's right. A big concert. I don't remember talking with you before now, but—"

Necrilda penned a few words more.

"Wait a minute," the Commander said, "yes, we've been talking about it for months. When would you like to hold the concert?"

"Halloween, of course," Necrilda said.

Red Eye gasped. "That won't work!"

Necrilda picked him up by his lapels and threw him into a stack of old boxes in a corner of the warehouse. "I'm sorry, I didn't hear you. What did you say?"

Red Eye brushed dust off his jacket. "Hagdallah is going to be in town Halloween and that's when she's holding her concert."

Necrilda wrote more in the script. Red Eye only shook his head.

"Editing won't do you any good this time," he said, backing away as she tried to grab for his lapels. He climbed up a stack of wooden pallets, out of her reach. "I hate to tell you this, but I've been doing a little snooping and I've found out that Hagdallah has just as much power as you."

"Impossible!" Necrilda raked at the pallets with her nails. "How can that be?"

"She's a sea-witch," the one-eyed man said. "She gets her power from the water daemons. So you can't hold your concert on Halloween and you certainly can't do it on a battleship. The water is her territory."

"Nonsense! I am an island princess. I've lived my life looking out over the ocean. I am not afraid of sea-witches or water daemons. I can do whatever I want, whenever I want." Necrilda stared up at her hunched henchman. "Come down from there. Where is this Hagdallah creature going to hold her performance?"

"She's big into charities," the agent said, climbing down but keeping a wary eye on his boss. "There's a big new amphitheatre downtown—the Keanu Reeves Memorial Arts Center—that holds ballet classes for the blind. That's where she will be doing her concert."

The singer turned toward Commander Swenson. "My good man, I would imagine your battleship is fully armed even in times of peace, yes?"

The military man nodded. "Certainly. We have to be ready to defend our nation at a moment's notice. Why do you ask?"

Necrilda shrugged her slender shoulders. "Just curious."

* * * *

Ongan Records spared no expense to prepare for the concert, which was to be the starting point of Abra Cadaver's ZOM BEE CEE DEE Tour. Commercials ran on all media for weeks, and the concert sold out quickly. They flew in members of the press from all over the country. Fireworks exploded and laser lights lit up the sky, spelling out NECRILDA in bright purple streaks. Arrangements had been made to broadcast the concert live on pay-for-view cable. Necrilda had claimed her rightful place among single-named celebrities, such as Cher, Oprah, Prince (before he changed his name into that inexplicable symbol), and Glugg, the talking dolphin and fashion consultant created by the scientists of Calvin Klein Industries in 2035. The concert started with a heartfelt love ballad, "ZOM BEE LAY DEE."

"Don't wanna star in a ZOM BEE MOO VEE," Necrilda sang. "Don't put me in no ZOM BEE TEE VEE. Just wanna sing on a ZOM BEE CEE DEE. It's a blast for you and a BLASPHEMY!" Her zombie flyboys, swirling gracefully around her, flashed big purple smiles as they joined in on the chorus—"ZOM BEE LAY DEE needs love tonight. ZOM BEE LAY DEE gettin' down tonight. ZOM BEE LAY DEE wants to feel so right. ZOM BEE LAY DEE gonna give you a bite!"

Song after song, Abra Cadaver rocked the boat. Necrilda belted out some of her newest material, including "Eat Your Meat To The Beat," "Rigor Mortis Mama," and "Zombie See, Zombie Chew."

Eventually Necrilda did what all divas do near the middle of their concerts: she quickly went to change costumes. The band played on. Jimi Hendrix played a blistering guitar solo so ferocious, so frenzied and so loud, it could wake the dead.

In fact, it did.

And because the program was being broadcast live, the wavelengths of the music were in the air everywhere.

Morgue cadavers, dead bums in alleys, recently buried corpses in graveyards and millions of other fresh stiffs were reanimated. They stirred, stretched, and turned purple. They opened their eyes, revealing shining star-white orbs. They grinned ravenously and hit the streets en masse.

Unfortunately for the folks at the Hagdallah concert, the Keanu Reeves Memorial Arts Center was on the same street as a hospital and an upscale cemetery.

Hagdallah was in the middle of her hit single, "Dirty Girls Do It In Public Toilets," when the zombies stormed into the amphitheatre. Dead, naked patients with toe-tags and deceased dowagers in silk gowns rushed to feast on pulsing, living flesh.

Johnny LaSynn, one of Hagdallah's back-up singers, grabbed the sea-witch by the arm. "My God, what are those purple creatures? They kind of look like that new singer, Necri—"

The albino woman punched him in the mouth. "Don't you dare say that name in my presence!" she cried. "Oh, I can't believe it. I was going to be a good girl and not make trouble for her, what with her being new and all—and look what she does! I wondered if she was a real zombie or not. Well, this sure answers my question. That purple bitch has sent an undead army to screw up my concert. Well, I'll show her!"

She grabbed Johnny by the arm and dragged him off the stage. "Come on, you. Help me cast a revenge spell."

She led him to the bathroom in her dressing room and pointed at the toilet. "Okay, you. Make pee-pee."

He bit his lower lip. "Right now? In front of you?"

She rolled her eyes. "It's a ritual, okay? You have to do your part while I contact the water daemons. Now squeeze that bladder before you make me madder!"

* * * *

Necrilda, unaware of the zombie outbreak on land, was thoroughly pissed off when hot torrents of urine began to fall from the night sky. Her entire audience ran for cover below deck.

"That Hagdallah!" she screamed. She was in the captain's cabin with Red Eye, and both of them were drenched with hot yellow stink. "Here I thought she was actually going to leave me be! Well, two can play at this game!" She pointed at her agent. "You! Fire the big guns at the Keanu Reeves Memorial Arts Center."

"Why don't you just write it in the script?" he said.

"The script!" Necrilda gnashed her teeth. "I left it in a duffel bag behind the stage."

"But it's an open-air stage. No roof." Red Eye whispered.

"Yes, Einstein, I realize that."

"Was the duffel bag zipped shut?"

Necrilda shook her head. "The zipper was caught on a little piece of fabric."

Red Eye winced. "I hate to ask this, but have you been using a fountain pen or a ballpoint with waterproof ink?"

A single tear rolled down her cheek. "I'm a princess. I like fountain pens. They're more ... royal."

"Oh."

They slowly walked to the window of the cabin and looked out. By this time, Hagdallah had thought up another revenge spell—one inspired by the calamari she'd had for lunch —and winged squids were attacking the battleship. One of the squids was reaching into a doorway, pulling out concertgoers and throwing them to the other winged monstrosities to eat.

"Is it my imagination, or is the room starting to spin?" Red Eye said.

Necrilda sighed. "This entire alternate reality is based on my notes in that copy of the script. And now those notes are being washed away."

The sky, the squids, the ship and everything in sight began to waver. The walls of the cabin faded away. Red Eye and Necrilda found themselves floating through a murky void of swirling mists. For a moment, Necrilda caught a glimpse of the script as it floated serenely back to the cloud daemons.

"I think I've had enough of the music industry," Necrilda said.

"Yeah. It's a big thrill at first," Red Eye said, "but in the end, you just get pissed on."

A moment later they were back on the beach of Zovemba. It was a sunny day, and another yacht-load of rich young thrillseekers were swimming ashore to inspect the island.

"Oh, look," Red Eye said. "Here comes your dinner."

Necrilda smiled. "Listen. What do you hear?"

The hunchback cocked an ear up toward the clouds. "The soundtrack has changed."

From nowhere and everywhere came the chorus—soft at first, then louder, much louder. Delighted, Necrilda and Red Eye began to dance.

"ZOM BEE LAY DEE needs love tonight. ZOM BEE LAY DEE gettin' down tonight. ZOM BEE LAY DEE wants to feel so right. ZOM BEE LAY DEE gonna give you a bite!"

ZOM BEE DEE VEE DEE

I. HellCo Cares

Helping.

Everyone.

Live.

Life.

That's what HellCo stands for.

Thank you for your interest in our company. As a potential investor, we feel that you are entitled to a special level of insight regarding our goals and philosophies. This DVD presentation has been prepared to answer any questions you may have about our wide range of products and services.

Because HellCo cares.

II. Meet Ms. Huske

Ms. Huske joined our company three years ago, but already her staff members think she has been their boss forever.

Or maybe it just feels that way.

Ms. Huske is in charge of Promotions. She is quite petite, but don't let her tiny hands and delicate features fool you. Her predecessor wore out like an old tire, coming part in strips. But Ms. Huske is made of sterner stuff. Her hard, black eyes are like those of a spider—glossy, pitiless and hungry. She works from eight to eight, then takes home papers to read and tells her child to please leave Mommy alone, because Mommy needs to concentrate. No clock-watcher, our Ms. Huske.

Ms. Huske used to comment on the light-purple cast of some employee complexions. She also used to ask why the televisions in the employee break rooms only show ZOM BEE MOO VEE, an old horror movie about the cannibal princess of Zombie Island.

Ms. Huske has since been told to disregard such observations. That knowledge will come to her in due time.

Ms. Huske's goal is to improve the department. The staff had a morale problem—they were all too interested in the world outside of work. So she gave them all more to do, and told them to enjoy it. Or else. Discipline, after all, is an important part of the big picture at HellCo.

The staff members hate Ms. Huske, but that is to be expected. At least their morale has improved. Now, they all get together after work and laugh over drinks, as they compare notes on the things they've dipped in her coffee and rubbed on the rim of her cup while she was off visiting the lady's room. They have discovered the joys of team spirit.

A few weeks ago, our surveillance cameras caught Ms. Huske staring at herself in an employee washroom mirror. No doubt she was wondering about the changing hue of her own complexion.

Soon, she too shall discover the marvelous benefits of team spirit.

III. Meet Fun-Time Fuzzy

Fun-Time Fuzzy is a man-sized purple kitten—the company mascot.

His job is to amuse the employees with his jolly antics, and to attend social events in the community, playing with the kids, letting folks of all ages know ...

HellCo cares.

Inside that fake-fur body-suit and oversized mask, you'll find a gentleman named Frank who doesn't mind the occasional drinky-winky.

Frank's had that job for fifteen years, and has had only two raises—small ones at that. But you know, he's lucky to have that job. Or so we tell him.

It sure is funny when Fun-Time Fuzzy staggers down the street. It's a good thing folks can't smell his breath behind that big mask.

HellCo cares, and so does Frank. He cares that five-thirty to six-thirty is Two-For-One Happy Hour at Ernie's Brew-Ha-Ha, the roadside bar two miles down from the city dump.

Deep down, Fun-Time Fuzzy is horribly afraid of the company that gives him his drink money.

But at least the booze helps him to forget.

In time, he shall make a very special contribution to HellCo.

Whether he likes it or not.

IV. Meet Mr. Scarr

Mr. Scarr is in charge of Distribution. He makes sure that all of HellCo's wonderful products can be purchased at stores everywhere. Because HellCo wants to Help Everyone Live Life.

All of those fine products are packaged in deep purple boxes and bottles with bright silver letters in a typestyle specially designed by a woman who now plays with her feces in a locked, padded room.

Mr. Scarr is rather short, rather fat, and rather old. And he'd rather be working somewhere else, but he's set in his ways, so he'll stay right where he is, thank you very much.

Sometimes Mr. Scarr wakes up screaming, because he knows that somewhere, out there, a child is putting pins in a doll he or she calls Daddy—because earlier that day, that precious urchin ate a high-protein snack bar that came in a purple wrapper.

Last week in his office, Mr. Scarr placed the wee round mouth of a pistol between his own lips. But he didn't pull the trigger. No, he simply put the gun away with a weary sigh.

Mr. Scarr knows—oh yes, he knows, he knows, he knows—that living or dead, he still has a job to do.

V. Meet Nurse Krumbell

Nurse Krumbell is named Employee of the Month at HellCo five to seven times each year. She isn't really a nurse, but she wears the outfit, and her name-tag says she's a nurse. It maintains that she's OLIVIA KRUMBELL, RN and that's all that matters.

Nurse Krumbell is a very tiny lady, about as tall and slender as an eight-year-old. But she has a very old face. She makes sure that all the employees receive their shots, and she checks everything served in the employee cafeteria. If necessary, she'll add a few vitamins to the entrees. Well, she calls them vitamins, and that's close enough.

HellCo provides such thoughtful employee health benefits: shots of purple ooze from purple bottles with silver letters, and vitamins in powder form—purple powder from purple envelopes with silver letters that don't get too specific regarding the contents.

At the end of the day, Nurse Krumbell crawls under her desk, goes to sleep and dreams of purple skies with silver stars.

Sleep well, Nurse Krumbell.

VI. Meet Our CEO, Mr. Pnugg

At the end of the Administrative Corridor is the office of Mr. Pnugg, the Founder and Chief Executive Officer of HellCo. He is ninety-seven years old, and yet in many ways, he still maintains the vitality of youth. His office is always kept jungle-hot.

One day, years and years ago, when Mr. Pnugg was a little boy, his filthy-rich Dad and Mama took him with them on a cruise, quite exotic, so lovely—or at least, right up to but not including the end.

The ship stopped at six different islands, and the last one was called Zovemba.

Zovemba had once been a delightful island paradise, but then something had happened. And that particular event had taken place just a few days before the ship docked there.

The island's ruler, the princess Necrilda Voltaire, had taken her own life, out in a field near a pretty stream. Then the cloud daemons—good friends of hers—had noticed her outstretched arms. Mistaking rigor mortis for a beseeching gesture, they'd given her something that wasn't actually life ... but still, it needed nourishment.

Generous Necrilda passed on this gift to all her subjects.

All the ship's passengers, the jolly fat businessmen and their wives, were eaten by the citizens of Zovemba, now known as Zombie Island.

All except one.

Little Winston Pnugg was spared. Because Necrilda wanted to try out an experiment.

Necrilda has purple skin, star-white eyes and silver fingernails. And she struck one of those slender, silver nails through her chest, into her heart, and then slid that bloodied, petite dagger into Winston's ear, all the way to his brain.

Since then, that ear has been able to hear the low, distant roar of the ocean, every minute of the day, every day of the year. But he's used to it. That ear hears one other thing, too. A woman's voice. It's only a whisper, really, but together with the ocean, it utterly fills his head.

He is rich. Powerful, too—in more ways than his underlings could ever guess. His desk faces west, toward Zombie Island, so far away. And he stares at the west wall for hours.

Every now and then he nods, as though being told what to do, even though he is alone, all alone, staring and sweating, sweating and staring. He sees something and it isn't a wall.

VII. Meet Scooter

Scooter is seven years old and he loves, loves, loves his Commander Crunch-A-Munch cereal. It's easy to spot on the shelf in the grocery store, since it's the only cereal that comes in a purple box. He gobbles down a big bowlful every morning, and he loves the way it makes the milk turn purple.

Scooter think Commander Crunch-A-Munch is so cool, with his big purple hat and purple coat with silver buttons. He wishes that the Commander was his daddy. He doesn't have a daddy—that guy left a few years ago. Now he just has a mommy, and she won't eat Commander Crunch-A-Munch cereal—at least, not on purpose. Scooter hides little bits of it in all the leftovers in the refrigerator.

He puts other stuff in the leftovers, too. Little bits of dead things he's found in the yard.

His mother's name, by the way, is Melissa Huske.

VIII. Meet Earl Jabowski

Earl Jabowski is sixty-three, bald, red-faced, overweight, diabetic—he has a hard time staying away from the doughnuts in the break room—and a chain-smoker.

He can keep a secret, too.

He has never told anyone about all the secrets he has seen and heard at HellCo over the years. He says to himself: I'm not one of those god-damn TV news pretty-boys. I don't have to yap about every goddamn thing I see and hear.

For the record, yapping is not encouraged at HellCo.

He died a week ago—fell down a staircase and broke his neck. But Nurse Krumbell gave him some medicine and now he's fine. His face is more purple than red.

And he doesn't say anything to himself any more.

He just laughs softly.

IX. Meet Necrilda Voltaire

On an island far away, in the Great Cave, the Princess of the Hungry Dead sits by a purple fire, staring into the flames.

She ponders weighty business matters as she stares, her star-white eyes rolling thoughtfully in their sockets. Her lips move ever so slightly as she whispers directives to—

To who? She is alone in the cave. Nevertheless, somewhere, someone is listening. Listening and nodding.

She doesn't have any real management training, but that's okay. She is a predator, and predators know their business.

X. Let's See How Ms. Huske Is Doing

Ms. Huske has been with the company for three years now and my, how her attitude has changed.

She's not a slave-driving bitch any more. She's happy and hungry and purple, just like all the other employees and most of the folks who buy products in purple packages. People love HellCo products. They just can't get enough of them—or of meat, living meat, rich with hot blood.

And speaking of love, tomorrow Ms. Huske is going to marry Mr. Pnugg. True, he's quite a bit older, and he calls her Necrilda sometimes, but still, she's pretty sure he's the guy for her.

It isn't going to be a customary church wedding. The ceremony—more of a ritual, really—will be presided over by Nurse Krumbell by the silver light of thirteen purple candles in the basement.

Afterward, the guests will eat Fun-Time Fuzzy.

HellCo.
We're changing the world one purchase at a time.
Helping.
Everyone.
Live.
Life. True, it's not Life as most people know it, but hey, things change. We've all got to push the purple envelope. Think outside the pine box.

HellCo cares. And woe to those who do not care for HellCo.

You, as a potential investor, have some key choices to make. Join us, or ignore us and find yourself on the menu.

Invest or die.

Eat or be eaten.

That has always been the way of the business world.

After all ...
You can't stop progress.

HUMANOID HORRORS

WHY COSMO USED TO WEAR A LAB SMOCK EVERY HALLOWEEN

As soon as Davis walked into the Celestial Bean Coffee Shop, he heard Cosmo's odd, sharp voice, rambling on and on, as was his way. Davis wanted to turn right around and leave. Quickly. But he couldn't, because Cosmo, who was dressed as some sort of doctor or maybe scientist, had seen him and was waving him over. Davis seemed to recall that he'd dressed that way last year for Halloween. And the year before that. And before that, too... Very odd. Cosmo was usually so trendy.

Cosmo always seemed to be surrounded by a group—always young people, always good-looking, always rich or at least well-to-do. Davis couldn't fathom why. True, Cosmo was extremely handsome, in a pretty-boy game-show-host sort of way. And Cosmo was smart—the author of three books of poetry from prestigious literary presses. He used to like Cosmo, and in a way he still did. The problem was, the man was so oblivious. So pretentious. And so in love with the sound of his own voice. The artsy set loved him in spite of—or who knows, maybe because of—those faults.

"My little man, I believe you were thinking of leaving," Cosmo said as Davis approached the table. "You hesitated. You kept looking back at the door. If you'd been Lot's wife, you'd have turned into a pillar of salt at least six times." Cosmo always picked the largest table at any restaurant or coffee shop, and the seats were usually filled long before the evening was over. It was Halloween, so everyone at the table was in some sort of costume. Cosmo's gang for the evening consisted of a mummy, a lady pirate, a Vegas-style showgirl, a French chef complete with puffy white hat, and Tarzan.

Davis hated it when Cosmo called him 'my little man'. What the hell was <u>that</u> supposed to mean? Davis wasn't little—in fact, he was downright large. Six-foot-four and heavyset. And more to the point, he didn't belong to the pretentious poet, or anyone else, for that matter.

"No, I was just wondering if I'd left my headlights on." Davis set his book bag on a spare chair at the table, then went to the counter and ordered a Mocha Supreme. Like Cosmo, he was also a writer—but he wrote books and articles on caring for cats. Not quite as glamorous as poetry.

As he waited for his beverage, it dawned on him that Cosmo was a lot like a cat. Vain and self-absorbed. Of course, one expected that sort of a behavior from a cat.

When he returned to the table, Cosmo was in the middle of another ramble. "Civilization—or do I mean society? Yes, *society*—has completely outgrown Christmas, but Halloween—! Halloween should and in fact will be with us forever. Davey, you're not wearing a costume. You should be dressed up like a cat. An enormous cat. Davey writes cat books, you know. A couple years ago he helped me pick out Wing-Wang, the cat I have now. I forget why I named her Wing-Wang. She looks like a Wing-Wang, though."

Davis' full name was David Harrison Davis, but Cosmo never called him David or Davis or even Harrison. The poet usually stuck with 'my little man', but sometimes he chimed in with 'Davey' or worse, 'Davey Jones'. Maddening. He decided to turn the tables on Cosmo for once.

"And why should Halloween be with us forever, Cocoa?" Davis asked.

Cosmo raised an eyebrow. "Did you just call me Cocoa? How clever, my little man! Society needs Halloween to help loosen up the stranglehold of all that is politically correct."

All of Cosmo's artsy, pretty friends nodded their agreement.

"For example," the poet continued, "last year, at the insurance company—my day job—management said we could wear costumes to work on Halloween. I went as Dr. Quest, the dad from the old Jonny Quest cartoons, because I always wear a lab smock on Halloween."

"Why's that?" asked the young man dressed as a mummy.

"Oh, that's a long story… Anyway, I was Dr. Quest but more importantly, the receptionist came to work as—get this!—a pregnant nun. Isn't that wonderful? Such an outrageous concept—maybe even blasphemous. I don't know, I'm not into religion that much. But no one gave the pregnant nun a second thought—because it was Halloween!"

The pretty people all laughed, all complimented Cosmo on yet another marvelous observation.

Out of the corner of his eye, Davis thought he saw a skull, or more likely, a Halloween mask of one. He turned, but saw only a group of slacker types at a nearby table, discussing some article in the local alternative newspaper, *The River City Prophet*.

Then he noticed the person sitting at the table beyond that one.

The man had a pale, angular, bony face with deep-set eyes—a face so stark, Davis had mistaken it for a skull. The man also had short, reddish-orange hair and wore an orange sweater. He seemed to be staring with keen interest—at Cosmo.

The bony man absent-mindedly tapped the handle of his coffee cup with a long, thin finger. Suddenly he got up and walked over to the poet's side.

"Hello," he said in a low, musical voice. "I overheard some of what you were saying. I see you still have a spare chair at your table. Would you mind if I joined you? I'd like to hear more."

"Sure, that's okay with me," Cosmo said with a hugely dramatic shrug. "Is that okay with everyone else?"

No one objected, so the man took a seat. "So you think Halloween is necessary…?"

"Oh yes, entirely." Cosmo returned to his ramble. "Like I said, it gives us an opportunity to be politically incorrect, which can be fun. Plus, it keeps us in touch with our fears. And all of you know my philosophy on fear and unhappiness in general."

"Yeah, yeah…" Davis mumbled. He could tell that the poet wanted to launch into his most tiresome rant. "Embrace your discontent."

The bony man's eyes grew wide. "Repeat that, please?"

"Embrace your discontent!" Cosmo said cheerily. He was obviously pleased to have a possible new disciple at the table. "In order to be happy, you must first figure out what makes you unhappy. If you'd like to be free of fear, you must wrap your arms around the monsters who are scaring you. Speaking of monsters, should P.C. lingo apply to them? Like, for example…. The Wolfperson? Gillperson? Little Green Persons from Mars?"

The bony man smiled. "The Boogeyperson."

"Exactly!" Cosmo laughed, and everyone else at the table followed suit. Even Davis. He liked the idea of a politically correct Boogeyperson.

Davis turned to the bony man. "I didn't catch your name. I'm David Davis, but you can call me Dave. Or David. Or Davis. But not 'Davey' or 'Davey Jones'."

The bony man smiled, revealing a mouthful of large, square teeth and very pink gums. "I'm Paul Skillet."

Cosmo cocked his head to one side. "Sounds like a really bad alias for Peter Pan." It wasn't one of his better jokes, so no one laughed, which pleased Davis immensely.

Cosmo then introduced himself, as did the others: Chad the mummy, Heather the lady pirate, Courtney the showgirl, Michael the French chef, and Lance in his Tarzan gear.

"So tell me more about this 'embrace your discontent' idea." Paul waggled a thin finger at Cosmo. "What have you—embraced—in your own life?"

Davis decided he had to say *something*. "Careful, Paul. Once you get Cocoa-Puffs started on this particular topic… Let's just say it's a long and winding road."

Cosmo shot him a sharp glance. "Cocoa-Puffs?" Then the poet proceeded to launch his favorite ramble. "I had a father who never talked to me and a mother who hated me, because I was an unwanted child. She told me so at every opportunity. They were both extremely abusive during my childhood. After I left home, I avoided them for years, but in time I decided to get in touch with my anger—rage, in fact, might be the better term—so I wouldn't have to carry all that mental baggage. Eventually, I talked with them and forgave them, and I'm glad I did. A few days after my breakthrough, they died in a car crash."

"Interesting!" Paul said. "What else?"

Cosmo thought for a moment. "Oh, there were a few bullies who used to pick on me when I was little… I lost track of them, so it would be pretty hard to forgive them." He glanced at the list of specials on the sign above the counter. "I think I'll try the Pumpkin Pie Latte. Be back in a second."

After the poet left the table, Davis leaned toward Paul. "I should warn you, Cosmo has about a million 'embrace your discontent' stories from his college days."

The bony man nodded. "Yes, he's always been… Unique. An extraordinary young man. Even when he was little."

"Oh! You two know each other?" said the lady pirate.

The bony man flashed that big-toothed grin again. "Certainly. He doesn't recognize me, though. But that's okay." He put a thin finger to his even thinner lips. "Don't any of you folks tell him I said that. I want to see if he'll remember me."

The costumed folks smiled and nodded.

Cosmo returned to the table. "Paul, I thought of another case of 'embrace your discontent' from my childhood. You know, I should just call the concept E.Y.D.—it would save excess syllables. Plus, concepts with initials seem to do well. Now where was I…? Oh, yes. My childhood. My sixth grade teacher, Mr. Burkle, was always extremely mean to me.

He thought I was really pretentious. I don't know where he got that idea. He used to say demeaning things to 'bring me down a notch.' He'd actually used those words. So much for encouraging a budding intellect! But a few years ago, I visited him in the nursing home and forgave him. Even gave him a big hug. He was completely addled, the poor guy—Alzheimer's, I suppose—but I do believe he recognized me a *little* bit."

"How sad. What else?" Paul said with a hint of impatience in his voice. Some of the young pretties at the table exchanged worried glances.

"I think that's about it, childhood-wise," Cosmo said. "Now, once we get into my *college* years—"

"But your childhood fears," the bony man said. "Are you sure you've covered all those? What else bothered you, made you afraid, back when you were a child? When you were little, so very little?"

Cosmo released a huge sigh. "Goodness! Let me think back. I've already covered a lot of ground. There's always that horrible scientist I used to dream about, but it never would've been possible to embrace *her*."

"A mad scientist?" Lance/Tarzan asked. "Were you scared by some old horror movie?"

"I didn't say *mad*," Cosmo corrected. "A horrible person can be sane, and vice versa. Besides, my parents wouldn't let me watch scary movies. They were very religious. They thought vampires and stuff were all manifestations of Satan, or were they Stan's imps...? Something like that. I used to dream I was in a huge laboratory, where everything was white, all white. The walls, ceiling and floor glowed with light. And there was a lady scientist who never said a word. She had long white hair and a broken nose. It looked broken, anyway—it twisted to one side. She had very thick lips, and she licked them a lot. In the dream, I was always hiding under a table, or behind some boxes in a corner."

"Fascinating," the bony man said.

The poet took a drink of latte and then wiped his lips with an orange napkin. "The scientist—she's the reason I always wear a lab smock for Halloween. In her honor, I guess. So in that small way, I'm trying to embrace that particular fear. She had these assistants—dozens of them. They looked like giant spiders with bulbous heads, and tentacles instead of legs, and batwings. Each one had eight orange eyes, and dripping mouths with huge mandibles. They would drag two or three people into the laboratory and hold them down, and the scientist would cut into her victims and pull loads of guts and organs out of them. She'd toss their parts onto big steel carts, and then she'd reassemble the people in different ways. Sometimes she'd even chop parts off of the spider creatures and splice those onto her victims."

He took another drink. No one spoke during the pause.

"The dreams went on for about three years," Cosmo said. "That lady scientist never stitched together the same kind of monster twice. Some of them had multiple heads, or eyes in weird spots on their bodies, or teeth where teeth had no business being. After she'd stitched them together, she'd bring them back to life by pouring a beaker of some chunky blue goop down their throats. They're come to life and then stumble around screaming, if they still had mouths to scream with."

"You have a remarkable memory," Paul said. "Simply remarkable."

"So the dreams stopped after three years?" Davis asked. "What happened in the last dream?" He was actually surprised to hear himself asking for more information. But then, this anecdote was actually intriguing. Who would have guessed that Cosmo had such a wild imagination as a child?

"Let's see…" The poet took a moment to think back. "Oh yes, now I remember. How could I forget? I had to be really quiet in the dreams, so the scientist and her spider creatures wouldn't notice me. I had to hold back my screams. But one night—I sneezed. Who sneezes in a dream, for Christ's sake? Yet I did. Then the spider creatures started chasing me. They chased me 'round and 'round the laboratory, trying to wrap their tentacles around me, and I kept screaming and screaming. At one point I grabbed a scalpel off one of the tables and started slicing at some of the tentacles with that. Finally I found a white door, shaped like a coffin lid, that led out of the laboratory. I opened it, ran through, woke up—and haven't returned since. But just before I slammed the lab door shut behind me, I looked back."

"And…?" said the showgirl.

Cosmo picked up another orange napkin and wiped the sweat from his brow. "The lady scientist had opened up the head of one of those spider creatures and had pulled out its dripping green brain. She shook that brain at me, like…like…"

"Like she was going to put it in another body so it could track you down?" Paul Skillet suggested. "Track you down, no matter how long it might take?"

For once, Cosmo was at a loss for words. He stared at Paul for almost a full minute. Then he looked at his watch. "I think I'd better get moving." He rose from his chair. "Good night, everybody. Happy Halloween." He walked out of the coffee shop.

Without saying a word, Paul Skillet left the table and followed Cosmo out the door.

Davis turned toward the others. "That's weird. That Paul guy took off right after Cosmo. Maybe one of us should follow him. You know, to make sure everything's okay."

The pretty idiots said nothing. They simply looked about the coffee shop nervously. None of them dared to look Davis in the eye.

Davis shook his head. "Whatever. Watch my book bag. Can any of you do *that?*"

He followed the bony man out of the shop.

He looked around Seventh Avenue. There was a full moon out that night, perfect for Halloween. A light wind swirled a few orange and red leaves around his feet. Across the road were a pizza parlor and a dry-cleaning business. His car was parked on that side. Trick-or-treaters and their parents were walking by on both sides of the street. One boy was dressed as a little businessman, complete with tie and suitcase. Davis couldn't see Cosmo or the bony man anywhere.

He decided to check the parking lot behind the coffee shop.

He walked around the corner and hurried along the side of the brick building. Soon he began to hear voices.

"Come along! It's time! Time to embrace your discontent!"

"No! Get away from me! No! No!"

"She's been waiting for you! Come along now!"

He approached the far end of the shop—he couldn't see most of the lot, but he could tell something was wrong back there. A strong white light was shining from behind the building.

He rounded the corner and stopped.

A door had opened up right in the middle of the lot. A coffin-shaped entryway, mounted on nothing, but leading into an abyss of relentless white light. Cosmo was hanging onto the fender of a nearby car while Paul Skillet tried to drag him into the light.

Davis ran to help Cosmo. As he drew nearer, he could see figures squirming in the blinding whiteness behind the bony man. Figures with bulbous heads and tentacles. One of the tentacles whipped out and wrapped around Cosmo's ankle.

"Get away! Stop!" Cosmo screamed.

Davis reached into his pocket and pulled a small jangling bundle on a silver chain. House keys, work keys, car keys... He held them in his fist so that all those keys were sticking out from between his fingers. He began stabbing the keys into Cosmo's attackers, alternating between the bony man's hands and the writhing tentacle.

"Let go!" Davis cried. "Let go of him! He never hurt you! He never hurt anybody!"

"Oh, God! Get them off me!" Cosmo cried.

Davis kept stabbing, over and over. The bony man's flesh was oddly soft, more like thick clay than flesh. It didn't bleed very much, and what little blood there was looked like watery green pus. At one point, he looked through the doorway and saw, bleached into a phantom image by the light, a gaunt, broken-nosed woman in a lab smock, standing with her arms crossed. Staring. Waiting.

He looked down at the green fluid coming out of the bony man. Cosmo had said something earlier... He'd mentioned a brain, dripping with green stuff...

He took the longest key—the one that locked the side-door of his garage—and stuck it into the bony man's eye, popping the wet ball of goo. He rammed the key in as far as it could go.

All the way to the brain.

He kept working the garage key, pushing and twisting, until a rush of green slime and grayish curds spurted out around it. He gave the key one final shove, lodging it in place. The rest of the keys, still attached by the chain, hung down from the bony man's face, dripping with ooze and bits of flesh.

Paul Skillet squealed like a dying hog. He let go of Cosmo's leg and clawed at his face with his hands, trying desperately to remove the key.

Davis pushed the bony man back through the doorway of light—

And the door disappeared.

He turned to look at Cosmo.

The poet was now sitting on the trunk of a car, crying. "Sorry about your keys."

"What...?"

"That guy, that—thing—has your keys. All your keys. I'm sure he's dead and all, but how are you going to get into your home tonight?" He kept on rambling and crying. "And your car, how are you supposed to drive now? I'm sorry about that, okay? I'm just really sorry, is all, and thanks for saving my life, I don't know what I would have done if you hadn't saved me like that, but now all your keys are gone and—"

"Will you please shut up? Keys can be replaced." Davis grabbed the poet's costume by a lapel and worked the garment off of him. "No more smocks. Next Halloween, you're going to be a monk. Vow of silence, the whole bit." He balled up the lab coat and threw it into a patch of weeds bordering the parking lot. "Okay?"

Cosmo wiped his eyes and smiled. "Okay, David."

TELL YOUR SECRETS TO THE SLIME

"Mom," I had asked her, "do you think we'll get back home in time for my birthday?"

Her reply? She said what she always used to say when she meant 'No,' but still wanted to torture me with hope. "Maybe yes, maybe no. Maybe rain, maybe snow."

I've never touched snow—in fact, I've only seen it from a great distance. All the settlements to which we'd ever delivered had been pretty warm, some even tropical. It never snows on my home planet—probably because it isn't really a planet. It's a space station called Capricorn 289, built upon a large asteroid. There, 'outdoors' isn't a grassy meadow or a forest or field of wheat. 'Outdoors' is a desolate landscape of ragged black rocks under a bleak night sky. No sunshine, no clouds—no air. You'll see plenty of pitted, dented spaceships and shuttles, though.

I have a few friends about my age, twenty-four, on Capricorn 289. We liked to throw secret parties in storage facilities and unused ships. Some of my friends would even steal stimulants from their parents—drugs, bottles of fermented v'raaka, brain implants, other goodies. Fun isn't something built into the system there. You have to grab it on the sly.

Mom's business was based on Capricorn 289. I say 'was' because I have a feeling that her business doesn't have much of a future. Basically, she owned and operated an interplanetary delivery service. Most of her crew members were ex-prisoners from nearby planets.

'Nearby.' That seems like a truly ridiculous choice of words when describing the proximity of worlds. I don't have what you'd call a formal education, but I still think I'm pretty smart. Yet I still find space travel hard to understand. How can space be laced with natural tunnels that create shortcuts through—itself? Impossible. And yet it does. Thanks to those wormholes, planets that are light-years apart can indeed be near each other. Neighbors. I once asked Mom to explain it to me, and she said, "It just works, that's all. Like eyeballs. How can a ball of goo see things? I can't explain that either. But that won't stop me from looking around."

Mom's name: Letitia Gannon. My name: Conrad Gannon. Our top ship: the Gaea. Whenever Mom decided to go on a delivery—because she was bored, or wanted to see an ocean (she loved oceans)—she always made the trip in the Gaea. And she always took me along to wait on her, because she was crippled. She never told me what was wrong with her. Probably because that would require her to admit something was indeed wrong. A fault? She could never confess to one of those. But basically, she had a problem with her bones that grew worse with age. Her limbs were weak and slightly malformed, and she was flabby, too, since exercise was out of the question.

Her company's last job had been a delivery to a stinking toilet bowl of a planet. It was heavily polluted, and global warming had melted too much of its polar ice, washing over most of its land. The vast majority of the people had gone away, so other planets began to use it as a dump hole. Its oceans became primal soup gone berserk, so schools across the galaxy liked to send academic missions to see what was cooking. One of these missions was an amphibious ship called the Perseus—it could travel through space, drive across land and through swamps, even cruise like a yacht. Mom used to say ships like that should be called Chitty Chitty Bang-Bangs, but she never bothered to tell me what that meant— though she did once say it was the best idea the ancients ever had. She had loads of old books, though most of them were preserved in a variety of quaint old electronic, sometimes even paper formats. I don't know why they didn't use recreational brain implants back then. I guess they were just stupid.

The job was to deliver supplies to the Perseus. Mom wanted to go, since it was an ocean planet. So of course, I had to go, too. To oozy, swampy, shitty old Earth.

* * * *

On our first day there, we had a little time, so Mom told the pilot to "take the scenic route." Basically, that meant we got to wander at a decent elevation, taking in the sights. I sat with her in her chamber and together, we watched the wall monitors. We ate fried gronth and had some chocolate fizz.

The waters of Earth were choked with pollution. A lot of the crap had congealed into islands of hardened foam and scum that floated along on the surface. Embedded in these islands, you could see skeletons of all sorts of animals, and people, too. Lots of metal and plastic artifacts were stuck in the goo as well. Rotted-out automobiles, washing machines, dolls, vacuum cleaners, TV sets... A friend of mine from Capricorn 289 used to collect old Earth junk, so I was able to identify most of the crap. Mom was pretty impressed.

That ocean scum was crawling with vermin. Big jumping things with shell-like bodies, dozens of spindly legs, and clusters of shiny silver eyes. Enormous slugs oozing with black slime. Glassy crystalline creatures shaped like pyramids with clear tendrils spouting from the points. And all over the garbage, worms of every color, texture and type—black and smooth, red and spiny, yellow and scaly, green and segmented.

At one point, Mom saw a creature that looked like a fuzzy bath sponge with three jointed legs, one big pink eye and a catlike mouth. "Look at that thing!" she said. "Isn't that bizarre? I want one of those. When we get to the rendezvous point, tell the crew to look for one of those."

"What do you think it's called?" I said.

"I don't think it's called anything," she said. "So I'll give it a name. I'll name it after you: how's that? A Conradoid. Looks just like you! Now fetch me some more fried gronth."

The rendezvous point was on a stretch of beach on the island of Vanna. I asked Mom what the name meant and she said, "Some ancient love goddess. She was also the goddess of good luck and prizes."

Later, as our "scenic route" was coming to an end, we did see something that made all the other freaky sea-things look as boring as shoes. It was an old Earth cruise ship, still drifting along after countless centuries. But there was something very wrong with it. The whole thing was covered with a sort of thick green tissue, veined with purple streaks. Here and there the tissue was swollen into thick, enflamed lumps.

"Look at that!" Mom cried. "That ship's covered with some kind of seaweed, just like an animal's covered with hide. And it's got bumps—jumbo pimples, do you suppose? I wish I could go down and pop one of them."

"That's disgusting," I said. "Besides, it can't be a pimple. Plants can't get acne."

"But still, imagine that those huge lumps were infections... What kind of germs would they have inside them? Germs as big as that Conradoid. Hey, maybe that's what the Conradoid is. A super-germ. Now I really must have one."

The cruise ship was also plagued by an array of parasites, big and small. The biggest of them was the size of a medium-sized Earth automobile. It had long, waving eyestalks, and its warty flesh was pink tinged with orange. It had six tentacles, all of which were sunk into the green tissue.

"I wish we had more time to examine that ship," Mom said. "Is that green stuff on the inside, too? I'd love to see it cut down the middle. A laser cannon would slice it up real nice—too bad we don't have one! Rub my feet, boy. They're so cold—rub 'em 'til they tingle."

I did as I was told.

"Ah, is it any wonder I love these wet planets?" Mom said. "They're so wild, so strange, so alive! And the creatures move so freely! Damn it, boy, rub harder! I can barely tell you're doing anything!"

I looked at Mom's moon-round, dark-skinned, tiny-eyed face, topped with a mop of curly black hair, and wondered for the millionth time how she could be my mother. I'm skinny, with straight red hair, a pale, thin face and big eyes. I never knew my father. Mom once said, when I asked who he was, "How should I know? The ship had a twenty-man crew back then. My arms and legs worked better in those days."

The Gaea only had twelve crew members on its last delivery. Thirteen, counting me. Crew members were hired and fired at a hectic pace, since Mom had little tolerance for laziness or subordination. Even mild subordination. She often had me plant various miniature surveillance devices in the crew's quarters. I didn't like doing it, but what else could I do? Mom had a problem with the word 'No.'

* * * *

As it turned out, that cruise ship was a preview of things to come.

Most of the island of Vanna was also covered with the green tissue. It was a terrible yet also awe-inspiring thing to behold. Trees, boulders, hills and valleys, all wrapped in that same puffy, purple-veined mess. It even had those lumps, too. Once we landed, Mom instructed Dr. Belvek, our smartest crew member, to analyze samples of the freakish growth.

"I wish we had better equipment," Dr. Belvek said. He was seated next to me on a couch next to Mom's bed/control module.

"Yes, and I wish I was the Queen of the Galactic Alliance," Mom said. "Now let's return to reality. Tell me what that stuff is made of. My guess is some kind of seaweed."

The doctor, an old, birdlike humanoid with light blue skin, nodded eagerly. "Very good, Letitia! Your powers of observation are admirable. It does indeed seem to be seaweed. And an incredibly advanced form at that! It doesn't even need to be submerged in water to thrive. I took large samples—each about as big as one of my hands—from three different areas. Incredibly, this seaweed has a sort of rudimentary nerve system. And tiny, almost imperceptible ocular organs—"

"*Eyes?*" Mom said.

"Yes, I was surprised, too." The doctor nodded again. "The seaweed grows at a hectic rate—almost like a form of cancer. I have never come across a life form quite like it. Highly mutated, most certainly. It can extract nourishment from—well, practically anything."

"What about the pimples?" Mom asked.

"Not quite sure what you're talking about..." The doctor said.

"The big lumps," I said. "Mom thinks they look like pimples."

"Oh yes, those." The doctor raised a feathery white eyebrow. "I do not think they are microbial infections, as the term 'pimple' suggests. I opened one up, but it was a small one, so I'm not quite sure that I can draw any conclusions from what I found. I'm tempted to say those lumps might house a form of symbiotic parasite."

Mom drew in her breath with a sharp hiss. I could tell she was impressed. "A symbiotic parasite! So what exactly was inside? What did it look like?"

"I found some underdeveloped organs, some nerve tissue, some cartilaginous material, and..." The doctor paused. Both Mom and I leaned toward him. "...and a lot of thick, yellow slime."

"The slime part sounds like a pimple to me!" Mom cried. She looked me in the eye. "We have a few hours until the Perseus gets here. Boy, go out with the doctor and find a really big lump. The biggest you can see. Cut it open and bring me one of those symbiotic parasites. But be sure to kill it first. Be sure to take Mugmei with you, in case there's any lifting that needs to be done." Mugmei was a large, docile, hoglike crew member who was extremely strong. "Oh," she added, "and if you find one of those Conradoids, bring that, too."

So the doctor and I found Mugmei, who had been napping in a storage room, and we explained to him the nature of our quest: basically, we were going out to find and open up an enormous lump.

The crew had already set up camp on the beach. The three of us had a quick meal and then we headed inland. I was actually pretty happy to be able to roam the island with Dr. Belvek and Mugmei. Both of them were friendly and interesting to talk with, each in his own way. They were ex-criminals, like all of Mom's crew members, but their crimes weren't as bad as those of the others. Dr. Belvek used to practice medicine without any form of licensure, and Mugmei had been caught eating an endangered plant in a botanical exhibit.

"This island place smell bad," Mugmei said in his squealing yet oddly boyish voice. "Smell like sweaty human with stink-gas coming out of the back part. Smell like little human baby who has made brown."

"Lovely. You do paint a picture with words," Dr. Belvek said. "Yes, it does smell rather ripe."

"Why everything got funny green skin on it?" Mugmei was in a talkative, inquisitive mood. I liked Mugmei. For a criminal, he was an exceptionally honest being. "I not going to eat anything I find on this place. I bet would make me be like this."

"What an interesting observation, Mugmei." The doctor then turned to me and said, "Our piggy friend has good instincts. He's probably right. Eating this stuff could result in a person being invaded from the inside by it. This seaweed has a tenacious will to live. Many creatures indigenous to garbage planets are that way."

We passed by some small lumps, but we ignored them, since Mom was very specific about size: she wanted, quite simply, the biggest we could find. It dawned on me that we were being very reckless, walking around on that foul, infectious island in our usual clothes, carrying only some cheap tools and a little medicine kit. But then, that's the way Mom's business usually operated. In her eyes, lots of fancy equipment would just cost a lot of money—and crew members were easily replaced.

"So what exactly is a Conradoid?" the doctor asked.

I told him.

"Your mother's sense of humor is..." He finished the sentence simply by sighing.

"That lump big enough?" Mugmei pointed ahead to a boxlike structure which, like everything else, was covered with the green hide. Half of one wall of the structure was covered with an enormous, swollen lump.

"I think so!" Dr. Belvek said. "That thing the lump's on—I'm sure that was once a building. The first one we've seen so far on this island." He tapped his chin in thought with a long-nailed finger. "Maybe that's why the lump is so extremely big. If it's a building, it would of course be hollow on the inside. That would give ... whatever is inside the lump ... more room to grow."

We walked up to the building. We could hear, coming from within, a sickening, bubbling, sloshing sound, like an oversized maggot flailing around inside a corpse. The doctor's face twitched with fear.

"Let's cut! Cut deep and see something now!" Mugmei said, pulling a long knife out of a sheath strapped to his leg. "I want to see what makes funny noises. I cut here, right in this crack." So saying, he tapped the tip of his blade against a long, liplike opening in the lump.

"No, not yet," the doctor said. He gave me a frantic look. "Do you think we should try to ... coax it out? If we simply go slicing into it, it may attack." He put his hand on the crack. "I think maybe ... maybe it would want to ... talk with us ..."

Suddenly—at the time, I didn't know quite why—I saw his point. "Yes, I think it wants to talk to... No! No, it wants us to talk. To it."

Mugmei dropped his blade. "Lump wants to hear our words. I feel it, too."

The sloshing inside the house grew faster. Almost eager.

"It wants to know..." The doctor's voice trailed away as he grabbed the lump with both hands. He began to rub it softly, tenderly. "It wants to know everything."

"Everything," Mugmei repeated. He stepped up to the lump and began to rub it as well.

I, too, felt a sudden urge to follow their example, to put my hands on that swollen mass and console it. Pleasure it... But I managed to resist. I'd spent my whole life being manipulated by Mom, so I knew when I was being mentally coerced. But the thing inside the lump didn't use mere words, like my mother—it had a greater power. I had to concentrate all my will to resist it. I couldn't run away, but I was able to just stand back and watch.

"I've never loved anyone," the doctor said in a low, dreamy voice. "I like others, but they scare me. I'm not very strong. I can be hurt so easily. I wish I had a strong body."

"I'm too stupid," Mugmei said in a slow monotone. "Just a big stupid animal. People make fun of me. I know they do. It makes me sad. I'm real lonely."

The doctor began to cry. "My people come out of eggs. Sometimes I feel like my brain is an egg and it will crack because I worry so much. I wish I was as strong as Letitia. She's mean but that excites me. I must be sick in the head, to be excited by someone so mean, so smart but so cruel, someone who wouldn't mind killing me and cooking me for her dinner."

"I want to find mud and roll in it," Mugmei whispered. "I want to stop trying to be like people. I want to just be an animal and be happy. Happy. Once I ate a dead man I found in a forest. Someone had killed him and left his body under some leaves. No one could see me, so I ate him. He was a little rotten. That made him taste good."

I wanted to scream, wanted to vomit—but also wanted to tell my secrets, too. But I did not—the urge was not overwhelming because I wasn't touching and rubbing and adoring that monstrous lump.

The crack in the lump slowly began to open. A large dollop of yellow slime blurted out, but it didn't drop to the ground. Instead, it spread out over the lump and flowed onto the hands of Dr. Belvek and Mugmei. The criminals continued to declare their secrets, and even more slime oozed out and slithered onto them, until the two were covered with the nauseating secretion.

Short, writhing lengths of tentacle and various odd lumps of flesh and cartilage emerged from the lump, carried forth by the slime, and these bits and pieces flowed onto Dr. Belvek and Mugmei and—grew onto and into them.

Then even more slime poured out, to create a new layer of coating over them both.

* * * *

The sun sank toward the horizon, and still I simply stood and watched, spellbound. The slime slowly hardened around each of the two crew members. Finally each, encased in his own chrysalis, fell over onto the island's surface. The lump they had been rubbing was now very small, and the sloshing sound was gone.

The hypnotic power of the lump faded away. I looked down and saw that the island's green hide was starting to grow over my shoes. I tore free and ran away. I had to return to the Gaea to tell Mom and everyone what had happened.

Eventually I saw the Gaea in the distance, and I ran even faster. By then it was night. But, the crew had set up lights around the camp, so the beach was almost as bright as day. Soon I saw something unexpected—something nasty and frightening—and I began to slow down.

The Perseus had arrived. And the academic ship was thickly coated with that seaweed hide—as well as a profusion of large, sloshing lumps.

I could see that Mom's crew had towed the Perseus onto the island with chains. The green skin was enflamed and mangled, bleeding a purplish gore, around the spots where the chains had dug into its surface.

I walked closer, but not too close. I did not want to fall under the mind-numbing spell of those slime-filled mounds.

Each crew member was standing dazed in front of a lump, rubbing it with disgusting tenderness, coaxing out the secretion.

All of the ooze-streaked criminals were dreamily uttering their secrets—some of the things they had to say were truly appalling. Secrets of violence, sexual abuse, greed, deception and more, more, more.

Mom was there, too, in her transport chair. Her seat in this small vehicle could be raised, so she could look a standing person in the eye. I imagine the prospect of viewing one of those big lumps up close had been too tempting to resist. She was rubbing one of those lumps as it coated her with slick yellow goo.

I didn't want to hear her secrets. I didn't. I tried to concentrate on what the others were saying. But still, I heard some of her words—I couldn't help it—and what I heard included this:

"He's not really my son. I bought him for cheap when he was a baby, from some poor woman who used to run errands for me. She died a long time ago."

She couldn't even remember my real mother's name. Just some poor woman. Someone who'd been expected to wait on her. Like me.

I watched as tentacles and organs and other wet chunks of tissue flowed out of the lump and became part of Mom. Even though I knew she wasn't my mother, I still thought of her as Mom. Mean, selfish, lying Mom.

I turned away from the Perseus and headed toward the Gaea. I didn't know how to fly the ship—at any rate, I was fairly sure that one person couldn't possibly operate it alone anyway. But at least I knew how to activate the distress signal. I went to Mom's quarters and hit two large red buttons on a control console at the same time. There were two so that the signal wouldn't accidentally be sent if one was bumped by accident.

I went to my quarters, took a shower and changed my clothes. Then I went into the food preparation area and made myself the best meal of my life. The best cut of gronth steak, some steamed vegetables—nothing green, though—and a couple glasses of fermented v'raaka... Everybody else was—busy—so I figured, why not?

Finally, I walked back to the Perseus to see what was going on. I felt strangely at peace with what was happening. It was strange, but at least it was a change. When your life is crap, any kind of change can be considered as an improvement.

Each crew member was enclosed in a yellowish-orange chrysalis. The surface of these casings had a distinctly crystalline structure. They looked like huge snot-diamonds. Mom's chrysalis was resting on the ground next to her transport chair. I activated the chair, turned it toward the ocean, and tapped the 'forward' control. I waved bye-bye as it rolled into the filthy water.

It occurred to me then that I'd never found a Conradoid for Mom. Oh, well. It wasn't like she was in any position to punish me.

I went back into the Gaea, sealed all the hatches and went to sleep in Mom's big bed. I figured that, like the chair, she wouldn't be needing it.

* * * *

In the morning, I prepared a lavish breakfast for myself. Then I went into the storage area and found a variety of cutting tools, some clear, flexible plastic sheeting, and a tube of adhesive.

Then I went outside and began working on Mom's chrysalis.

It took some time, but eventually I removed a long strip of the casing from the length of the chrysalis and replaced it with the sheeting, which I glued into place. That way, I could observe the changes going on inside.

I then destroyed all the other chrysalides on the beach. But I didn't go inland to the skin-encased house to destroy the two chrysalides there. The doctor and Mugmei had been nice to me. Maybe they would enjoy their transformations. Maybe the doctor would feel less vulnerable, and Mugmei would feel smarter. Maybe.

I figured it would take about a month for some ship to detect the distress signal and come to rescue me. The Gaea had suffered breakdowns on different planets before, and rescues usually took that long, give or take a few days.

Mom, for all her faults, had at least instilled in me a curiosity about nature. And it was fascinating, watching her turn into something new and startling. Her arms and legs became chitinous and angular, with tentacle groupings where her hands and feet used to be. Her body slimmed into a scaly, segmented greenish-blue cylinder. Her head grew wider at the top and her eyes became enormous and multi-faceted. Veined, diaphanous wings sprouted from her upper back. She was becoming an insect-like creature with a streamlined mix of humanoid and aquatic traits.

The symbiotic parasite that brewed inside the seaweed hide needed to find yet another creature to complete its life cycle. In this case, that creature was Mom. Once it found that creature, it hypnotized it, joined with it, and became an altogether different being. A bizarre DNA mingling of different life-form traits found on Earth.

Therefore, Mom was becoming the ultimate Earthling. A garbage beast without parallel.

But still, I wanted to add my own personal touch.

I looked around in the Gaea's medical supply room and found a large syringe. I then took some of my blood, peeled back the plastic casing a little, and injected me into her.

We hadn't been related before, but we would be now. But I wouldn't have her traits. She would have mine—and, those of the poor woman who used to run errands for her.

In a few days, straight red hair began to sprout in tufts here and there on her body. Her eyes became even bigger. The color of her body changed from greenish-blue to dark pink. Her diaphanous wings soon were covered with bristly orange fuzz. The tentacles that were her hands and feet became thinner and longer. She was not as eerily beautiful as she had been, but I found that I liked her more this way.

One day, I heard a loud buzzing in the sky. I looked up and saw two enormous creatures flying far overhead. The buzzing was the sound of their frantic wings. These beings had to be Dr. Belvek and Mugmei in their new bodies. I waved to them, but they didn't see me. I figured that if they were already hatched, then Mom's rebirth couldn't be too far away. She had loved oceans. Well, soon she would have plenty of ocean, and strange creatures, and maybe she'd even find a Conradoid, too.

I decided to throw a little party. I made a cake, took it to the beach, and waited for Mom to come out of her chrysalis. My own birthday had been overlooked, so if I couldn't be the guest of honor at a party, at least I could be the host.

Eventually I got tired of waiting and ate most of the cake myself. But not all of it.

At last Mom emerged from her casing.

I'll tell you this now: the next day, I was rescued. The ship that picked me up was a delivery ship, like the Gaea. But that ship was part of a more prestigious service. It was in the process of delivering a new wife to an alien emperor on a planet I'd never heard of. I got to meet the new wife—her teeth were dark purple and her eyes were bright red. But to someone—I suppose that emperor—she was the very vision of delectable beauty.

The timing of my rescue was perfect, because after Mom emerged—and did what she did—I felt that I really needed to leave that planet. I had to grow up and move on. I had to figure out who I was, and what I wanted to do with the rest of my life. I don't have all the answers yet.

Will I ever have all the answers?

Maybe yes, maybe no. Maybe rain, maybe snow.

It didn't take Mom long to escape the chrysalis, since it had a natural fault in it—the plastic sheeting. She ripped her way out of her birth-envelope and stumbled around the beach on her angular limbs, gasping and making a strange humming sound. It make me shiver, because its tones reminded me of my own voice. She rested for a few minutes, and then crept up to me and looked at me. She cocked her head to one side, then the other. I still had a little piece of birthday cake left, so I put it on the ground in front of her.

She studied it briefly. Finally she seized it in her mandibles, gnashed it up and swallowed.

A moment passed. A breeze blew over the beach, carrying with it a stench from some distant, long-dead sea-thing that made me want to throw up.

Mom reached out a forelimb, and ran her long hand-tentacles slowly over my face.

Suddenly I knew ... I knew, I knew, I knew, deep within me ... that the real Mom—that crippled, controlling, eccentric, impossible woman— had loved me. As much as someone that twisted was capable of loving anyone.

And then she flew away.

MELINA MAVRODAKIS AND THE FIVE SOMETHING-OR-OTHERS OF THE APOCALYPSE

Spencer, along with everyone else at the party, was afraid of the hors d'oeuvres.

Melina would throw a cocktail party once every seven months, give or take a few weeks. That was how long it took for her to do one of her enormous soft sculptures. This particular soirée took place a few days before Christmas, and Melina had cooked up a variety of disturbing red and green tidbits. Spencer, the hot young poet, stood by the snack table with Buster, the hot young model, discussing whether or not Jake, the young playwright, could really be considered hot, since his work was so painfully *obvious*.

"He just needs more life experience. He's as green as this piece of dried seaweed." Buster picked up one of the hors d'oeuvres by the corner. "What's this in the middle? Smoked salmon, and—? I have no idea what these things are."

Spencer took a look. "I think they're candy sprinkles. Are you going to eat it?"

At that moment Melina drifted up to them in a cloud of red and green lace, and Buster didn't have a choice. His eyes rolled up a couple times as he choked down the vile morsel.

"I'm so glad the two of you could make it," she rasped. Melina was a tiny, bone-thin woman; one would have expected a voice like a twittering sparrow. But she was also a heavy smoker. Spencer used to sleep with her years ago, and she started and ended the day with a cigarette, with four packs in between. That was probably why her cooking was based on colors: her taste buds were coated with tar. Why she even bothered setting a foot in the kitchen was beyond the poet's understanding. She certainly had enough money to hire caterers.

Spencer cocked an eyebrow toward the other end of the studio, where her most recent masterpiece stood draped under red and green bed sheets. "Your biggest one yet. What is it, about fifteen feet tall?"

"Close. Fourteen feet, seven inches," Melina said around a mouthful of maraschino cherries and spinach. "Thirteen feet, nine inches wide. And it's already sold."

"But it hasn't been on display anywhere," Buster said. "Was it commissioned?"

"Yes and no. I was at this birthday party a while back, and there was this guy ..." She started twirling her index fingers at shoulder level, which meant she was remembering things. "I was really drunk, and he was too, and at one point, he said, 'There are five Something-or-Others of the Apocalypse, right?' And I said, 'No, there are only four,' and he said, 'No, I'm pretty sure there are five.' Did I mention he was rich? Anyway, we started naming Something-or-Others of the Apocalypse, like, 'The Seven Dwarves of the Apocalypse,' and 'The Three Little Pigs of the Apocalypse' and then, off the top of my head, I shouted out the silliest one yet and he said, 'Do a piece of art with that title and I'll buy it for a million dollars.'"

"So you did?" asked Jake. He had joined the group in the middle of the anecdote.

"I did indeed. He gave me the check this morning. It's cashed and everything." Melina pointed toward the punch bowl, where a bald man with a boyish face was ladling a drink. "That's him. He hasn't even seen it yet."

"So what's it called?" Spencer said. "*What* of the Apocalypse is it?"

"You *know* she's not going to tell us." Buster said. He then turned from the poet to their hostess. "So is Cue Ball your new boyfriend?"

"I wish. But he's as gay as—well, *you*. His first name is Strohm. Isn't that ghastly? His parents must have been Nazis. Oh, I'm sorry, Jake."

"You can say 'Nazi' in front of a Jew, Mims. We're not made of spun sugar." For some reason, Jake always called her 'Mims.' He waggled his fingers at the hors d'oeuvres. "So what are you trying to poison us with this time around?"

While Jake and Melina were talking, Spencer took Buster's hand and together they escaped the snack table, weaving their way through the crowded party. Spencer used to sleep with Buster, too. And Jake. He supposed that some might consider him slutty. But he preferred the term *polyamorous*.

"So are you going to go after Storm?" Buster said.

"That's not his name. But yeah, I think so. He's cute. He's rich. He'll buy something on a whim for a million bucks. I'd be a fool not to. What about you?"

"Things are back on with Darien." Darien was Buster's intermittent boyfriend, a film producer who would ignore him for weeks and then shower him with gifts to win him back. "I'm going to mingle. See ya when I see ya."

Spencer scanned the room and saw Strohm standing in front of the blanketed sculpture, looking up at it with his head tipped to one side. The poet pushed and shuffled through the crowd, picking up two glasses of champagne on the way.

"Oh ... hello," Strohm said as Spencer handed him a drink. "Are you ... a waiter?" The bald man looked around as if the answer to his question could be found floating in the air. Spencer usually didn't find bald men attractive, but this one was definitely an exception. Strohm was young—probably in his late twenties. He had an angular yet gentle face, with big, sleepy green eyes and a mouth that twisted slightly to the right when he talked.

"I'm Spencer. A friend of Melina's. She was just telling me that you've already bought—" He waved a hand toward the sculpture. "—Whatever-It-Is of the Apocalypse."

Strohm continued to search the air around his face. "And?"

Spencer couldn't very well say, *And you're a cute millionaire. Take me to Paris and spend lots of money on me.* So instead he said, "And I know everyone else here and I'm bored. So tell me a joke. A recipe. A dream. Anything."

The bald man finally looked him in the eye. "Well, let's see. I can't cook and I always give away the punch line. So that leaves dreams. Do you want to hear about the Red Nurse? It's pretty weird."

The poet nodded. "Weird is good. Hit me."

Strohm downed half of his champagne. "When I was little, my father belonged to a sort of freaky mystical society. Their meetings consisted of outlandish cocktail parties—with rituals, yet—presided over by an overbearing foreign woman."

"Like Melina."

"No, no, no! Melina's a Christmas tree angel by comparison. Miss Zarachenska was a huge scary *truck* of a woman, each tit as big as her head. They called her the Red Nurse—I forget why. She died years ago, after falling down a flight of stairs. Anyway, I dream about her sometimes. I dream she's reaching out for—" He looked to the side. "I'll tell you the rest some other time. We're about to start."

Melina had walked up to the sculpture and was now climbing onto it, until at last she settled on a flat spot about four feet off the ground.

"Attention, everyone!" she rasped out. She'd had a bit more to drink and her words were now slightly slurred. "Gather 'round! It's time! It's time!"

The partygoers obediently surged forward.

"We have a very special guest this evening." Her arm shot out and for a moment Spencer thought she was pointing at him. But then she said, "My dear, dear friend Strohm Krepp. Come forward, darling, let everyone look at you."

The millionaire did as he was told, nodding and smiling bashfully.

"This morning, this gorgeous man bought this monstrosity, so he gets to unwrap his big new Christmas goody. Strohmmy, help me down, please."

Laughing, he helped her climb out of her perch.

"Okay!" Melina cried out. "Give those sheets a good tug! You know how to tug, you naughty boy! Tug! Tug! Tug!"

Soon, the whole party was chanting *"Tug! Tug! Tug!"* So, the bald man stepped up, grabbed a handful of fabric, and began pulling. It took some doing, since there were so many sheets, but within a minute he had removed all the coverings.

And the chanting stopped.

For at least thirty seconds, no one said anything.

Then Strohm whispered, *"I love it."* Soon he began wiggling and jumping up and down, clapping his hands. "I love it I love it I love it *I LOVE IT!*" He grabbed Melina and spun her around, and soon the whole party was laughing and clapping.

No one really knew what Melina's works were made of, but the main ingredient seemed to be some kind of soft, flexible, slightly fuzzy pink plastic. She somehow formed or molded this material into life-sized human figures, and then dressed these figures and arranged them in interesting tableaus. This one, however, was more than just interesting. It was *awe-inspiring.*

Melina strolled up to her latest masterpiece. "Ladies and gentlemen, I present to you: The Five Drag Queens of the Apocalypse."

The five figures were shown sprawled on a segment of staircase, so that some were on higher levels than others. She placed her hand on the shoulder of the nearest figure, a young Asian man wearing a platinum-blonde wig, pearls and a white silk dress. "Regard the Starlet," she said. "She never knew Mommy, and Daddy loves her too much. She doesn't blame him, though. She blames her beauty, this horrible beauty that drives men mad. She drinks, she smokes, she whores, and still she wears white because she wants so *badly* to be a good girl, Daddy's good little angel-girl. Sometimes the pills make her feel that way: like a sweet, perfect angel. Don't worry, precious Starlet—you'll earn those wings yet!" Melina's deep laugh brayed forth.

She moved on to the next one, a pouting Goth-boy in a black spider-web dress. "Regard the Vamp. This dark beauty hides in the shadows, hides behind funeral lace and sunglasses with midnight-green lenses. How sad this is, for you see, the Vamp would like nothing better than to play the debutante! To skip about, wearing bows and frilly dresses! To drink mint juleps while boys in sweaters fight over her! But no, that will never happen. For you see, when the Vamp throws the dice, she only gets snake-eyes. Cadaver-eyes. Demon-eyes. She knows her lot in life, this poor spider with a butterfly in her heart."

She pointed to the top of the stairs. There sat a muscular black man with his arms held out to embrace the heavens. He wore a wig of pink feathers, cobalt-blue pumps, and a spangled pink-and-blue body stocking. "Regard the Dancer. How she loves to strut and swirl her feather boas. She can kick high, this nimble darling—sometimes her shoes go flying off into the night. It's hard to believe she used to weigh almost three-hundred pounds. To lose the weight, she bought a postcard of a Las Vegas cutie, put it on the fridge and said 'the me to be, the me to be,' every time she saw it. Our Dancer lost her appetite and gained an appreciation of glitz and glamour and stretch limousines. There's a tiny spoon in the glove compartment, but she doesn't eat with it."

Jake brought Melina a glass of something—probably a gin-and-tonic, her favorite—and she drank it all down before continuing. "And this," she said, standing over a slender, bony older man in a billowing red wig and beaded evening gown, "this regal songbird ... Regard the Chanteuse. She has a pretty voice, but her face, her body—not so pretty. Enticing? Not to most, but at least to some. Even so, she wants to bewitch the world! Our songbird drinks a lot. When she is singing and when she is drinking, she is the prettiest bird that ever soared among pink cotton-candy clouds. Brilliant plumage and perfect pitch."

Finally she came to the fifth drag queen, a delicate, thirtyish man wrapped in furs. His long, shining corn-silk hair was swept up into an elaborate coiffure. "Regard the Playgirl. She has always been rich and has always gotten her way. Pater wanted her to be a lawyer or a doctor, but she just shook her dainty doll's-head. One day she looked out her window and noticed the minimum-wage boy who cleans the pool... She now spends her days flying here and there, flirting with princes and

potentates, seeing and being seen. She won't go home, she simply *won't.*
That's where the pool boy is. She's desperately trying to forget about
him—trying to forget she is deeply in love with *a man without money.*
The horror! Oh, the horror!" She laughed again as she played with a curl
of the figure's hair.

Melina moved toward the audience. "Why are there five, you ask?
Because a hand has five fingers, and it takes that many to grab hold.
These five sweethearts have seized the steering wheel of fate, and together, they shall drive this tired old world into a glorious new dawn of
mystery, magic and tragic beauty." She bowed to the partygoers, and
they responded with frenzied applause.

Behind her, the sculpture's stairs seemed to light up from within: first
red, then a deeper scarlet.

Strohm wiped his eyes with a handkerchief. *"Fantastic,"* he breathed.

Spencer's mind wandered for a split-second—he found himself
thinking about a buffet table stocked with live insects. But why? Had he
read that in a book, or seen it in a movie, a foreign film maybe?

When he turned his attention back to the partial staircase, the glow
was gone.

* * * *

After Melina's performance, her guests swarmed toward the hors
d'oeuvres. Spencer formulated a theory regarding this inexplicable pil-
grimage: they must have decided that if her art was that wonderful, her
food *had* to be haute cuisine.

He managed to find a few edible bits and pieces at the table—it was
getting late, and he had to nibble on *something.* Buster started talking to
him, but Spencer managed to keep the conversation short. It wouldn't
do to leave a millionaire unattended in this teeming nest of cuckoos and
culture vultures.

He grabbed a half-full bottle of white wine off a table. As he threaded
his way through the crowd, a few more friends tried to involve him in
conversation. By the time he found Strohm, his shiny-headed new friend
was most definitely drunk.

"Spency, old pal," Strohm said, clapping a hand firmly onto the poet's
shoulders. In his other hand he held a Manhattan with extra cherries.
"Ain't that Melina something? Do you think she was making all that up
as she went along?"

"Yes, I'm sure she was." Spencer found it best to agree in such situations. "So, where are you going to put something that big?" He took a swig from the wine bottle.

The millionaire smiled wickedly. "Hmmm...?" Then he nodded. "Oh, you're talking about the sculpture. By the piano in my dining room. Away from the windows. All that sun would fade the colors."

"And there's nothing sadder than a faded drag queen," Spencer said. The wine was making him light-headed, but that was okay.

Strohm looked around the room. "So where did Magda go?"

"Magda? I don't think I've met Magda."

The bald man closed his eyes for a moment. "Oh, I meant—what's her name? Our hostess... I've got to talk to her."

"Why? Is something wrong?"

"No, I just wanted to know if she *signed* the thing anywhere. She has to sign it, you know." He finished his Manhattan. "Did they sign Dad? I'll be right back. Gotta get another drinky. I'll bring you one, too. One, two, one, two. Hold onto these." He handed his cherries to Spencer and disappeared into the crowd.

The poet ate the cherries, idly wondering what "sign Dad" meant.

Jake came up to him. "I see you've hooked up with Magda's millionaire."

Spencer considered correcting him, but he couldn't put his finger on the actual mistake. "Yes, I've hooked up, so take those yummy puppy eyes elsewhere."

"Oh, I'm not interested in your hairless boy. The Cat Man finally showed up!"

"The Cat Man's here?" At first, the poet had no idea what Jake was talking about. Then the knowledge came to him in a rush, like a package tumbling down a flight of stairs. Yes, the Cat Man, the *Cat* Man. "He is *so hot.* Good luck there, dude." He chugged more wine.

"He might let me hold the Moon Scarab," Jake whispered. "Wouldn't that be awesome? Then I'd be able to see everything and not even use my eyes."

As Jake walked away, Spencer wished he'd asked if the Cat Man would be using any of his magick powers tonight. Then someone tapped him on the shoulder. He turned around and Strohm put the straw of a drink up to his lips. "Want a taste?"

The poet had some. It tasted like a mix of cheap whiskey and pureed caterpillars. "Fabulous," he said. "Is this mine?"

"Of course, I got one for both of us. Hey, there's Magda! Magda, over here!"

Someone was moving through the crowd toward them. For a split-second, Spencer thought it looked like some bony little woman in a silly Christmas outfit. But of course, he'd had a lot to drink. Magda Zarachen-ska swept closer, majestically tall, her arms outstretched and trailing scarlet lace.

She hugged Strohm to her enormous bosom. "My darling boy! Are you having all the fun in the world?"

He nodded blissfully.

"It was very naughty of your Daddy to push me down those stairs," she said. "But my friends taught him a lesson! They put a clock in his belly, like one of those funny Buddhas. My boy, it's so good to be back."

"Did the Cat Man use the Leech Magick?"

Magda shook her head and pointed to the soft sculpture. "No need. I used my own Stair Magick." She stroked his smooth head. "I've been waiting on the Steps of Time. Ever since you were a little boy."

The millionaire laughed softly. "Stairs go up, stairs go down."

"They do so many things. They take away, but they give, too." Magda took Strohm's hand and Spencer's and led them toward the soft sculp-ture. "Now let's get to work."

* * * *

The guests chatted and chewed on their insects as Strohm and Spen-cer arranged the figures in a circle, about thirty feet wide. While she waited, Magda removed Jake's left ear and cauterized the wound. There was nothing wrong with the ear, but being a Nurse, she liked to keep in practice.

The Cat Man ran his claws across the hardwood floor between the figures. He was about three feet tall and eight inches wide across his bony shoulders. He wore a tight-fitting black leather bodysuit with gold zippers and a golden mask. By the time he was finished with his task, he had scratched out a five-pointed star, edged with astrological symbols, foreign phrases and equations.

Magda stood in the center of the configuration and began a complex series of hand gestures, constantly murmuring, whispering, pointing from one figure to the next. The figures warmed to her persuasion, re-turning her gestures and chanting responses.

Spencer watched for a few minutes. Then he realized that Strohm had wandered off. He found the millionaire with Buster and Jake under the buffet, drinking vodka and eating whatever bugs crawled off the table. So he joined them.

"Are we ever going home?" Buster said.

Jake sighed, fiddling his fingers over his fresh burn-scar. "I don't really have much to go home to. A couch. A wok. My VCR." He pouted. "I don't think the Cat Man is interested in me."

"So Strohm," Spencer said, "why did your dad push Magda down some stairs?"

"Because ..." the bald man closed his eyes and thought. "Because Dad said she was ..." He huddled closer to the poet. "She was ... *is* ... intrinsically evil."

Buster crunched down on a grasshopper. "That's not a very nice thing to say about the hostess."

Strohm nodded. "I shouldn't have opened my mouth. I'm sorry."

"Is somebody doing wash?" Jake said.

Spencer listened and heard a sort of rumbling sound, just like a washing machine. They all crawled out from under the table to see what was going on.

Magda was now floating, slowly spinning, over a thunderous, swirling maelstrom of scarlet light that had opened up in the center of the star pattern. The Five Drag Queens of the Apocalypse chanted and sang and waved their hands joyously in the air. The partygoers watched silently, mesmerized.

"Thumb!" Magda cried out.

With a breathy giggle, the Starlet jumped into the light.

The Red Nurse spun faster. "Forefinger!"

The Vamp dove in with a dejected moan.

"Naughty Finger!"

The Dancer twirled as she flew in.

"Ring Finger!"

The Chanteuse walked in gracefully, allowing the whirlpool to sweep her away.

"Pinky Finger!"

The Playgirl turned around, spread out her arms and fell in backwards.

Magda Zarachenska lowered herself inch by inch into the red maelstrom. All the while she repeated, over and over, "A hand has five fingers, and it takes that many to grab hold."

Finally she was swallowed up by the light. Spencer and his friends kept watching to see what would happen. The Cat Man scampered here and there, chasing crickets and cockroaches across the floor.

"What are we waiting for?" Buster said.

"That," Strohm replied.

An enormous writhing mass sprang up out of the maelstrom. It stood about eight feet tall and smelled of musk and mad desire. It squealed madly as it leaped around the party, trampling people and overturning furniture. This frenzied creature was a grotesque yet undeniably stylish hybrid: an enormous hand—a woman's hand, well-formed and perfectly manicured—with the head of Magda Zarachenska sprouting from the wrist. The Cat Man pounced on top of the hybrid just before it crashed though a large plate-glass window and shambled off, into the night.

Strohm shook his head sadly. "The world will never be the same."

"The beginning of the end." Spencer put an arm around the millionaire's waist. "So what the Hell. Take me to Paris and spend lots of money on me."

I shall always miss Ong'ponth. Even now, the littlest things remind me of my stay there. Sunlight shining through the curtains brings to mind the membrane-clouds, spinning through the morning sky. And the telephone wires outside my window ... not unlike the network of ichorous veins stretched across the Living City. As for my appliances—I must constantly resist the urge to call them by name.

—Regina Osborn, "Dimension of Splendor"
New Vistas Magazine, Issue No. 22

"Hmm hmm-mm ... hmm hmm-mm ..."

Anne sighed as she glanced over to her husband. Whenever Paul started humming his little song, she knew something was bothering him.

"I hope there aren't any cops around," he said, looking out over the traffic. "Everybody's passing us. You're going to get a ticket for going too slow."

She glanced at the speedometer. "I'm already five miles an hour over the limit. What's the big hurry?" She instantly regretted her statement—she knew too well why Paul wanted to rush home. And she knew he was now going to launch into his Aunt Regina spiel for the seventeenth time since their vacation in Chicago began two weeks ago.

"Your Aunt Regina is the big hurry. Wacky Aunt Regina from beyond the cosmos. We should never have left her in charge of the house. The place is probably teaming with Poopalumps by now."

"Poopalumps?" Anne couldn't help but smile. "Last week they were Oompa-dinks. Before that they were Dingy-poos. The term is Ong'ponthoids. Try not to sound crazier than the person you're trashing."

"Regina has already trashed herself on every talk show around." Paul said. "And what about that stupid magazine article? She might as well have branded a big O on her forehead for 'Out To Lunch.'" Paul lit a cigarette but didn't crack his window open. Out of spite? "And the clothes she wears! Hippy dresses and a tin-foil purse. No one in the neighborhood is ever going to invite us over again. They'll all be afraid we'll bring her along."

"That's not true," Anne said, fanning a ribbon of smoke away from her face. "I talked to Aunt Regina a few days ago on the phone and she said Darlene had invited her over for coffee. Darlene thinks she's a celebrity. Could you please open your window a little?"

They drove for several minutes in silence. Soon a sign came into view—BENTON, 30 MI. Home was less than a half-hour away. This, Anne hoped, would put Paul in a better mood.

"You know why I asked Aunt Regina to stay over," she said. "Her whole life has gone haywire. For God's sake, the woman disappeared for three years!"

"So you really think she was kidnapped by Ontarians?"

"By a gang of Canadians? No." They both laughed at that. "The thing is, Aunt Regina thinks she was taken to another dimension filled with freaky monster-brains. Plenty of people who believe in UFOs and that sort of thing don't even know what to think about her story. It's important for her to have people in her life who trust her. Who treat her like a normal member of society."

"It's going take more than a couple weeks of house-sitting to bring her back to normal. You humor her too much."

"I suppose I do. It's not easy—she tells such long stories. About Ong'ponth, and all about her ex-husbands. All total losers: Number One gambled, Numbers Two and Three drank, and Number Four had a big temper. Once she had to fight him off with a frying pan."

"There's one thing I never understood. If that alien place was so special, why'd she ever come back?"

"According to Aunt Regina," Anne said, "they took her away to learn more about humans. After a while she became friends with them, and they decided to let her come and go as she pleased. Who knows where she really was? The point is, I don't want her to decide to go off again."

Later, as Anne turned the car into their driveway, Paul put a hand on her knee. "Don't worry. I'll be nice," he said. "I feel better now that I can see the place is still standing."

Aunt Regina's ancient Volkswagen was parked by the side of the house. "Wait here a minute. I'll go in first," Anne said as she turned off the engine. "Regina once told me she likes to do housework in the nude."

She walked up to the house, rang the doorbell and waited a minute, just in case Regina needed to throw on some clothes. Then she unlocked the door and went inside.

The first thing she noticed was that the entry hall floor was waxed. There were fresh flowers in the vase on the side table, too. Yellow roses from the bush in the back yard.

She barely recognized the living room. The furniture and pictures had all been completely rearranged—for the better, she had to admit. The sofa looked so much better by the north wall. Plus, the drapes were cleaned, magazines were put away, even the ashtrays had been scrubbed.

A folded piece of paper stuck out from the wax fruit centerpiece on the television. As she removed the paper, Anne noticed that the artificial apples, oranges and bananas, once furry with dust, were now shiny-clean.

As she read the note, she realized there was something wrong with Aunt Regina's strong, angular writing. The words were scribbled, as if written with the wrong hand.

Anne—
Something terrible has happened. I couldn't move my right side when I woke up this morning. I was about to call the hospital when some of my friends came by. They're going to take my (here two lines were smeared and completely illegible) will stay behind to look after things. Gugu will be using materials at hand (Anne could not make out the next several words) I'll be okay. Nothing to worry about! See you soon.—R

A knock sounded at the front door. "Are you decent in there?" Paul called out.

Anne rushed to meet him. "Something's happened to Regina. She left a note, but I can't read some of it."

Paul looked over the message. "She must've had a stroke. Who are these friends of hers? And who's—" He squinted at the paper. "Bugu? Is that what it says?"

"It looks like Gugu." Together they walked into the living room. Paul sat down in an easy chair, still examining the note.

"That doesn't make any sense," he said. "The name must be Gigi." He looked around the room. "Maybe that's who cleaned up the place."

"I'm going to look upstairs to see if I can find anything else," Anne said. "This Gigi must be staying here. Could you start calling the hospitals and find out where Regina's been admitted?"

Paul nodded, got up and began to look around the rearranged room for the phone, humming, "Hmm hmm-mm ... hmm hmm-mm ..."

Upstairs, Anne found that the second floor had been cleaned as well. Aunt Regina's dresses had been hung up in Anne's closet, but there was no sign of a third woman's clothes. She looked in her jewelry box, and was relieved to see that nothing was missing. In the bathroom, Aunt Regina's countless bottles of pills were still lined up on the top shelf of the medicine cabinet. She hoped her aunt's friends had supplied the hospital treating Regina with a list of her prescriptions.

Suddenly she heard Paul call to her. Racing down the stairs, she found him standing in the kitchen looking down into their large plastic wastebasket.

"Look at this," he said. "They're all dead."

Anne gasped—the wastebasket appeared to be almost three-quarters full of insects. Cockroaches, crickets, grasshoppers—all dry and shriveled. An indescribable stench rose from the pile, so Paul took the edges of the trash bag lining the container and tied it up at the top.

"Jesus, you wouldn't think bugs could stink like that," Paul said. He put a hand on Anne's shoulder. "Aunt Regina hasn't been admitted to any of the hospitals. I called the police and they're sending over a couple officers. We've been robbed, too—the word processor in the study is gone. So's the answering machine."

Anne looked around the kitchen—one look told her that the wall-mounted hand-vacuum was missing. "I don't understand," she said. "I checked my jewelry box and everything's fine. Why would anybody steal the hand-vac and leave behind my diamond earrings?"

The doorbell rang and Anne and Paul went to the front door. There they found their neighbor, Darlene Sturn, wiping her brow with a tissue. Her heavy make-up was beginning to trickle down her face.

"I'm so glad you're home," Darlene said. "I'm terribly worried. I haven't been able to find my boy Keith since this morning. I tried calling earlier but there was no answer. Would you know if he's with your aunt?"

"You'd better come in, Darlene." Anne led the tall, heavyset woman into the living room. "We just got back from Chicago a few minutes ago and we haven't been able to find Regina. We think she's had a stroke. She left a note but we weren't able to read most of it."

"I'm so sorry," Darlene said. "I feel just awful, bothering you at a time like this."

"We called the police," Paul said. "When they get here, we can tell them about your boy." He thought for a moment. "You had lunch with Regina. Did she mention a woman named Gigi?"

She managed an uneasy smile. "You know about her—experiences, of course. Well, she did tell me about one of her friends in that ... place. Something called Gugu. I'm sure that's not who you mean, though. Gugu isn't anything you could call a woman. They split in half like amoebas there. Regina liked that idea."

"Actually, the note looks like it says 'Gugu.'" Anne said. "You're sure Gugu isn't somebody ... human?"

Darlene rolled her eyes. "She tried explaining the whole deal to me, but it was all over my head, I'm afraid. She said this Gugu was some sort of cyber-thingy used for domestic work. Kind of a fancy space maid, I guess. I remember she said they made them big and strong, because—"

At that moment, a clattering noise erupted from below. Then came the sound of heavy footsteps on creaking stairs.

"Did you check the basement?" Anne asked Paul.

"I haven't had time." He took a couple steps toward the kitchen. The door to the basement was in there, right next to the refrigerator. But then he stopped. "It could be a burglar. Maybe we should wait for the police. Or it could just be Aunt Regina's friend."

"I hope not!" Darlene said. "I mean, I know they're not real, but the description sounded perfectly horrible. They eat whatever vermin they come across. And over there, vermin comes in all shapes and sizes. Oh, maybe it's Keith!" She walked over to Paul's side. "Keith!" she called. "Is that you making all that noise? Keith, answer me right now!"

They heard a sharp noise from the kitchen—the door to the basement, slamming. There was a moment of silence, then six booming steps echoed, each closer than the last.

Anne screamed as a misshapen figure pushed through the kitchen door.

The creature had the body of a sixtyish, full-figured woman—Aunt Regina, to be exact. A word-processor monitor served as the creature's head. The screen was filled with spark-streaked yellow and pink flesh, dotted with green slit-eyes. The monitor was held onto the body with wires, extension cords, and reddish meaty cables. The answering machine sprouted at an angle from the upper chest. The hand-vacuum had grown into Regina's torso. It seemed to be working, too—pumping blood through pulsing veins into the living monitor.

"Good day, friends-of-Regina," the answering machine purred in a metallic voice. "I hope you haven't been too worried. Right now Regina's head is on Ong'ponth, receiving the best cerebral care available. My name is Gugu and I've been assigned to look after her dwelling. I am employing her body to sustain my corporeal presence here. Her flesh-hands are so clever for small tasks. Much better than my usual metal ones."

Gugu stepped forward, unbuttoning the top of its tie-dyed hippy dress. A long, pink fleshy stalk tipped with three chitinous needles shot out from beneath the word processor and began to waver toward Paul. "Have no fear, friends-of-Regina. I shall dispose of this vermin shortly."

"That's not vermin!" Anne shouted as the needles stabbed into Paul's neck. "That's my husband! My husband!"

A faint, strangled "Hmm hmm-hmm" escaped Paul's lips. Darlene blinked twice, fainted and fell to the floor.

"Husband? Husband?" The green slit-eyes squinted behind the glass screen. "Aunt Regina told us that husbands are men ... and men are pests. Vermin." Paul turned a sickening shade of gray as the hungry stalk did its work. Anne picked up a poker from the fireplace—and then set it down. What could she do? Aunt Regina would need this body when the Ong'ponthoids were done repairing her head.

"I have been so very busy today," Gugu confided as Anne sank into the easy chair. "I took care of a smaller bipedal husband in the backyard much earlier today. I put the husk in the trash under all of the tiny six-legged husbands."

The creature withdrew its stalk from Paul's desiccated flesh and then shambled to the window. "I see two husbands in blue garments approaching the dwelling," Gugu said. "So much to do. My work is never done."

THE RICH, MEATY TASTE
OF VENGEANCE

"Would you care for something to drink? Iced tea? Coffee?" Mr. Belt-hor's thick finger hovered over the intercom button. "Something stronger?"

"Whatever you're having will be fine, thank you," said the woman seated in front of his desk. She turned slightly to glance at the clock on the wall.

Mr. Belthor stabbed the intercom. "Meg? Two Manhattans. And a cold-cut tray." He turned back to his guest, started to say something, then stopped. "I'm sorry. I'm afraid I've forgotten your first name."

"You haven't forgotten. At the group meeting, I was introduced simply as Ms. Tetrarch." A scarlet smile slashed across her thin, sleek face. "Agadora. Not Aggie, not Dora. Agadora."

"What an unusual name. But lovely, lovely. You can call me Edgar. I take it you're here about Meaty Boy ..."

Agadora flicked a stray blonde lock out of her eyes. "I understand you've cancelled the campaign, and after only two weeks. I think you are making a mistake, Edgar. Public reaction has been favorable. Sales were showing gradual improvement. A campaign takes time to build—we told you that at the very beginning. I can't understand why you pulled the plug."

A heavyset, middle-aged woman wheeled a small cart into the office. She removed a glass from the cart and set it on the desk. "Your drink, sir. Your cold cuts. I thought you might like some Brie." She handed a glass to Agadora and left the room.

"That was Meg," Mr. Belthor said. "Meg has been with Perfect Pet Products for fifteen years. Meg knows what I like. She knows I like Manhattans. She knows I like cold cuts and Brie." He took a long pull from his glass. "She also knows I hate Meaty Boy."

Agadora took a sip. "Then why did you approve the storyboards?"

"Usually, that's all I do. O'Hara, Stern & Finlay has been my agency for years. I'm a busy man—I find people I can trust and let them do what they do best. The storyboards did seem kind of odd, but I thought, perhaps their savvy new creative director knows something I don't. And maybe you do. And yet... Can I be frank?"

Agadora nodded.

"I watch a lot of late-night TV," Mr. Belthor said. "A few nights ago, I was watching a talk show. I was just about to fall asleep in my chair when the commercial come on." He selected a slice of pimento loaf from the tray. "I almost shit my pants. It caught me off-guard. That commercial you made is a nightmare come to life. A little boy made out of red dog food? Being chased by beagles and poodles? And the look on his face: that was the worst. Like a soul in Hell! I know commercials these days have to be edgy, but my God! I don't like being frightened in my own home. I can't remember the last time I'd had such a scare. Perhaps when I had eye surgery a few years ago... I will admit that Meaty Boy is slightly less frightening than a scalpel."

"Really, Edgar. He's only a piece of animated clay."

"Ah! Then why did you say 'he' instead of 'it'? Meaty Boy is far too *realistic*."

"We could redesign him. Stylize him." Agadora rose from her chair and crossed to the window, where she stood looking out over the city. Mr. Belthor studied her: slim, fashionable, really quite stunning. Mature, but she wore her age well. It was hard to believe this perfect woman was the creator of that grotesque meat-devil.

Strange, but there was something familiar about her pose by the window, hand on hip, chin thrust forward. Familiar and yet disturbing ...

"I'm sorry, Agadora, but the problems I have with this concept go beyond mere design. I want to see new storyboards next week. This time, keep it light. Lively. Irish setters catching frisbees. Got it?"

Agadora studied the cold-cut tray and popped a strip of rare roast beef in her mouth. "I'll see to it personally, Edgar."

* * * *

After work, Mr. Belthor stopped by the Red Rhino, a yuppie nightspot with an eclectic assortment of weekly promotions. He found a seat at the bar and ordered a Manhattan from MacRae, the manager.

"So, what's on tonight's agenda?" Mr. Belthor said, lifting his glass. "None of that dance music crap you had last week, I hope."

"'Fraid so, Edgar," MacRae said. "But don't worry, the college kids won't start showing up for another couple hours. The girls are still putting up decorations."

Mr. Belthor looked across the bar, where a trio of waitresses were pinning up campy movie posters by the dance floor. He read a few of the titles: *Attack of the Wasp Women, Voodoo Death Vixens, Nightmare Boudoir*—the same posters he'd seen last week. Hopefully this promotion would die out in a month or so. He didn't like being driven out of his favorite bar by a pack of college brats.

Nightmare Boudoir ... he kept glancing at the poster. Had he ever seen this movie, on the late-show, perhaps? The poster depicted a leggy redhead in a black negligee, hand on hip, chin angled up to catch the light—

He rose from his seat and walked over for a closer look. He had to step right up to the poster; his eye operation hadn't returned him to perfect vision. The woman in the negligee—was that Agadora Tetrarch? Much younger, with a different hair color, but yes, undoubtedly her. He had no idea she'd ever been an actress. He searched the credits and found what must have been her pseudonym: *Featuring Real-Life Witch CATHEDRA TARRAGO as Countess Orgasmia.*

He returned to the bar, caught MacRae's attention and pointed to the poster. "That movie, *Nightmare Boudoir*. Have you ever seen it?"

"Sure. Years ago, at a drive-in. Some spooky Italian soft-core crap. It even had a couple sequels: *Orgy Dungeon* and *Tomb of the Love Countess*." MacRae smiled at the poster. "A real-life witch. The closest I've ever had to that was my ex-wife—a real-life bitch."

"That actress, did she ever make any other movies?"

MacRae shrugged. "Just some porno flicks. I've got an old magazine in my office with a spread on her. And I do mean spread. Do you want to take a look at it?"

"If you don't mind." Mr. Belthor paid for his drink with a hundred-dollar bill. "You can keep the change if you'll let me have the magazine. The poster, too."

* * * *

That evening, Mr. Belthor pinned up the poster in his den. At the end of their meeting, Agadora had given him a business card listing home, work, car phone, and fax numbers, as well as an e-mail address. A few minutes earlier he had left a message on her answering machine, commenting on her lively and athletic career as an actress and model. With any luck, she would be returning his call shortly. What would Ms. Tetrarch do to keep her past a secret? He could hardly wait to find out.

He decided to have another drink. The day's events were certainly cause enough for celebration. He went to the liquor cabinet, poured himself a glass of white wine, and settled down in his favorite easy chair.

He picked up the remote control and turned on the television. He flicked through the channels: a sitcom, a cop show, another sitcom... What was this? Some sort of documentary? A group of young people dressed in black were tramping through a weedy cemetery. Several were carrying burlap sacks. The picture quality was poor: grainy, with bleached-out colors. Maybe this was a foreign film.

The group gathered at the side of a grave. Mr. Belthor couldn't quite make out the name on the stone. Shovels were pulled from the sacks and two burly men dug vigorously at the grave.

A young red-haired woman in a black leather jacket separated from the group and moved behind the tombstone. She carried a large book bound in dark red cloth, which she rested on the top of the stone. She began to read aloud in a foreign language. Latin?

Then it hit him—the young woman was Agadora. Or Cathedra, for this had to be one of those Italian movies MacRae mentioned.

Soon the young men scrambled out of the hole they had dug. The red-haired woman came from behind the tombstone and knelt by the side of the grave. Pulling a small curved blade from her jacket pocket, she slit the palm of her left hand and allowed the blood to trickle onto the coffin below.

The next shot zoomed in tight on the red-haired woman. Cathedra looked into the camera and smiled. "I'll see to it personally, Edgar," she said.

Mr. Belthor choked on his wine. What the hell was this? Some sort of bizarre joke? The screen suddenly darkened, so he leaned closer to see what was happening. All he could make out was a brown, whorled pattern. Wood grain, that's what it was. An extreme close-up of the coffin's lid—

With a sharp crack the lid split open. Meaty, glistening cylinders poked through the cracked wood; red fingers, followed by a searching red hand. Then the wood fell away, revealing a raw, insane face.

That moist, chunky flesh—that toothless maw. It was Meaty Boy, squealing and twisting and groping, reaching out—

Heart pounding, Mr. Belthor grabbed the remote control and turned the television off. For a long moment he sat staring at the blank screen.

At last he turned the television back on. The cemetery scene was gone. In its place was a news program about the homeless.

He left the den and went downstairs. Earlier that evening he had been sorting through some invoices and contracts on the long table in the dining room. His briefcase was in the midst of the paperwork, with Agadora's business card inside.

He opened his briefcase, then stopped. Even if he did call her again, what could he say? *You've put a curse on me, haven't you? Marvelous. Let's do lunch.*

A movement outside the window caught his eye. He reached into the briefcase and removed a small German handgun from a zippered pocket. He moved closer to the window, but saw nothing. Nothing except a large greasy handprint on the outside of the glass.

Mr. Belthor put his own hand against the stain. The fingers of the imprint were three inches longer than his own.

He returned the handgun to the briefcase. This foreign peashooter might do for muggers and other urban vermin, but it was no match for what was lurking outside.

He went into the hallway, opened the closet, pushed aside sweaters, jackets and raincoats and then opened a smaller, hidden door. It was a tight fit, but he managed to squeeze through.

He turned on the lights and looked around. Monitors, gauges, rows of toggle switches and buttons... God, but it was beautiful. What he had said to Agadora earlier was too true: he did not like being frightened in his own home. That was why he had installed this elaborate home security nexus several years ago. The system had cost him hundreds of thousands of dollars, but it had done much to allay his fears.

He sat at the control panel and switched on the various monitors. He looked in, via hidden cameras, on the driveway ... the front and back entrances ... the swimming pool and tennis court ... the main hallways, first and second floor ... even the basement. No sign of an intruder.

As a precaution, Mr. Belthor flicked on the laser sensors. In a half-second, each of the monitored locales was spiderwebbed with thin beams of light. The disruption of any beam would set off alarms both in the house and at the police station.

Opening a drawer under the control panel, he withdrew a bottle of whiskey. He took a pull from the bottle and glanced over the monitors. He had no idea what sort of powers Agadora could summon—but at least he could summon a fleet of squad cars, if the need arose.

A hulking form materialized on the driveway screen. It lurched silently through the laser beams toward the house. The same dark shape appeared on every monitor.

In the basement—

Beside the pool—

At both entrances—

—Cutting through the lasers without setting off the alarms.

Mr. Belthor screamed with rage. Each Meaty Boy was shambling toward or through the house. A death-troop of rampaging dog-food behemoths! Their hands were raised, huge fingers clenching eagerly, as though those juicy digits itched to strangle him to death. The raw, writhing lips of the creatures seemed to be mouthing obscenities at him. Infuriated, he raised the whiskey bottle to take another swig.

There was a little Meaty Boy inside, clawing at the glass.

He poured the whiskey on the floor, his foot raised to squash the tiny horror. But it wouldn't come out. When he looked into the neck of the bottle, Meaty Boy appeared to be clinging to the bottom on the outside. Yet when he held the bottle any other way, it was still inside.

Mr. Belthor started to laugh.

Like any television image, Meaty Boy was a harmless optical effect: a ghost in glass. Whenever he had seen Meaty Boy, it had been through a transparent medium. Even the handprint had appeared on the other side of the window.

He turned off the monitors and left the control room.

Returning to the den, he ripped the poster off the wall. Strangely enough, he was actually disappointed in the B-movie sexpot and her grade-B witchcraft. Was this evening's journey into the macabre the best this 'real-life witch' could conjure up? True, there had been some especially tense moments. But so what? His eye operation had been ten times scarier.

At that moment, twin red shadows sprang to life in his artificial corneas.

THE PRINCE OF DREADFUL MAGICK

They had the perfect life together, or at least, as perfect as one might reasonably expect (for perfection is such a relative concept): both were fit and tanned and tolerably intelligent; they bought the right cookbooks, ate the right foods with the right wines, and even flossed; at parties, they hinted and cooed about their constant lovemaking, and rightly so, for they coupled regularly, energetically, adroitly; but they were not in love. Let me share what I know, for I know much: some knowledge comes to me so easily and yet sometimes, I am blind to the most obvious of truths.

And now I'm thinking about the first time: not the first time I had sex (it took an hour and a half!), but rather, the first time that I was seized by the urge to make magick. I couldn't help it; I think I was about nine at the time. I softened the wax from a candle-making set in my hands and mixed in pubic hairs from my brother's bed, some dead flies, and bits of chocolate. And I found myself muttering over and over: "Here you shall stay and never be free. Nothing for you and all for me." My burger-flipping brother never moved out of our parent's house; he never even learned to drive; while I became a $35-an-hour results-oriented dervish of a public relations consultant and surprise, surprise, many of my clients were known to call me a wizard. Tee hee, ha ha.

And I hasten to repeat that I couldn't help it. Not everyone can do magick (I should know) and often, those who *can* know not what they do—but still, they simply cannot help it; and it may be hereditary. Grandma did magick, too; this I realized years after her death; she never said a word about it and in fact, she surely didn't know. I remember this: she was in the habit of constantly twisting, twiddling, playing with her cocktail rings (she wore one on each finger); turning them in a specific order; and if she was mad at the husband du jour, she would mutter under her breath—"That bastard, that bastard, that chintzy bastard"—and twist the diamonds 'round and 'round on her fingers and wonder of wonders, that husband, that bastard, would develop so, so, so many tumors (one, I think, for each turn of the diamonds, or perhaps, for each repetition of the word 'bastard').

When I was eleven, something happened and I couldn't help it: I was playing basketball with my best friend Carl in his parent's driveway and I threw the ball into a nearby group of trees. He went to get the ball and

I went too, whispering "This is going to be good. This is going to be just like it should." I picked up some weeping willow twigs; I whipped the air with them as I followed Carl; the twigs were damp and flexible, and I was able to tie them into a large knot which I slipped over Carl's head as he stooped to pick up the ball. I didn't hurt him; I simply slipped the loose knot over his head; a second later, the knot came free and the twigs fell to the ground. Carl called me a dim bulb (his father used to call people that) and we finished our game. After that, Carl began doing my homework; he brought me cookies that his mom baked; he was popular and with his help, I became class president; he gave me the skateboard that his dad bought him for Christmas; eventually he bought a gift for me with his own money (it was only a cheap plastic chess set; he wanted me to teach him to play) and it was this gift that tightened the knot, the willow knot that no longer was. In college, we became lovers and he was extraordinary (like I said: the first time took ninety minutes) and it was fun to play chess my way: his pieces moved according to the rules, while all of my pieces were queens.

That was the year that I had my first vision: it happened while I was taking a bath, leaning back in the tub and reading some lurid, cheap-ass paperback. I found myself walking through a desert of silver sand; furry vermin were being torn apart by glittering metal insects; a misshapen sun boiled orange and green in a phlegm-yellow sky. An enormous face of quavering vapor stared at me from the horizon: pale flesh, a wide nose, lavender eyes; fleshy, pointed ears; wide cheekbones. Thin, cruel lips parted, revealing needle teeth, and I heard a voice, thick and slow like poisonous honey: LEARN CONTROL AND I SHALL COME INTO FOCUS FOR YOU. And the vision ended; it popped like a bubble and I found myself in too-cold bath water with a soggy paperback half-floating, half-resting against my belly.

Magick has nothing to do with good vs. evil; rather, it's more a matter of longing vs. fate. We want one thing, but fate provides another (and always, a poor substitute). For some, magick comes to the rescue; in my case, the results could not be controlled.

From that day forth, I noticed this: others like myself! in nightclubs and malls and on the streets, with high cheekbones and dark hair and wicked smiles; there was an unmistakable intelligence in their eyes; when I talked with my kindred, there was always a sense of understanding beyond mere words. Ours was a family (to paraphrase the insouciant dead) that dared not speak its surname.

In time, I grew oh! so! tired! of Carl's doting: that may be why (but then, who can say, when magick is involved?) I took one of his dirty sweatshirts and sprinkled it with salt; then I cut it into ribbons and tied these together into a crude doll of knots: and I stabbed my finger with a pin and smeared lips of blood onto the face of this doll and said these words five times: "This is exactly how. Make him yours! I'm done with him now."

And so he met a pretty girl and they became a couple and I should have moved on, should have left them alone, but I couldn't. Magick had compelled me to end my romance with Carl; and yet the magick would not allow me to start anew. Nothing else in life worked for me; I tried to find work in some other part of the country, but phone numbers disappeared; letters got lost in the mail; potential employers went out of business within days of talking to me; incredibly, one fellow was struck by lightning. And so I lingered; and the pretty girl, blonde and dark-eyed Miranda, found me interesting and knew only that I was Carl's best friend (for he had never found better).

One night, quite spontaneously, I fried onions and garlic in peanut oil; I dug cockroaches out of the trash basket and threw them in the hot oil; they burst like popcorn kernels and I muttered utter gibberish: "What could and should be is for me: we shall see what there is to see." Then I took a claw hammer from my tool kit, smashed a hand mirror, and tossed the bits into the oil. I had no idea what I was doing, but it felt exquisite. The next morning, Miranda invited me to her apartment for lunch; Carl would be there; I was lonely, so I decided to go. I was curious, too; I wasn't sure how Carl felt about me; and an intrigue surfaced: had magick wiped the slate clean, or had it only written over the message? I was determined to find out. (Of course I realized this: I seemed to have no control over my powers, and yet, the results were often to my benefit. There had to be a degree of subconscious desire involved; and yet how much of anyone's fate, good or bad, is brought about by suppressed needs?)

Miranda had prepared baked salmon with dill sauce; Carl was hail-fellow-well-met; our lunch led to dinners to movies to weekend trips out of town. Miranda was well-read; middle class, but still fun to talk to; I wasn't sure what to make of Carl, so I took him at face value: we chatted, smiled; no knowing glances, no innuendo, nothing. I soon realized that Miranda found me attractive: there was no mistaking those glances, bold and accommodating.

My next vision happened while I was trying on pants in the dressing room of a menswear shop. Again I was walking through the silver desert: rats and rabbitlike creatures writhed in the sand, bleeding and screaming; in their wounds, oversized copper ants and golden beetles stared up at me, and metal maggots sparkled like tiny diamonds. And again, the vaporous face loomed on the horizon: only this time, the features were sharper, more catlike, and the honey-slow voice oozed forth: YOUR TIME IS COMING, MY LITTLE ONE. And I could only say, "Who are you?" The reply was this: THE GREATER PART OF YOU. When I awoke, I found that I had soiled the slacks I had been trying on; a frantic clerk was standing over me, trying to put a pencil in my mouth so I wouldn't swallow my tongue.

Another day, another lunch (this time at a restaurant): "It's funny," Miranda said. Carl was at work and I was downing my third mimosa. "You and Carl have known each other since you were kids, right? But he never talks about his childhood. He just skims over it. At the most, he'll say, 'we played basketball a lot.' Did he have a lot of problems?"

"Not that I know of." I rolled the stem of my glass between my fingers. "Is it all that important?"

"Of course it's important." Her eyes grew large; it was as if I had dared to question ancient wisdom. "What if I wanted to have kids someday? He might not make a good father if he hated his childhood."

I had to perform a ritual there and then (I couldn't control it; you might insist that I could have, but I should know): I continued the conversation, fiddling with the salt shaker, the silly miniature pepper grinder, the napkins; I made little scenarios with my food (the potatoes are mountains! the carrots are dwarves!) and Miranda laughed and laughed; she thought I was just being charming; and in a sense, I was indeed charming her; and I asked her what she would want to name a baby, and suddenly—a *revelation!*—two Names popped into my head: and certainly they were not names for babies. The face of vapor has many Names, and AZU is one; another is The Prince of Dreadful Magick.

I wondered: What would my table ritual yield? It was a tiny spell in that I didn't have to do so very much; it was an enormous spell in that it involved another. I had a thought that made me laugh: Miranda heavy with a child of AZU. That surely would be a waste of time; AZU has many, many children (I should know), yet He did not need to father them; rather, He found ones with talent, and claimed—and shall always claim—them as His own.

Whenever I went out in public, I felt the eyes of my kindred upon me: their hot, lusty eyes; but for me, the heat was curiously subdued; it was a warm glow that held a curious degree of hope (the most unexpected of longings) and I was vaguely frightened: nothing had been said, nothing had been promised; and yet I felt utterly responsible.

I spent more time—far too much time—with Carl and Miranda. We drank waaaay too much; we talked about sex practices in foreign lands; Carl began resting my hand upon my leg now and then, and whereas the gesture did not thrill me as it once had, it did comfort me with its familiarity. In a tiny corner of my brain, a sluggish toad of a beast whispered: oh, how sad that he does not remember the pleasure.

As I have said: I had no control over my magick; perhaps my subconscious was at work; and I pondered this: maybe my secret brain was in league with the Prince. I hated to think that I was a puppet! a mere pawn! (for I have always cherished my individuality); but of course, one must make sacrifices.

Carl and Miranda began preparing my meals and doing my dishes and laundry and I found myself collecting things! Things! THINGS! You cannot imagine so I shall tell you: gears from old clocks; springs and lenses and antique scissors; parts from broken televisions and radios; and more! I put these things in my basement; I arranged them in a cunning fashion. SO MANY THINGS! Velvet ropes from abandoned theatres; boxes of claw hammers; party favors and the dried and/or rotted husks of jack o' lanterns. Occasionally one of my wild-eyed siblings would stop me on the street and press a curio into my hands: a brass key, perhaps, or a molar with a filling.

I abandoned my work but that was fine, since my siblings began to hand me loose change and twenty dollar bills and stolen credit cards. I didn't doubt and I didn't question and I didn't hesitate; I simply DID. Days passed and the basement collection grew to fill the entire house; and Carl and Miranda and I spent hours each day (for they had quit their jobs too) coupling, or rather tripling; and my siblings began stopping by to join us: each day, different siblings: there was Agatha, an older but incredibly agile woman; hare-lipped, lean Ingrid; vicious Paxton, he of the curved black nails. My vision grew blurry around the edges; high-pitched noises hurt my ears; and I found myself repeating a phrase as each visitor entered the house: "Any day now, any way now. Soon I shall know what to do and say." Every now and then, Carl would put his hand on my chest and say "Mine, mine, mine."

Days melted into weeks into months and still the siblings gave me money; Carl grew prone to possessive, babyish fits; he would wrap his arms around me and scream at Miranda to GO AWAY; and Miranda grew smaller, paler, leaner, crueler; she watched our lovemaking from the most shadowed corner of the bedroom, all the while muttering, her eyes glowing silver; often I would catch her tentatively trying to magick against Carl, fashioning little dolls out of filth; so I instructed several of my siblings to watch, constantly watch her, to distract her, to hide her loathsome dolls.

And it was clear to me that we were forming archetypes: not Father, Son and Holy Ghost; not Maiden, Mother and Crone: but surely there were vague, disturbing similarities: I was the True and Guiding Light (brilliant, relentless, searing); Carl was the One Who Had Returned to Grace; and Miranda, my sad, oddly shrunken, horrid darling, was the Plotting Worm (and even now, I know—as I know so many things—that someday, followers of the abhorred but completely necessary Miranda will test the resolve of my minions).

And this morning: I gazed into the sun and knew it to be a single cell of my brain; I felt the talons of AZU tearing raw doors into my soul; I set into motion (unthinkingly, yet instinctively) the collection/amplifier/deus ex machina of my house/church/tomb; and as AZU entered my psyche, I allowed the parasite Miranda (my wormy infant of perfect wickedness) to enter my flesh, to riddle my meat with the tunnels of her Everlasting Objection; and Carl! O my Carl. Yes, Carl had to die; yes, I had to bathe in his blood (that is and shall always be the way); and YES, he did rise from death.

Worldwide, my siblings—by the thousands!—are burning, bombing, intoning, cursing, cleansing with fire and magick; I can hear them, and not only their voices: surely I can hear all, all, all of their frantic heartbeats. And the slender, passionate ghost of Carl is gazing at me with complete adoration; for you see, at last I was able to initiate and execute a ritual with utter *intent,* and I know that I can (and will) perform this particular act of magick again and again: I only hope that future siblings do not take to worshipping my bloody claw hammer; but we shall see what we shall see. Even now, several of my favorite siblings are drawing near, to worship and more; and I find myself thinking: Just how many Saviors can one religion endure?

THE BLOODY WOMAN AND THE CHAMELEON MAN, ALSO KNOWN AS MOM AND DAD

I loved them, and love them still, though I'm not sure if that's in spite of—or because of—their status as semi-mythical urban legends. I've even written poems about them. The poem about Dad was called "The Guy Who Never Leaves The Mall" and the one about Mom was entitled "Follow The Bleeder." I write a lot of poetry. I do other things, too, but most of them are pretty boring. Well, I don't think they are, but you probably would, so...

Never mind.

Back to my parents. First let me tell you about Dad.

His big problem was, he blended in too much when he was growing up. His parents weren't mean to him. But they weren't especially nice to him. He was simply <u>there</u>.

His older siblings were much more accomplished. His younger siblings were much better looking. Oh, he did a lot of things, and looked just fine—not that anyone noticed. He was of average height and weight, with brownish-bluish-hazel eyes and blondish-darkish-sandy hair.

He grew up accustomed to not being seen. Eventually, attention just made him ... uncomfortable. Itchy.

His friends called him Mr. Average—while he still had friends. Eventually they all lost track of him, and he of them.

He loved going to the mall because it was so easy to become just another face. Or better yet, a part of the scenery. In fact, if he stood completely still, people often would mistake him for a mannequin.

He didn't like having to work for a living. What a rigmarole. It just meant having to show up regularly. To strive. To be evaluated. Who needed the scrutiny? Not him, that's for sure.

One day, during his lunch hour, Dad had to go to the mall for some gloves. It was getting cold outside. He found a nice pair in a department store and stood by the counter, waiting for a clerk.

They ignored him. And ignored him.

Finally, he just walked out with the gloves. These days, most malls have those sensor thingies to detect shoplifting. But back then, not too many stores had that kind of ritzy technology.

Dad never went back to work. He decided to just stay at the mall. It was easier that way.

He ate the food left behind on trays in the food court. Eventually, he took to crawling around in the air ducts, so that after hours, he could go into shops and get soft pretzels and corn dogs and really big cookies.

He changed his clothes constantly to fool guards and clerks. He avoided security cameras almost instinctively—they were, after all, watchers, and he could not abide being watched.

Years passed, and he enjoyed the streamlined simplicity of his chosen lifestyle. He had no desire to meet or talk to or even touch anyone.

Until he fell in love with the Bloody Woman.

She showed up at the mall rather abruptly. One night she was just ... there. Some say she had been a lovesick customer, who had fallen in love with a shoe store clerk who couldn't care less about her. He broke her heart, and broken things are usually leaky.

Others say she was a blood-drive donor, and that she died after an over-zealous attendant took way too much from her.

No matter what her origins, the results were the same: every night she walked the mall, bleeding and bleeding and bleeding, leaving her gore everywhere. The security cameras would catch her trying on gloves, dresses, shoes, saturating the goods with crimson. But at dawn, the blood would all evaporate like magic, leaving no stains, no wetness. Nothing.

At first Dad was a little upset (he never really got mad) that someone else was invading his territory. But on the other hand, it was kind of nice to have a lady around the place.

She was pretty. Very pale, with long black hair and lustrous black eyes. And she was classy. She only tried on the very best merchandise.

My Dad got to see what happened to her in the morning. She evaporated along with her blood. She was, after all, a ghost.

And yet she wasn't your average ghost. She could pick things up, move things around. She had a flesh and blood body, and an endless supply of blood at that.

Why didn't security guards ever arrest her? Well, some tried, but her touch made those poor fools die. Of brain hemorrhages. So the guards were told to just ignore and avoid her. They were also told not to mention her to anyone—but they did. Usually in bars. Their drunken anecdotes started rumors, and the rumors grew into the legend of the Bloody Woman.

Every now and then, her mall wanderings took her through areas without any security cameras, and Dad would go and chat with her. She never answered, so Dad had to do all the talking. An eavesdropping guard once heard what he had to say, and so Dad eventually became a legend, too—the Chameleon Man.

Fortunately, the Bleeding Woman could control her fatal touch, which was lucky for Dad. They fell in love and had a baby. And the Bleeding Woman became Mom.

Dad once told me that when my pregnant mother evaporated in the morning, her belly bulge—me—evaporated along with her. But when closing time rolled around and she returned, there I'd be, too, bulging just a little bigger.

I hate to tell you what killed Mom ... or rather, what killed her a second, permanent time. Sad to say, it was me. Dad told me the only thing that kept her going, kept her moving, was the hurt. When she looked at me, the hurt went away—and so did she.

I never knew her, but I do love her.

So Dad went back to being a normal guy with a home and a job and an identity again. Because he had a kid. It's hard to live in hiding with a crying baby. But being visible turned out to be too much stress for him, and when I reached an age more or less considered the beginning of adulthood, he died of a heart attack. I think he wanted to die.

"Dad," I once said to him in my youth, "do you miss being the Chameleon Man?"

"Of course," he said. "But I'm not sorry that I stopped. A person really ought to leave something behind. Something substantial. More than just cookie crumbs."

I guess that makes me something substantial. I hope so, anyway.

My family history may seem outlandish, but really, every family has its share of eccentrics—and worse. Drunken fathers. Vicious mothers. Brutal, thoughtless siblings.

So now you may be asking: what about sonny-boy? What's the deal with me? Am I invisible, simply walking around, ignored by everyone else? Or am I constantly bleeding, reminding others that ours is a world of hurt?

Such silly questions.

I do a little of both, every day, every week, every year.

Just like you.

HELLO! MY NAME IS HALJA

Gumm wondered why the door of his whitewashed hospital room was locked. He wondered why the window of his room opened into perpetual darkness, and why his medicine was such an awful shade of green, and why his doctor never stopped by to check on him.

He especially wondered how his nurse—a cow-eyed, shiny-faced creature—could have gone through life without developing a personality.

The woman brought Gumm his meals, spoon-fed him ghastly dollops of green syrup, and tended to his various bodily peccadilloes. Her name tag read HELLO! MY NAME IS HALJA. She always turned away from him before she spoke. Gumm guessed that she was hiding a mouthful of crooked, or perhaps discolored, teeth. The nurse's conversation was utterly boring; often, he would fall asleep while she was talking.

Once, after the nurse had left, Gumm opened his window and peered down into the darkness. He heard a lapping sound, a slapping of— Waves? He threw a mug into the abyss and waited for the splash. Instead, he heard a distant, high-pitched squeal.

He went back to bed and slipped under the covers for a nap. He felt tired and sad. He suspected that the hospital was keeping his family away from him, and for no good reason. Surely Elizabeth was a nervous wreck by now. Surely poor little Anthony was crying himself to sleep each night...

He heard a faint clink. He looked to the window and saw the cup, resting on the sill.

He returned to the window. The cup was filled to the brim with green syrup. He poured the ooze back into the darkness.

Later, when the nurse brought him his supper, Gumm asked for the hundredth time if he could take a walk in the hallway.

Nurse Halja turned away from him. "Oh no, Mr. Gumm. You need rest. You took a nasty fall. Yes, you certainly did, and I'm afraid that your treatment plan does not include exercise. Wouldn't want to jostle your poor, sore brain. Do you want your condition to evolve from acute to chronic? I think not. Now forget about the hall and eat your cutlet like a good boy." She turned back, and her smooth face glowed in the fluorescent lighting.

"I want to see my family," he said. "I want to see Elizabeth and my little Anthony. It's been so long."

"What a fuss you are making, Mr. Gumm." The nurse *tsk-tsk*ed under her breath. "I hope that you are not experiencing a relapse."

Gumm unfurled his napkin and his plastic tableware clattered out of its folds. The spoon missed his meal tray and fell to the floor. The nurse stooped to pick up the spoon; in doing so, she momentarily lost her footing and leaned against the bed to regain her balance.

Gumm ate his cutlet and his rice pudding. Out of the corner of his eye, he glimpsed a small rectangle of plastic caught by its metal pin on his bed cover.

* * * *

Days and weeks and months passed. Gumm ate his cutlets and swallowed more teaspoons of green syrup. His nurse performed her duties with polite boredom. Eventually she replaced the name tag she had lost with a new one, which read ASK FOR HALJA. THANK YOU!

Gumm would often try to pick the door lock with the pin on the nurse's misplaced tag. He would twist bumps and bends into the pin, hoping to replicate the actual key. He failed each time, but found the endeavor to be a pleasant, even exhilarating diversion.

During one meal period, Nurse Halja informed him that there was to be a change in his medication. "We favor an aggressive pharmaco-dynamic approach, Mr. Gumm," she said. Gumm noticed that the back of her neck was heavily speckled, but couldn't tell if these were age spots or freckles. "From now on, you shall take your medicine by the tablespoonful."

"What exactly does this medicine do for me?" Gumm said.

The nurse sighed with either impatience or indifference. "It helps you to get better. You had a nasty fall, you know. You have experienced severe physical and psychological deconditioning. Take your medicine and rest. Rest is so important, Mr. Gumm. You wouldn't want to addle your brain all over again."

"How long have I been here?"

The nurse sighed again. "Not long enough, I'm afraid."

Gumm stared at his half-eaten cutlet. "I want to see my doctor."

"Your doctor is a very busy man. Simply too busy for words."

The nurse turned and moved his meal tray to the nightstand. She leaned over him and felt his jawline and forehead with her cold hands.

Never before had Gumm been this close to her. Her flesh did not appear to have pores. A faint, foul current of air issued from her nostrils.

She touched the lower lid of his right eye and tried to push it down. Gumm shook his head a bit. She tried the left eye next, but he slapped her hand away.

"I'm not a puppet," he said. "I demand to be treated with respect." He stared up into her shiny face with defiance. Then he saw the shadowed gaps between her eyeballs and their lids, and he gasped.

The nurse spun away from him. "With or without respect, you shall be treated," she said. She stood completely still for a moment, thinking or perhaps waiting for a comment, before leaving the room.

Gumm's heart pounded so fiercely that it pained him. So the nurse wore a mask. Was she ugly? But why did she turn away from him to speak? Perhaps she had a facial deformity, and her mouth didn't move well with the mask. Or perhaps her mouth didn't move at all.

He removed the name tag from its hiding place in one of his slippers. He shaped the pin into a new configuration (three tiny bends instead of four), inserted it into the lock and twisted. Nothing happened, so he twisted again with more force.

Within the lock's workings, a decisive clack sounded.

Gumm eased the door open.

The hall outside of his room was long, white-washed, and lined with doors. Across the hall, twenty feet to the left, he saw a half-open door, leading into darkness.

He moved slowly and quietly through the hall. He peered warily into the shadowed doorway. He saw dozens of jackets, coats, dresses... Only a closet. He reached in and grabbed a dark green overcoat. He tried to shut the closet door, but the catch was broken.

He continued down the hall. Soon he would be with his family! He wondered how old Anthony would be... He heard a faint scratching behind him. He turned just in time to see a black and white cat emerge from the closet. Gumm found this terribly amusing. A cat in a hospital? How woefully unprofessional. The piebald creature began to slink toward him.

Gumm walked for several minutes. In the distance he saw a red sign hanging in front of a door. He walked faster—yes, the sign read EXIT. The cat had caught up with him and was pacing by his side. Gumm didn't want to carry the animal, but he hoped that it would follow him out of the building. He could give it to Elizabeth. Elizabeth loved cats! He remembered that Elizabeth used to call her cats her real family, since Anthony was so damned moody and she needed someone, something to love her—But no, no, no, that memory couldn't be right. Gumm took a deep breath. He felt dizzy now, even a bit nauseous. He suddenly realized that he was standing in front of the red sign.

He slipped on the overcoat. It was far too big for him; its owner had to be an incredibly fat fellow. He was about to open the exit door when he heard a sound...a sort of bubbling.

He listened closely: yes, something was bubbling and gurgling in the room to his immediate right. He thought for a moment of the lapping sound he had heard beyond his window. He looked up and down the hall—no sign of Nurse Halja. He bent down for a quick peek through the keyhole.

He saw the back of a woman in white. Was this Nurse Halja? Why, yes: even from this distance, he could detect the spots on her neck.

Evidently she was on excellent terms with this gentleman. She had seen fit to remove an item of personal attire in his presence. This smooth, rubbery item stared at Gumm with eyeless sockets from atop a side table. The nurse was pouring green syrup directly from the bottle down the throat of the patient. The poor fellow appeared to be suffering from some sort of severe skin condition. His flesh was green, puffy, damp—actually, a bit *frothy*...

Gumm recoiled from the keyhole with a cry of revulsion. He staggered to the exit, opened the door, and rushed down and down a stairway lit with small red bulbs.

"Mr. Gumm!" The voice of Nurse Halja echoed above him. "Mr. Gumm! Come back here immediately! Think of your condition! I insist: forget this foolishness and return to your room!"

Gumm ran down stairs of carpeted wood, then bare wood, then stone. "Elizabeth!" he cried. "Anthony! I'm coming!" Tears were running down his cheeks. Strangely enough, his impending escape did not cheer him. In fact, he felt sadder than before.

The red bulbs were soon replaced by small metal lanterns. He came to the base of the stairs; from this point on, all was darkness.

He took one, two, three steps into the dark. How sad he felt...he found himself clenching his fists. Clenching and unclenching. Squeezing.

"Oh God, Elizabeth," he whispered. "Oh God, Anthony. My poor little Anthony."

He heard a ferocious slapping of waves. He returned to the staircase and removed two lanterns from their hooks on the walls. He then walked back into the darkness.

He found himself standing on the banks of a roiling green river. He could see long arms rising from the waters, only to melt and fall back into the current. Countless faces swirled in the green river. Each face was happy, deliriously happy.

A tap on the shoulder startled him and he dropped the lanterns. They rolled a short distance before they were pulled into the waters by green hands. Gumm was enveloped in endless night.

"Oh, poor Mr. Gumm," Nurse Halja whispered. "We're beyond secrets now, aren't we?" She pressed her mask into his hands. He felt the sleek nose, the rubbery lips.

"I'm sorry," Gumm said. "I'm sorry, sorry, sorry."

"You know now, don't you, Mr. Gumm?" The nurse sighed with emotion. "Memory can be such an awful inconvenience. You were not a nice man, Mr. Gumm. If only you had completed your medicinal regimen. You could have had oblivion. Lovely, lovely oblivion."

Gumm caught a whiff of the nurse's animal breath. "What's going to happen to me now?" he whispered. He felt something moving around his ankles, and heard a low, velvety purr.

"My pretty kittykins." Nurse Halja's voice turned childish. "Mama's precious little baby." The movement at his ankles went away. He heard the purring again, closer this time; he guessed that the nurse had picked up the cat.

"To answer your question..." Nurse Halja continued, "we shall proceed with another form of treatment. A more radical procedure, perhaps; but we shall see what we shall see. I want to help, Mr. Gumm. And so does your doctor."

Gumm felt the rasp of a dry tongue on his chin. He couldn't tell if he had been licked by the cat or its mistress.

The nurse took hold of his elbow and began to lead him through the dark. He thought that she would escort him back up the stairs; but after a moment, he noticed that the lapping of the green waters was coming from his left. She was leading him along the river. It then occurred to him that the nurse did not need light to see.

As Gumm walked with Nurse Halja, he tried not to think of poor Elizabeth, poor Anthony. What a wicked, wicked man he was. He resisted a sudden urge to gnaw off his own hands...

"Here we are," the nurse said at last. "On the table, please."

Gumm reached out and felt a hard, cold platform, waist-high, before him. Tapping it with his knuckles, he heard the dull, echoing clang of metal. He removed the overcoat, folded it, and set it on the ground. He then climbed onto the table and laid on his back.

Gumm felt something brush by his arm...his shoulder...his neck. The cat was walking around his body. Hands began to unbutton his shirt; other hands removed his shoes.

"Who else is here?" Gumm said.

"Your doctor," the nurse whispered in his ear. "It was very naughty of you to take his coat. Do not speak to him. From this point on, you must be silent. Absolutely silent."

Hands removed his clothing, piece by piece. Hands swabbed his body with a soft, wet wad that reeked of chemicals. The cat curled up next to his head and began to purr, purr, purr. He found the purring quite soothing. So soothing, in fact, that he really didn't mind when the slicing began.

He wanted to ask Nurse Halja whether they going to put something in or take something out. Of course, he dared not; he had been warned. And really, there was no need for him to worry. He was in the hands of caring medical professionals. He smiled as the purring dissolved his thoughts into a lazy vortex of liquid sable.

BUZZ

The mid-1980s dance music scene was a giddy, rollicking kaleidoscope of fashion, attitude, and iridescent hair glitter. Glam-pop groups like Men Without Socks and Duane-Duane were riding high on the charts, and there was even talk of the latter group's lead singer, Duane LaRoo, receiving the first Nobel Prize for lip gloss.

Many of the groups of the time introduced a playful sense of androgyny into their make-up and outfits. For example, many music video viewers were not completely sure if Petey Bones, leader singer of Undead Sex Organ, was a man or a woman. In the video for the hit single, "You Twirl Me 'Round (Like A Dead Cat)," his haute couture ensemble brought to mind a high-spirited cross between a Supreme Court judge, a black-leather dominatrix and a bedroom-comedy French maid.

In an interview published in *Mega-Groovy Hits* (Vol. 3, No. 9, 1986), Petey Bones explained: "Basically, I'm trying not only to reinvent music and fashion, but also the concept of masculinity. I mean, if a woman goes shopping wearing a man's trousers and a blazer, no one blinks an eye. But if a man goes out in public wearing ... oh, let's say, fish-net stockings, a whale-bone corset and black velvet robes, and carrying a whip and a feather-duster ... people automatically start pointing and saying, 'Ooooh, isn't that rather unusual!' or 'My goodness, there goes that terrible Petey Bones!' or even 'Heavens, that whole outfit makes me question his or her sexuality and perhaps mine, too.' It's just awful, and I really do cry about it sometimes."

But certainly, the most outrageous pop icon of that decade, and perhaps of all time, would have to be the legendary Coco Vidal.

This is his story.

Coco Vidal was born Clarence Kevin Butts in 1963, at St. Agnes' Holy Redemption Hospital in Purity, South Dakota. The son of an insurance salesman and an insurance saleswoman, he had difficulty fitting into the Purity scheme of things. For one thing, he had a British accent, even though no one else did within a seven-hundred mile radius. Plus, he often went to school wearing false eyelashes and his mother's favorite bib coveralls, which were embroidered with purple butterflies and phrases like KEEP ON TRUCKIN' and THE DEVIL MADE ME DO IT. Plus, he wore his auburn hair in two long braids, which he moussed heavily so they'd stick straight out on each side of his head like insect antennae. In high school, he was voted 'Most Likely To Be Ostracized.'

In an interview published in *Super Pop Darlings Magazine* (Vol. 3, No. 5, 1984), Coco Vidal had this to say regarding his upbringing. "Growing up in South Dakota was an unbearable nightmare. Every night I woke up screaming at about 3:15 a.m., wishing to God I could be a normal boy, like Peter on *The Brady Bunch* or Gilligan on *Gilligan's Island*, or maybe the Robot on *Lost in Space*. Surely my horrible childhood was more unbearable than any amount of torture in a Nazi prisoner-of-war camp, like the one on *Hogan's Heroes*. Basically, I was not happy."

At their collective wits' end, his parents and all the citizens of Purity finally decided to send the boy to England on his eighteenth birthday. They all contributed to a fund to buy him an airplane ticket and an apartment in London for one year. Hopefully that would give him enough time to settle into a new life.

It was, after all, a one-way ticket.

Clarence Kevin Butts was delighted by his new home and surroundings. He soon befriended pop music producer and fashion designer Mephisto MacDervish, who saw a great deal of potential in the young man.

In an interview published in *Ultra-Fab Chart-Toppers* (Vol. 9, No. 7, 1985), Mephisto MacDervish said, "I first saw young Clarence washing his frocks at a launderette near my flat, and I knew at that very instant that he had the makings of a pop super-star. His cheekbones were so incredibly high, like those of a praying mantis, and all any would-be star needs to start out with are some fantastic cheekbones. I can teach a budding talent anything they need to know from there. It's not that hard, being a fabulous international star. I could teach a monkey to do it, but primates just don't have the right cheekbones for the job.

"I convinced Clarence to change his name to Coco Vidal, after Coco Chanel and Gore Vidal, two really marvelous, classy, sexy celebrities. I had thought about naming him Gore Chanel, but with those cheekbones, he really looked more like a Coco than a Gore."

Mephisto decided to form a new group with Coco as the lead singer, and so he held auditions for the rest of the band members. Priority one: they had to be able to play some sort of musical instrument. And if they had great cheekbones—all the better.

In an interview published in *Mondo Music Frenzy!* (Vol. 10, No. 2, 1986), Coco Vidal said, "We found a nice bloke named Derek who knew how to play the guitar, and then we found another bloke, also named Derek, who could play the drums. But we didn't want to be like

Duane-Duane, where all the band members were named Duane—so we had to turn away Derek the drummer. Fortunately, we soon found a bloke named Chris who could play the drums, and we thought Chris would make a rather nice name for a drummer, since it wasn't Derek.

"At a club in London we met a bloke named Andy who could play guitar—a different sort of guitar from the one Derek played, which we thought was important—and then at a freak show in the village of Horseshoe-On-The-Wold, we met Siamese twin blokes named Simon and Nigel who could play synthesizers, and we decided, 'Hey, now we've got a band!'"

And so the group Roach Klip was born.

Their first single, "I'll Stumble Toward You" (1983), climbed the British charts to No. 3 in less than a week. But it rose no higher. The hit single "Set The Alarm Before You Am-Scray" by the pop duo Whomp was locked into the No. 2 position for three months, while Kyla Minotaur's high-energy dance-mix of "Itsy-Bitsy Spider" ruled the roost at No. 1 for a full year.

The video for "I'll Stumble Toward You" was a perfect mix of Coco Vidal's natural flamboyance and Mephisto MacDervish's outrageous fashions. Coco wore a black-satin evening gown, opera gloves, bright-red galoshes and a puffy chef's hat as he and his band members danced through an operating room where actual open-heart surgery was taking place.

In an interview published in *Funky Pop Vibes Magazine* (Vol. 3, No. 9, 1989), Chris Clark the drummer reminisced about the shooting of that video. "I'm not sure who decided to set it in an operating room during open-heart surgery—but the whole concept was brilliant. Extremely fabulously brilliant. We found a doctor and patient who both had showbiz aspirations—and a hospital that needed funding—and the rest was history. At one point, Coco slipped on some blood that had spritzed out of the patient, and he fell right onto the operating table, face-first into that big incision. We didn't put that in the video. Fortunately, the patient wasn't hurt—Coco has very small features, so he couldn't really have done much damage. We just washed off Coco's face and went right on with production.

"But you know, Coco wasn't the same after that. That same night, we all stopped at Club Pants-Rocket and Coco kept saying things like, 'That fresh human blood didn't taste too bad' and 'Actually, fresh human blood tastes pretty good' and even, 'Boy, I sure could go for some fresh human blood right now.' It was really rather unnerving. I mean, it's not unknown for pop stars to drink human blood—Mick Slagger of the Cascading Boulders, for example, drinks about a quart a day. It's always been a trendy pop-music thing to do. Must musicians do it just to be fashionable, but still, they get the stuff from reputable blood banks. As for Coco—! It sounded like he wanted it super-fresh—you know, straight from the source. That sort of thing could lead to trouble. I mean, think about it. Fresh blood. That kind of implies that some person is still using it. It's still flowing around in all their little body-tubes... Veins, I think they're called."

The video received ample exposure on the music channel VPTV—Video Party Television. The channel soon began to receive thousands of viewer letters and phone calls asking about the charismatic performer...

"Is Coco Vidal a man or a woman?"

"Is Coco Vidal straight, gay or bi?"

"Is Coco Vidal seeing anyone at the moment?"

"Coco Vidal dresses like a transvestite chef who's afraid to get his feet wet. Why is that?"

Soon teenagers all over England were buying puffy chef's hats, evening gowns and bright-red galoshes at trendy boutiques. Most of these shops were owned by Mephisto MacDervish, always the consummate entrepreneur.

Roach Klip's first album, *Dare To Be Fabulous* (1983), became an international sensation. In addition to "I'll Stumble Toward You," two more songs from the album rose high on the charts—"Destiny Iguana" and "Cathedral Of The Toxic Brain."

During that time, Roach Klip began their first tour, which included concerts throughout England as well as in France, Germany, Italy, Japan, Australia and seven cities in America. The tour was a complete success—except for the fact that each concert usually ended up with a dead body found somewhere near the parking lot.

In an interview published in *Conjoined Twin Monthly* (Vol. 6, Double Issue No. 7 and 8, 1992), synthesizer players Simon and Nigel Fairwood shared their memories of the tour.

Nigel: "Yeah, it was really weird. Right after every concert, Coco would suddenly disappear for about twenty minutes. When he'd eventually show up backstage, he'd have all this blood on him, and always a different excuse for it, like he'd cut himself shaving, or he'd received an especially deep paper-cut. They weren't the best excuses, really. But none of us boys in the band cared anyway, because quite frankly, we were all on drugs."

Simon: "Nigel is quite right. At that time, the hot new designer drug was a combination of lion tranquilizers and platypus hormones called Happy Zone 3. We were all blissed out on HZ3, so whatever Coco did was—as the Americans say—'A-Okay' with us."

Nigel: "HZ3's worst side-effect is a complete loss of bladder control, so we all had to wear adult diapers. To hide those bulky diapers, us boys took to wearing Hawaiian grass skirts, and soon every teenager in every country we visited was wearing a grass skirt."

Simon: "Mephisto was the one who suggested the grass skirts. He also sold them in his boutiques. In fact, he was the one who provided us with the HZ3. A real schemer, he was. And an enemy of the platypus, since he grew up on a platypus farm and had to shovel their runny orange dung. Those drug labs have to grind up the whole platypus to extract its hormones, you know. Yes, I feel dreadfully sorry for all those dead platypuses."

Nigel: "My God, Simon, sometimes you say the stupidest things. Personally, I feel sorry for all those dead people. The ones Coco killed after the concerts. Stupid, that's what you are."

Simon: "Don't call me stupid! You're much more stupid! Utterly, catastrophically stupid! I feel more sorry for the platypuses because they're so sweet and funny-looking, and people should leave them alone. They're really very vulnerable and quite endearing. And they lay eggs. But you wouldn't know that, since you feel asleep while we were watching that platypus documentary."

Nigel: "I'm sorry. I shouldn't have picked a fight like that. How can I make it up to you? I know! Would you like a platypus for our next birthday?"

Simon: "Yes, please!"

The bodies of the victims, always hidden in a dumpster or under some rubbish, were usually discovered a few days after the band had left town. Suicide notes, later revealed to be forgeries, were found pinned to the corpses.

An anonymous police officer, quoted in the newsletter *Pop Cop Comments* (Vol. 3, No. 17, 1994) had this to say about the bodies of the victims. "In retrospect, it's amazing that those fake suicide notes threw off the police for as long as they did. I mean, the victims all died of blood loss from numerous bites and cuts, and yet there was never any blood spilled near the bodies. That's just not possible for a suicide. And how could a suicide victim hide his or her own corpse? Plus, all the notes had suicide misspelled in capital letters—SEWASIDE. In the same handwriting, too."

In late 1984, Roach Klip released their next album, "My Urine Smells Funny After I Eat Asparagus." In an interview published in *Radio Ruckus Magazine* (Vol. 2, No. 7, 1985), Coco Vidal explained the album's unusual title. "This is a very personal album—all the songs are very personal, because I have some very personal things to say to all my very personal friends and fans. So while writing the songs, I decided to hold nothing back. Nothing!"

Perhaps that comment helps to explain the lyrics to the album's first release—a single entitled "Do I Really Want To Kill You?"

> *Do I really want to kill you?*
> *Do I really want to make you die?*
> *Here's some news that might not thrill you:*
> *In a coffin, soon you'll lie.*
>
> *Blood will spurt out of your body*
> *as I stab you with a knife.*
> *You will think I'm awful naughty*
> *when I terminate your life.*
>
> *Then your blood I will be drinking*
> *once I've sprung your mortal coil,*
> *and your corpse will be left stinking—*
> *in a dumpster it will spoil.*
>
> *If it's life you want to live,*
> *don't hang around with me.*
> *If your veins have blood to give*
> *I'll drink it—wait and see...*

In an interview published in *True Crime Escapades* (Vol. 6, No. 2, 1995), Mephisto MacDervish commented on those lyrics. "I remember warning him not to release that song. I mean, he pretty much confessed to being some sort of stabbing vampire. And that bit about the dumpster—that told the tale right there. Still, people didn't figure it all out until long after the song's release. Because really, who actually listened to the lyrics? And who would take them seriously?

"Besides, people were paying more attention to what was going on in the video. Coco and the Roach-boys were all hooked on HZ3, so they were all wearing grass skirts, spray-painted blue and red and aqua. Also, Coco wore a bridal veil and boxing gloves. He looked lovely—that gorgeous face, lightly framed in lace. First the boys danced through a sort of futuristic sci-fi battlefield, filled with robots and tentacled monsters. Then suddenly they were dancing with cavemen, and showing them how to make fire by rubbing some old sticks together. Then they were chasing John Wilkes Booth across ancient Egypt. So the lyrics could have applied to any of those scenarios. Well, except maybe the words about the knife. And the dumpster. And the blood-drinking."

In early 1986, Coco Vidal disappeared from the public eye. In an interview published in *Chatty Guitar Players* (Vol. 9, No. 4, 1993), band member Derek Hastings had this to say. "Looking back, I would have to say that Coco Vidal was a victim of the pop machine. I mean, those concerts can be so exhausting. So right afterward... Maybe that's when he needed some fresh human blood the most. He probably wouldn't have even developed a taste for it if he hadn't gotten some in his mouth while we were making our first video. The poor bastard.

"The irony of it all is, he had thousands of fans who would've gladly given him a bit of fresh blood every now and then, if only he'd thought to ask. I'd have been only too happy to give him, say, a pint or two every week. But, Coco Vidal was a proud man. Proud, I tell you! He couldn't admit to having a weakness. Better to just stab a complete stranger and lap up their blood."

Coco Vidal may have disappeared, but new victims kept popping up on a regular basis. They were always found in dumpsters behind record stores. All were customers of those stores who had just purchased records by Roach Klip. So in that regard, Coco was still loyal to his fans.

The killings sprang up in different countries, and eventually it became clear that a pattern was emerging. If the authorities in one country advised its record stores to stop selling Roach Klip records, Coco would simply move on to a new feeding ground.

In an interview published in *Cute Pop Dudes! Magazine* (Vol. 4, No. 13, 1996), guitar player Andy Young spoke of Coco Vidal's capture by authorities. "At last there was only one place in the whole world where a person could buy Roach Klip records. That place was a combination coffee shop, record store and tobacco emporium called Coffee & Records & Smokes & That's It, located on Yappog, a steamy-hot jungle island in the South Pacific. I was making a video with my new band, Green Monkey Twist, on Yappog when they finally caught Coco.

"My band members and I were in Coffee & Records & Smokes & That's It, enjoying some coffee and cigarettes and talking about buying some records, when suddenly we heard somebody scream. The scream came from the other side of the plate-glass window to the left of the table where I was sitting with the band, so we all turned that way. And there he was. Poor addled Coco was so desperate for blood, he didn't care that he was stabbing somebody in broad daylight. He had a big butcher knife and he was stabbing some poor cross-eyed tourist-type guy in the chest, over and over. I don't suppose the guy was naturally cross-eyed. I think the pain from the stabbing must have made his eyes cross involuntarily.

"Most people don't know this, but the Yappog police department has a trained monkey squadron that roams the city, ready to toss coconuts at folks who are up to no good. That's why we were on the island—those monkeys are very smart, and we wanted to put them in the video. One of them even joined the band for half a year. Great little drummer. Anyway, soon those monkeys came scampering, and they began pelting Coco with coconuts. He instantly backed away from them and crashed through the plate-glass window. He staggered for a bit and then landed on our table, tipping over my mint-mocha smoothie. The glass cut him up something terrible, and before he passed out, he looked up at me and whispered, in a sad little-boy-lost voice, 'Sorry about the smoothie.' That Coco! At heart, always a gentleman."

The monkeys of Yappog carried Coco Vidal to the police station. An island doctor tended to the pop star's wounds, and arrangements were made for Coco to be flown to a private asylum in France—the Matapathamos Institute for the Reality-Challenged. The staff at this particular asylum specialized in treating high-profile psychopaths: they had even cured child-star Bucky Blanchard of his inexplicable propensity for swallowing live baby hamsters. It was hoped that they might be able to rehabilitate Coco Vidal.

In an interview in *Celebrity Sickos! Magazine* (Vol. 8, No. 17, 1997), Dr. Emil Matapathamos made this statement: "I object to your use of the term 'sickos' in the title of your magazine. True, approximately eighty-seven percent of the celebrity population has difficulty dealing with the subtle nuances of the here-and-now universe—but that's no excuse for name-calling. I will not reminisce about Coco Vidal until such time as the name of your magazine has been changed."

In an interview in the newly renamed *Celebrities With Unfortunate Mental Disorders! Magazine* (Premiere Issue, 1997), Dr. Matapathamos explained the true nature of Coco Vidal's blood-thirst. "Everyone in the mental health field knows that the brain produces a hormone called serotonin, which regulates a person's moods—indeed, their actual happiness levels. But there is another, more obscure hormone which also fits into the equation, which I have discovered only recently. I call it matapatha-tonin. The brain doesn't make much matapathatonin—a few drops now and then. It doesn't really need that much. But that small amount spells the difference between a life of happiness and a dreadful existence of utter misery.

"In rare cases, certain individuals experience a massive increase in their matapathatonin production when they ingest a specific combination of enzymes and proteins—a combination found most readily in fresh human blood, and also in green k'harr tea, a delicacy brewed from vari-ous tree barks and beetle squeezings by a secluded tribe in the Brazilian rainforest.

"Coco Vidal is one of those rare cases. He has become hopelessly ad-dicted to the matapathatonin produced by his own brain when he drinks fresh blood. But he is not beyond hope. I could give him blood donated by his fans, but even that might not help, since transported blood might not be fresh enough to activate matapathatonin production. So, Coco must be weaned off of blood through the expedient administration of green k'harr tea. But this venture will be extremely difficult—and costly. Coco's Swiss bank account savings will not be enough to cover the in-credible expense.

"Plus, Coco Vidal will have to contend with huge legal expenses, what with him being such a busy serial killer. He has killed people all over the world, so he may have to stand trial in each and every one of those countries—even on the island of Yappog, where the penalty for murder is ritualistic execution by the police monkeys.

"Frankly, I don't know where he is going to get the money. So far, I've been helping him out of the goodness of my heart. I'm a big Roach Klip fan, you see. Listening to their lively pop ditties helps me to relax after a hard day of untangling the tricky Gordian knots of the human psyche."

Fortunately, Mephisto MacDervish had not forsaken his prodigy. In late 1997, he produced a charity album to help pay Coco Vidal's astro-nomical medical and legal expenses. This album, released in mid-De-cember, was designed to appeal to both American and British audiences and was entitled, "Does Coco Vidal Know That Santa Claus And/Or Father Christmas Is/Are Coming To Town?" It was hoped that the public would be sympathetic to the cause during the holiday season.

All of Coco's pop contemporaries sang on the album: the boys from Roach Klip, Men Without Socks, all the Duanes in Duane-Duane, Whomp, Kyla Minotaur, Mick Slagger and the Cascading Boulders—even Green

Monkey Twist joined in. Petey Bones was unable to attend the recording session, since it was held on a Thursday and that was his regular pedicure day. The first release from the album, "Cure For A Killer," was released two days before Christmas. The lyrics explained Coco Vidal's tragic condition:

> *It's always a shock*
> *when a bloke in a flock*
> *starts killing because he's insane.*
> *But before we all blame him—*
> *point fingers and shame him—*
> *remember, he's got a bad brain.*
>
> *We'll fill the prescriptions*
> *to stop his conniptions*
> *and save him from ruin and grief.*
> *His body is moanin'*
> *for matapathatonin*
> *to give his poor brain some relief.*
>
> *We are his friends,*
> *we're thinking of him.*
> *Coco's trying to make amends,*
> *so learn to love him.*
>
> *He just needs k'harr tea—*
> *then he won't stab and slice.*
> *No one's perfect, so join the party!*
> *Let's all be nice!*

The song was a huge success, as was the album. With the funds raised, an expedition into the Brazilian rainforest was launched, and great quantities of the appropriate tree barks and beetle glands were harvested and/or squeezed, and then shipped to the Matapathamos Institute for the Reality-Challenged. Meanwhile, a team of international lawyers was assembled to see what could be done to defend Coco Vidal.

In an interview published in *Rock & Pop Has-Been Memoirs* (Vol. 4, No. 1, 2000), Petey Bones discussed the results of the efforts to help Coco Vidal. "I really did want to sing on that album, but they held the recording session on a Thursday—I tell you, they scheduled it that way on purpose. All the world knows that Julian works on my toenails on Thursdays! It turns out that smelly jungle tea they brewed up did the trick for old Coco, and he stopped slashing at people and drinking their blood. Then all his fancy lawyers found out that those Yappog police monkeys never read Coco his rights, and so eventually all the charges were dropped.

"And now Coco Vidal is back in show-biz! He has a regular gig at the Lucky Nugget Casino in Las Vegas these days. He's scheduled between the Amazing Pierre, who turns into a giant croissant, and two wild animal trainers, Schweinhund and Hans. Plus, they're staging his life story as a musical on Broadway called 'Roach-Mania.' Apparently stabbing folks left and right is a sure-fire career booster. Too bad nobody told me. I've had some agents who I'd have been happy to slice up."

Certainly one would have thought that Coco Vidal deserved a little peace and quiet at that point in his career. Unfortunately, such was not to be. Because little was known about his unusual condition and the long-term effects of k'harr tea consumption, mistakes were made in figuring the correct dosage of the medicinal beverage.

In an interview published in *Famous Medical Boo-Boos Digest* (Vol. 14, No. 3, 2001), Dr. Emil Matapathamos explained what went wrong with Coco Vidal's treatment plan. "Basically, we were all pretty pleased when we figured out how much k'harr tea to give Coco to make him stop killing people and drinking their blood. Unfortunately, it turns out that such a high dosage of k'harr tea has some unexpected side effects.

"Medical science isn't one-hundred percent sure what functions are served by the seemingly dormant pineal gland, located in the back of the brain. But it turns out that the elevated levels of matapathatonin—brought about by k'harr tea consumption—in Coco's blood caused his pineal gland to grow exceptionally large.

"Coco is back at the asylum in France now. His growing pineal gland has sprouted three fleshy shoots. One has emerged from the back of his head and the other two have traveled down the spine, emerging from under his shoulder blades. Those two seem to be growing into new appendages of some sort. At least Coco is feeling no pain—all that matapathatonin keeps him quite happy."

The final chapter in the Coco Vidal saga was revealed in the pages of *The One That Got Away: The Journal Of Unrequited Love* (Vol. 13, No. 13, 2002). In an exclusive and extremely candid interview, Mephisto MacDervish revealed his true feelings for Coco Vidal. "When I read in some magazine that Coco had funny parts growing out of him—well, I just broke down and cried. My poor Coco—so many troubles! I then realized just how much I cared for him. How much I loved him. I flew to France as soon as I could. I had to tell him just how I felt about him.

"I'll never forget the moment I stepped into his medical suite. It was a very nice suite, with a hot tub and a balcony. And he was out there, standing on the balcony rail, looking up toward Heaven.

"That one gland-stalk of his—the one popping out of the back of his head—had grown into a sort of circular glowing thingy, gently bobbing up and down a few inches over his head, just like a halo. The other two stalks—the ones on his back—had grown into huge insect wings. They had dozens of little multi-colored panes on them, like stained-glass windows in church. Kind of pretty, in a horribly mutated sort of way. He was flapping those big freaky wings ... lightly. Testing the air.

"I called out to him, 'Coco! What are you doing? Come down from there! I love you! Come down!'

"He turned toward me and shook his head with a laugh. 'I love you, too, my friend. I love everyone and everything. Hate to disappoint you, but the way I feel right now, I don't think I'm ever coming down.'

"He flapped his wings faster, faster, faster, until they began to buzz. A low, powerful buzz, louder than thunder. A moment later, he was airborne. He smiled, gave me a wink and soared away. Into the blue and out of my life.

"I miss you, Coco, wherever you are."

Currently, numerous South American newspapers regularly report sightings of Coco Vidal, buzzing majestically above the Brazilian rainforests. Reporters in helicopters have tried to follow the buzz, but they're never able to catch it. Coco is way too fast for them.

He hasn't attacked anyone recently, which probably means he has learned how to brew up his special bark-and-beetle concoction. So apparently he does come down every now and then.

Around tea-time.

GLOVE

A TALE OF THE KING IN YELLOW

I loved Miranda and love her still. But she moved out of my house after seventeen years together because she needed to be her own person. In doing so, she left me with no one. No one meaningful, anyway. I avoided my sullen, cruel family. I had a few casual friends, coworkers, various other people with whom I did business... Not a rich life. Not a full one.

A week after leaving me, Miranda returned crying, but only to drop off something she had acquired but could not keep.

It was a small, dark-gray kitten. She had adopted him out of pity, because his right front paw was deformed. The toes were too long—almost like fingers. A friend of hers who worked at an animal shelter had told her about the poor thing.

The deformed paw didn't have much hair on it. The skin was pink with small grayish splotches. The claws were flat and shiny, like human fingernails. It was a beautifully creepy thing to see.

The kitten was a noisy little man, and his constant mewing kept her awake at night. And so one day she came knocking on my door, holding a cardboard box with the kitten inside. She didn't want to take it back to the shelter, because she was afraid no one else would adopt it and so it would be put to sleep. She knew I loved cats, and like her, wouldn't want a poor kitten to be killed. Especially one with such an interesting paw. Plus, my house was bigger than her apartment, so she thought his noise would be less of a bother to me.

I love cats, but I'm also mildly allergic to them, so I emptied the spare room of my house, scattered some pillows, blankets, and a few large boxes and branches, and made that the cat's room. That way, his dander and hair would be kept mostly to one room. The boxes and branches were for his play—things for him to crawl into and upon. It was a large room with a closet in one corner. The closet had a laundry chute leading down to the basement. I kept the door closed, since I didn't want the poor thing to fall to his death.

I kept the kitten in his room while I was at work. When I came home, I let him go out on the enclosed porch, where I would play with him for up to an hour every day. It took some time for me to come up with a good name for him. Finally I decided upon Glove. The color and texture of his strange paw's skin reminded me of an old pair of suede gloves I'd once lost.

As Glove grew older, his deformed paw started to resemble a little hand. Slender, like that of a child. Sometimes he even used it like a hand, wrapping it around his toys, as though preparing to pick them up. But he didn't have enough strength in his grip to actually lift anything.

One rainy late afternoon, while Glove was playing, I noticed he had stopped batting around his little toy mouse and was sitting on the window sill. He was staring toward the street, which was down the hill from my house.

He slowly lifted his deformed paw and pointed out the window with his longest claw. He appeared to be pointing at someone at the bus stop on the corner. The man was flat on the ground, and for a moment I wondered if he was ill or perhaps even dead. Then he quickly scrambled to his feet.

"Who's that? Some old friend of yours?" I asked. I didn't expect a reply, of course. I was very surprised by Glove's behavior, though, since it seemed so human.

The cat looked toward me with his golden eyes, then—still pointing—looked back toward the figure at the bus stop. The figure turned toward us.

It was a young, very pale man dressed in black, standing in the rain without an umbrella. Wet locks of his long black hair were plastered against his face. He looked ghastly, like the corpse of someone who had drowned at sea.

A bus pulled up and the doors opened. He stumbled toward it. There seemed to be something wrong with the way he moved. He hopped inside and the door banged shut.

Glove lowered his paw, jumped to the floor and continued to torment his toy mouse.

Later, I called Miranda to tell her what the cat had done. We still talked on the phone every now and then. Sometimes we'd have lunch at our favorite coffee shop, or go see a movie.

"He can point, just like a person?" she said. "I wish I'd seen that. So who was he pointing at?"

"Oh, I don't know. Some idiot, too stupid to buy an umbrella. You should pay us a visit someday, see how Glove has grown. That funny paw of his looks so much like a hand. Tomorrow's Saturday. You could stop by around noon. I'll make you lunch."

"Tomorrow's out. I'm going to an estate sale." She paused, then said, "I know you're not wild about antiques, but you're welcome to go with me. Maybe they'll have some old books."

"Sure, I'll go. I don't have anything else planned."

She then told me she'd pick me up at ten the next morning.

I wish I'd said no. But then, I'd had no way of knowing what was going to happen at that sale. Ultimately, I suppose I was meant to go there.

I was meant to buy that old pine crate filled with dusty, battered hardbound volumes.

I was meant to own *The King In Yellow*.

Miranda didn't buy anything at the sale. She was surprised that I'd spent so much on the crate—I hadn't even looked at all the books inside before buying it.

I have since come to understand that *The King In Yellow* is a very special book. Actually, it's probably not even a book—or at least, not *just* a book. In a way, I think it is alive, in the same way that the Earth is alive... Teeming with occupants.

Perhaps the book picks who is going to own it. That would explain a lot.

On the way back from the sale, I sat in the back seat of Miranda's car, where we'd put the crate. I wanted to look at all the books inside while she was driving.

"You know," I said as I sorted through the crate, "I just realized something. I don't even know who's sale that was." I looked into the rear-view mirror to see Miranda's reflection. She was concentrating on the road, so she didn't know I was looking at her. She looked especially pretty that day—her olive skin, usually a little sallow, had more of a golden-brown cast to it. A bit of a tan.

"Some rich dead guy," she said. "His name was Kilbane. He died in a car accident. I hear he drove right into a tree—suicide. I talked to his widow for a few minutes. She's not doing very well."

"Emotionally? Financially?" I continued to sort through the books. A few of them were foreign—French, German, Spanish. I couldn't read any of those languages, so I figured I'd probably donate those books to some library.

"She's in denial. Doesn't even think her husband is dead." She sighed with what I suppose was pity. "She thinks he's off visiting some place called Carcosa."

"Never heard of it. Sounds like an island." That was the moment I lifted up a torn, half-burnt copy of the Bible and saw, just under it, *The King In Yellow*.

Miranda stopped for a red light. "Why is that guy wet?" she said, pointing out the front window.

"Wet? Who? Where?" I said. I looked to the street corner, and caught a glimpse of someone thin and pale, with wet, serpentine locks of black hair. People seemed to be steering clear of him, though from that distance, I couldn't see why. Suddenly he hopped on a bus and the door banged shut behind him.

The traffic light turned green and Miranda drove on. I didn't tell her that the young man looked familiar.

The King In Yellow was filthy—caked with dirt, as though someone had once buried it, or dropped it in mud. "That Kilbane guy didn't take very good care of his books," I said. "Most of these books are in awful shape. Well, who knows? Maybe there's some long-lost goodies in here somewhere."

"You haven't changed," Miranda said. "Always looking for some strange rare treasure. Remember that big box of junk you bought at that yard sale, two or three years back?"

"That was a good deal. There were some really nice silver spoons at the bottom." Her talk of rarities made me think of Glove. "Speaking of all things unusual, do you want to visit Glove? You haven't seen him for some time. And you have to drop me off at my place anyway."

"Sure, why not?" Miranda stopped at another red light. "Why was that guy so wet? It's not even raining. What's his story? I can't stop thinking about him."

"Probably just some weirdo," I said. I picked up *The King In Yellow* and tried to open it, but most of the pages were stuck together.

Once we were back at my house, I made some tea for Miranda and coffee for myself. She was impressed by how big Glove had grown, and agreed that his paw looked even more like a hand now.

"It looks like a little boy's hand," she said. "A freaky little boy with funny skin."

I had set *The King In Yellow* on top of the TV. Miranda saw it and snatched it off. "This book's got dirt all over it. You're going to get dirt inside your TV. It'll get in those ventilation slots."

"Ventilation?" I looked at the TV more closely. "So that's what those slots are for. They're the kind of thing you see but you don't know what the deal is."

"Yeah, I think they let the heat out from all the electronic stuff inside." She'd walked into the bathroom with the book. Suddenly I heard water running in the sink.

"What are you doing?" I called. "You're not washing that book, are you?"

"Well, yeah. It's pretty much ruined anyway. I can't hurt it any more," she called back over the light roar and splash of the water. I could hear another roar, too—a loud engine, like that of a bus, somewhere outside.

I was about to see what she was doing when I noticed that Glove had jumped up on a window sill. He raised his hairless paw and pointed through the glass.

I turned my head in the indicated direction and—didn't have to look far. The wet young man was right outside the window, his black hair plastered in thick, soggy locks on his chalk-white face. His eyes were as yellow as egg-yolks, or perhaps pus. He smiled at me with a mouthful of broken, rotted teeth. Behind him, the sky darkened, but not with night—it was a different sort of shadow. Then his lips ... his hideously thick, pale lips ... began to move, and these words rolled off of his tongue and right into my brain:

"It's time to visit Carcosa. Lovely Carcosa. Lovely Carcosa."

Then I felt a hand on my shoulder and thought for just a second that it belonged to Glove, but no, it was Miranda's. In her other hand she held the book. The wet pages fanned out like impossibly bloated butterfly wings.

"It's a play," she said. "A lovely play. Lovely play."

The room began to slowly fill with mist, the sort of mist that writhes across Lake Haajir, which I'd never seen and yet suddenly knew existed, for he who wears the royal tatters is fond of strolling on the shore and watching the viscous green waters as they lap upon the rocks and bones. I heard the slight creak of the screen-door of the enclosed porch, followed by the louder creak of the door into the house.

Miranda's words began to mingle with those of the wet young man, so that I couldn't be sure who was talking: "It's time to play. See the lovely play. Time for the play in Carcosa. Time for Carcosa to play. Play-time in Carcosa. Lovely Carcosa. Lovely play."

Not a rich life. Not a full one. That's all there is to know about me. Glove walked out of the room and I followed him, for what else was there for me to do? Perhaps he was in search of royalty—they do say a cat can look at a King.

I followed him back to his room, with Miranda and the wet young man trailing close behind me, the two of them babbling, completing each other's sentences. The way to the cat's room seemed impossibly long—ordinarily my house is very small, but the mists made it seem like it went on forever. By the time we reached the iron doors of that special room, Miranda and the wet young man had perfected their dialogue, like performers rehearsing lines from a play. I think they had needed to dredge the words up from an abyss much deeper than mere memory.

The creak of that looming metal door echoed like thunder, and the cat's room stretched out before me, as spacious as a ballroom. The walls were draped with red and black curtains, all emblazoned with yellow symbols.

I suddenly noticed a shape standing in the recess of a doorway. It appeared to be a slender man dressed in dark-grey velvet. His golden eyes glowed back in the hollows of their wide sockets—his face was very large and angular.

"Careful, Glove," I said. "That closet behind you holds a laundry chute. Wouldn't want you falling in."

With a well-shaped, beautiful gray hand, the slender man opened the door for me. Then Miranda and the wet young man grabbed me and tossed me down the chute.

I fell and fell and fell through mist ... lovely mist, lovely mist ... until I was very wet indeed. I fell for such a long time that my hair grew into thick, soggy locks. Suddenly I found myself flat on my back. I scrambled to my feet as the bus pulled up to the curb. Out of the corner of my eye, I saw—sitting on a window sill up on a hill—some little grey thing pointing at me. Then the bus door flew open and the driver beckoned for me, yellow tatters flapping from his arm.

Not a rich life. Not a full one. But better than nothing at all.

I hopped onboard and the door banged shut.

FEEL THE SPIN

Dear Diary,

Philippe told me today that his parents were a space monkey and a dollop of cosmic ooze. If he has to make up a personal history, he could at least give it a little more glamour. Philippe is luxuriously handsome. His skin is so creamy and golden and his ice-blue eyes are so piercing. No doubt his parents are gorgeous jet-trash transsexuals.

I am dizzy with love and sometimes, I cannot contain myself. This morning, we drank mimosas by the hotel pool, lounging and sunning and chatting. Philippe fed Dunsott dozens of cucumber sandwiches—no wonder the poor thing is so fat. Every now and then some young lovely would stop and sit with Philippe and I must confess, I felt a bit jealous. I'm afraid my sharp tongue drove most of his admirers away.

Speaking of admirers, a blue-haired old woman recognized me in the lobby and asked for my autograph.

After lunch (sushi), we drove down to De Brou Productions, where we watched the shooting of a porn video. Of course, Philippe had to bring Dunsott, but at least he didn't bark. Philippe owns the studio, so everyone treated him like a god. Which he is. Was he born filthy rich? Perhaps he's the son of a politician, or an oil billionaire.

When we returned to the hotel, a hysterical, heavyset woman was screaming at two police officers in the gift shop. Sharkey, the desk clerk, told us that somebody had snatched her baby from its carriage.

I can still see the shining flesh of Philippe's video troupe, slick with spermicides, assorted lubricants and mutual juices! The entire studio had the delicious coffee-reek of sex.

It pains me to think of Philippe tangling with any of them. Jealousy is such a childish, petty emotion.

* * * *

Dear Great American Novel,

I can't get enough of Philippe's tigerish body. After a leisurely morning of lovemaking, he asked (jokingly?) if he should join the cast of the video. I'm sure he already has, off-camera. I was showering at the time, so I pretended not to hear him.

I wouldn't want him to think me prudish... I might ask if I can bring Sharky to our bed. He flirts incessantly with us, but his teeth are so crooked. No competition there.

Philippe and I drove down to the studio again. There are at least a dozen performers in the video (an ambitious production). I noticed dozens of small blue tubes scattered about the studio. I opened one of the tubes and squeezed out a little of its contents—a yellowish-white cream that turned to golden oil when I rubbed it between my fingers. Some sort of lubricant. None of the performers were using it; the slickum du jour was butter. I slipped three tubes in my pocket while no one was watching.

We ran on the beach this afternoon. Even though Dunsott is as wide as he is long, he was able to keep up with us. I should get a pet of my own... It would have to get along with Dunsott. Philippe takes the dog everywhere.

* * * *

Dear Spicy Paperback,

Sharky rubbed up against me by the pool. He has a wonderfully sinewy body. His teeth really aren't so bad—they give him character. A feral quality. He said that when he was in college, he used to watch me on *Passion for Tomorrow* and dream about making love with me—or rather, with that impetuous-young-law-student-struggling-to-uncover-his-family's-dark-secret, Biff Richards. Shall I make his fantasy come true? If I did, I'd even put on my Biff jacket—the one with the leather patches on the elbows.

What a monster I am: one minute, declaring my love for Philippe—the next, contemplating Sharkey's navel.

* * * *

Dear Pulp Thriller,

I was going to use some of the lubricant from the blue tube, but Philippe stopped me. He even took the tube away from me and wouldn't say why. I didn't bother to mention that I had more.

Later, he loaded Dunsott in the car and went to the studio without asking if I wanted to come along. I found one of my other blue tubes and called up room service a la Sharkey.

The golden lubricant must contain some sort of hallucinogenic. Sharkey turned into a hairless, noseless thing with silver skin and eyes like a jungle cat. A pattern of cobalt-blue splotches sprang up on my own flesh. Our reflection in the dresser mirror was perfectly normal. Both of us were screaming and laughing like devils. There was another sound, too—a shrill squeaking. I have no idea where that came from.

The entire mindfuck lasted about twenty minutes. Later, Sharkey told me that my eyes had turned into pools of black ink. We soon realized that we had experienced the same hallucination. Is that possible?

Why didn't Philippe want me to find out about the drugged slickum? I can only assume he's saving it for a special occasion.

* * * *

Dear Science-Fiction Epic,

Philippe went to the studio again without inviting me. I think he's afraid I'll steal a blue tube. While he was gone, Sharkey and I did the nasty again—and the lubricant made it very nasty indeed.

Like before, I was spotted with blue and Sharkey was silver-skinned. We found ourselves making love in a moonlit rain-forest. Black caterpillars the size of my thumb crawled on our steaming bodies. The sky was filled with giant insects and shrieking albino bats. A large, fish-scaled rat with human hands squeaked in the branches overhead.

My orgasm lasted for at least three minutes.

After Sharkey left, I ordered up dinner (steak) and took a nap. When I was awoke, I put a little of the cream on my hand and began to fool with my tool. Soon I was transported back to the rain-forest, where the rat climbed on my shoulder and smiled a mouthful of silver-needle teeth at me. "I love the smell of baby-fat," it said.

It wanted to know where I got the lubricant, so I told it all about Philippe.

It cocked its little head to one side. Then it shrilled "de Brou!" and began to laugh.

The rat, whose name is Iaak, claims that Philippe is over 350 years old, and that he is the son of Father Urbain Grandier, who was burned alive in 1634 for the bedevilment of the nuns of Loudon. Phillipe's mother was a young penitent, Madeleine de Brou. Iaak had served an accomplice of Father Grandier—a cleft-lipped old woman who had been betrayed by the priest and burned as well.

The rat also told me about the cream: it contains juice of aconite, cinquefoil, nightshade, and soot in a baby-fat base.

I can't believe I'm quoting a hallucination. And a rat at that.

That night, Philippe and I ran on the beach again with Dunsott. I had to rest several times—the stars seemed to whirl overhead.

* * * *

Dear Forbidden Tome,

A thousand pardons for ignoring you for an entire week.

Sharkey and I have made five visits to the rain-forest. I have gone by myself seven times.

In my visions, Iaak has taken me beyond the rain-forest to other realms of splendor. I have looked upon living geometric configurations of crystal floating through the primal mists of a young planet. I have walked among metal children with glowing needles for fingers, who must pleasure/shred the exposed brain of the giant leech that is their master. I have soared on the back of a horrid winged mollusk through skies alive with veined, pulsing clouds.

It is hard to return to normal life after such visions. The drugged lubricant has sharpened my senses. I now can detect the yeasty whiff of Dunsott's genitalia from across the room. When a bird flies by, I smell the ammonia tang of its feces-streaked tail. During meals, I taste the bacteria on my food. I can feel the mites and other minute life-forms that crawl on my flesh.

Sex with Philippe or Sharkey is like an act of exquisite torture. The greasy rumble of their intestines squirming in their abdomens thunders in my ears. At night, I can see the rings of Jupiter without a telescope. I constantly feel a strange spinning sensation.

Iaak has explained the nature of Philippe's power. The witch-hunters may have burned Urbain Grandier alive, but they pulled his carcass from the fire too soon. The magick had its own heart, and this had not been destroyed. In time, Grandier might have returned to life; too bad for him that his son had been told where he was buried. Philippe dug up the pauper grave of his father and made the magick his own—by swallowing it.

How many companions has Philippe had? Dozens? Hundreds? His ice-blue eyes have seen his aged lovers lowered into the ground. His skin is creamy from the fat of countless little ones... I'd like to think it's all a deliciously wicked fantasy: reality would require too much thought.

But still—one dozen performers in the video, with Philippe as mentor...

Iaak has told me what must be said and done. My first task is to mix the baby-fat mixture into a jar of Philippe's lubricant of preference. Then, we shall see what we shall see.

* * *

Dear Book of the Dead,

The rat was right.

The Sabbat ointment revealed Philippe's true form to me. My lover was a coven-master of great power: a horned satyr with the eyes of a blowfly and the beak of a vulture. Philippe was enraged, and would have torn me apart with his hooked claws had not Iaak whipped him across the eyes with a thick black vine slathered with snake venom. As I screamed the Scarlet Words, the rat ripped open Philippe's belly with its teeth. I tore out and ate Philippe's liver, and a surge of power coursed through my body.

When I returned to this world, Iaak materialized as my familiar in the form of a white ferret. It found Dunsott cowering behind the toilet and ripped the little butterball's throat open.

I can't say I am sad that Philippe is gone. Tomorrow I shall go to the studio and declare my mastery to the Twelve.

It is evening now. I am writing this by candlelight on the balcony. The tiny flame dazzles me with its brilliance. I can sense the earth spinning beneath me—and so much more. The gyrating planets hum with mind-less, majestic power. I delight to the frenzied music of all-consuming supernovas. The titan whirl of our galaxy has me dizzy with insatiable desire. And yet—despite this glorious barrage of sensations—I can still detect a soft, thrilling voice, velvety as a boywhore's tongue. Make no mistake: though soft, the voice is imperious. And it is repeating my name.

Mammon, Belphegor, Asmodeus—you are but servants to the Dark Reveler who is my God. When I look into the night sky I can see His eyes, and they are ablaze with hunger.

A knock at the door. My God and I shall feed together.

Coming, Sharkey.

A QUERY REGARDING THE WHEREABOUTS OF GRANT EMBRY

The following story originally appeared in issue No. 14 of Hella-cious *magazine. A copy of the issue was mailed to me anonymously three months after its publication. A short note was taped to the last page of the story. I have contacted the editor of* Hellacious *regarding the where-abouts of the story's author, Grant Embry. His last known address was a rented room in Brooklyn, New York. He has since moved without leaving a forwarding address.*

I wish to contact Mr. Embry. I would truly appreciate it if anyone who knows of his whereabouts would contact me with his address, care of this publisher.

LORING'S LUMP

by Grant Embry

One morning, Jason Loring awoke to find that he had developed a small lump on his forehead. He felt a bit queasy, too. Before leaving the house, he covered the lump with a flesh-colored bandage.

The swelling worried him. He had never been sick a day in his life: no childhood illnesses, not even an upset stomach. Why did his first af-fliction have to be so eye-catching? It seemed everyone he encountered that day kept staring at his forehead. Fortunately, it was a Saturday and he only had a few errands to run. He stopped at a drugstore and bought some skin cream. He thought that he could medicate the lump away—hopefully by work time, Monday morning. He didn't want to show up at the bookstore looking like a pimply teenager.

When he returned home, he removed the bandage. The lump was slightly larger. A shade pinker, too. He rubbed a dab of cream on it and went on with his day.

Loring did the dishes, vacuumed, and cleaned the litter box. He put away the books and magazines scattered around the apartment. He gath-ered his dirty clothes in a basket for the laundry. He found his suede gloves under a seat cushion of the couch. He wondered why he had bought suede—black leather would have been far more dramatic.

He spent the day drawing nudes in his sketchbook. He wished he had a model ... drawing from memory wasn't much fun. For dinner he cooked up a steak, rare instead of his usual well-done.

Before going to bed, he examined the lump again in the bathroom mirror. It was now much wider at the top, like an inverted triangle.

* * * *

The next morning, Loring was a little taller. A little thinner. Much paler. His hair was longer and his eyes, once dark brown, were now pale green.

He debated whether or not to see a doctor. Actually, he was pleased with the changes. He felt so much more receptive now... Even the lump had a unique charm.

Arla, an older lady from the bookstore, stopped by around noon. Her light knocks on the door tapped out a little song. Loring didn't know her very well, but he was sure she had a crush on him. He once asked to borrow a book of hers and on Friday, she had told him that she would be dropping by over the weekend to give it to him.

Loring answered the door without a word.

"Oh. Hello," Arla said, holding the book in front of her like a shield. "I'm looking for Mr. Loring. Are you his brother? I see some resemblance. Is Jason home?"

He said nothing. He simply studied the pudgy, too-tanned creature before him. Her hair was frizzy, with grey streaks. She'd had a cold for the past week, and her nose was red and shiny.

The woman stared up at him with frightened, owlish eyes. Finally, he took the book from her and shut the door.

He glanced down at the book—*Coping with Adoption*. Loring had tried to track down his real parents a few years ago, only to find out he had been a foundling, discovered in the bushes of a park. At age sixteen, he'd fathered a child that the mother's family had put up for adoption. He had hoped the book might help him to sort out his feelings ... but for now, his reading would have to wait.

Loring went downtown for a walk. He ate plenty of raw squid in a sushi bar. He visited several boutiques and bought a new outfit—black leather, with a few black rubber accoutrements. In one store, he spotted a magnifying mirror at a counter and stopped to glance at the lump on his forehead. Thin, raised lines of redness extended from the points of the triangle.

He put on his new clothes in a public restroom and threw what he had been wearing in the trash. After dark, he visited several interesting clubs—places he'd heard of, but never before dared to visit—where he drank amaretto and tequila and, to his delight, made many new friends. Loring did not know his real mother, but he felt sure she probably wouldn't have been too proud of him that night.

In the last club he visited, Loring ran out of money, and the bartender was not an understanding sort. Loring had to fend off the bouncers with a broken beer bottle, also injuring several other patrons. He despised violence, but what else could he do when people stood directly in his path?

Eventually he crawled into an alley to sleep. He dreamed that his skin was as soft as cream cheese and that eyes were bubbling up all over his body.

When he awoke, he noticed that a filthy old man was sleeping in a large cardboard box a few feet away. He oozed over to the box and began to fill the man's lungs with Loring-flesh. He sent hollow tendrils through the old man's body to inject the brain and organs with digestive juices. He never felt so hungry.

He poured up the side of the nearest apartment building and slipped through an open window into a bedroom. The man in the bed had a great many moles, some of which were cancerous and slightly bitter.

Along one wall stood a dresser with a mirror. Loring didn't need the mirror to check his appearance. Many of his new eyestalks extended more than two feet, long enough for him to examine himself.

His flesh was still pink—only now there was so much more of it. Tentacles and pincers and flapping waddles issued from his thick, shapeless trunk. The consistency of his flesh changed constantly. It could be as resilient as rubber or as runny as molasses.

The lump on what used to be his forehead was now quite prominent. It resembled a cluster of pink bubbles and tiny blue pyramids. Loring decided it had to be a gland ... yes, a long-dormant gland, now as large as a baby's head, pumping strange new secretions through his body.

Suddenly he heard a door creak open, then slam. He flowed out of the bedroom, down a hall and into the living room. A woman had entered the apartment carrying a sack of groceries. He cascaded over her like a wave, washing the flesh from her bones.

He engulfed her groceries, too, digesting paper, raw meat, oranges, broccoli, and cheese. An undigested glass bottle of aspirin caught in his flesh. He tried to spew it forth but it stayed firm. The sides of the bottle were too slick for his inner tissues to grasp. Finally, he reached into himself with a pincer and caught the bottle by the lid.

As he pulled, the lid came off and his juices poured into the bottle, digesting its contents. He pulled the lid and the bottle out of himself and collapsed to the floor. His flesh began to thicken. Several of his eyestalks and tentacles retracted as his insides churned painfully.

Loring rested for hours, barely moving. Night came and he slept dreamlessly.

* * * *

In the morning, Loring crept into the bathroom. In the medicine cabinet he found some cold capsules and vitamin C tablets. He had come to realize that it was the combination of oranges and aspirins that had started the reversal of the metamorphosis.

For the first time in his life, Loring had caught a cold; Arla must have given it to him. He didn't know if he was an alien or a mutant. All he knew was that his body had its own special method of fighting off sickness—a method that entailed astonishing transformations.

He stayed in the apartment for several more days, napping and taking vitamin C. He watched a few soap operas. In time the lump disappeared, and he regained his true form.

Loring rummaged through a closet and found a plaid shirt, trousers, and some old tennis shoes. Once he was dressed, he looked out of the living room window. Lead-gray clouds filled the sky. Across the street, he saw an attractive young couple, laughing as they chased a wind-tossed piece of paper. They appeared to be in their mid-twenties. The child he had given up years ago would now be about their age.

He turned from the window. The floor before him was littered with half-dissolved bones.

Before leaving the apartment, Loring searched the closet for a sweater. It wouldn't do for him to catch a chill.

* * * *

Like the protagonist of this story, I have never been sick a day in my life. I am also adopted. The adoption agency refuses to tell me the names of my real parents.

Perhaps I am the victim of a practical joke. Until I talk to Grant Embry, I cannot be sure. I need to know if his story is based on personal experience. If so, we have some important matters to discuss.

The handwritten note taped to the last page of the story said this:

Truth can be stranger than fiction, my boy. Are you taking your vitamins?

AND NOW, OUR FEATURE PRESENTATION

I. The Story So Far

He is beautiful and skinny and insane and he has written a screenplay entitled *Six Antichrists in Search of an Apocalypse*. He lives in his grandmother's basement (Grammy passed away five years ago—since then, the house has been sold three times and it's funny, no one can ever find the key to that little room behind the furnace) and please don't ask what he eats. The basement boy loves to dig tunnels. He has been in everyone's house, and wherever he goes, he peels off bits of his nails and throws them in the shadows while muttering something that includes the words, Wish I may, wish I might. The townspeople are only vaguely aware of his existence: they do suspect, in some far-off corner of their collective consciousness, that a semi-mythical ne'er-do-well may or may not be on the loose.

His screenplay—his neo-cyber-absurdist screenplay—is actually a series of obliquely interconnected vignettes: brief character studies, with random notes on setting and imagery. There is no dialogue because he so despises idle chatter. The first vignette is entitled:

Claws of the Depopulator

Out of the ears of the Boy Electrocutioner spool sparkling crystalline cables ending in wee copper jaws. A slender grey rope of frothy acid twists down from his hungry lips. His fingers have been crushed one by one with heated pliers.

On the tomb-world of Snegkuthu, tatter-fleshed unbeings wrap their deceptively thin, impossibly strong twig-limbs about the heads of unwary travelers and squeeze and squeeze and squeeze. Cadavers rot like wet papier-mâché, with greasy clockwork in their bellies and neon-pink fetuses in their brainpans. Something hums as it picks scabs off the walls of an open grave. Pyramids of flaming glass send extra-dimensional vibrations through leprous bodies, reducing the bones to grey-red sludge. Crickets crawl on a smiling face. An eclipse bleeds. Ropes of baby hair. Books bound in oily green cloth. A shiver-handed, smirking youth.

II. On With The Show

Our nameless basement boy searches the trash bin of a certain adult movie house for old video boxes. He takes these boxes to his basement hideaway, via his cunning tunnels, and cuts up the glossy depictions of hot sloppy. He then glues these salacious bits to a collage which will someday be integrated into the credits of his cinematic opus.

Sometimes, our (anti)hero sneaks into the aforementioned movie house and waits, curled up very small, under the bench in one of the little booths where men go when they want to take in a short but undeniably energetic motion picture. Soon the show starts: our skinny little friend starts muttering under his breath—so soft!—and before long, the ersatz film patron falls asleep. Later, the patron wakes, shuddering with satisfaction. He then notices odd little scratches here and there, and says to himself, Why am I itching like this?

The second vignette is entitled:

Bylaws of the Copulator

A mad cosmetologist sculpted the petite Incubelladonna from a pillar of living makeup: compressed rouge and lipstick and mascara, vitalized by an alien virus. Incubelladonna is the queen of Tantillasia, a funworld of hypersexual amusement parks with self-lubricating phalli and a variety of eager orifices built into the seats of the rides.

Drag queens gossip incessantly in mad gibberish. In a penthouse steamroom, living sexdolls of decayed purple latex keep pestering room service. A fat man with plucked eyebrows shaves a baboon in black lace. Cracked paint on cold eyelids. An eyestalked pleasureboy applies corpse-fat between his buttocks. Black-red lipstick. Callused penis of an aging porno star.

III. Meanwhile, in Another Part of Town

Midnight, and an itchy lawyer opens his filing cabinet. He gasps as a pair of pale, supple arms snake out and wrappity-wrap around his neck while a low, cooing voice murmurs something about *Making a deposit.* The next day in court, our attorney-on-a-journey pulls a big smelly gun out of his briefcase and begins shooting.

After several rollicking hours of Movie-of-the-Week drama, including shouts of You'll never take me alive, the attorney is indeed taken alive and thrust into a cell, and what do you know, there's a neat little something/somebody curled up under the bed.

You see, basement boy whisssssspers, I never wanted to be this way but what could I do? Life wouldn't let me sprout straight. I grew into myself like an infected fingernail.

The next morning, the cops gawk at the mess in the cell: a few gobs of white, LOTS of gobs of red. A potbellied officer hands his cruller to a pink-cheeked rookie and says, I'm not all that hungry.

The third vignette is entitled:

Tropic of the Oscillator

Dr. Xaxiphygra wears a pinstriped business suit and a barbed wire crown (the suit comes off). His bulbous doe eyes see all. In his pants squirms a coil of semi-cartilaginous flesh that could write a week's worth of haikus in the snow. But then, snow never falls on the businessworld of ZugCo: a mad electro-globe of rampant electricity, of fax machines and photocopying machines and modems, all interconnected by a network of obscenely knotted, pulsing veins.

Reed-thin secretaries tear a robot baby apart. Videotapes ejaculate ribbons of bar-coded goat-flesh. A book with razor-edged metal pages opens to cartoons of war atrocities. Syrup of electric fire. Test tubes filled with liquefied flesh. Rubber gloves coated with burst lung. Digitally controlled thumbscrews and a gentle voice that keeps repeating, I told you so.

IV. Just as They Had Feared

Pecs-of-granite personal trainer tells the attorney's widow, Feel the burn, as she pumpity-pumps stainless steel barbells. Hot and sweaty she is, and so lovely, and she really does miss her husband but you know, she's not getting any younger.

Moonlight pours like milk-gone-bad through the curtains as the not-so-merry widow pushes her beefy beau away. Words pour like baby poop from her lips, What-am-I-DOING-he's-not-even-COLD-yet-for-Christ's-sake, and Mr. Power-Pecs shrugs: Your loss, baby.

1, 2, 3 a.m.: widow wakes up from a nightmare about ants crawling out of her naughty zones. She soon discovers that ants aren't really crawling out of her (what a relief!): rather, little bits of torn-off fingernails are crawling *into* her. She also discovers that someone skinny and beautiful is sitting on the edge of the bed.

Who-are-you-What-are-you-DOING-here? she exhales, pupils as wide as black moons. Basement boy strokes her jawline with his gentle thumb and as her eyes roll back he says, You'd make a lovely bagwoman.

The fourth vignette is entitled:

Optics of the Teratoma

Weedfellow wanders the streets of a dying city of porous bricks and worm-riddled, soggy wood. Broken sidewalks are choked with creepers, and haggard Weedfellow loves to eat the pretty blossoms. Thin magenta petals thrust out from between his green, jagged teeth.

The city lost out against the jungle of Krekkuni: at night, catmen and dogwomen and insectbabies plip-plop, plip-plop on suction-cup hands along the looping, flexing cobalt-blue branches of enormous catalpa/mango trees.

Leeches sip from infected nipples. Scorpion tails drip with lime-green venom. Grasshoppers crawl through the intestinal yardage of a disemboweled ape. Out of a pile of lopsided skulls grows a rose with ticks in its petals. Rubble sweats slime in a blue-lit nightscape. Cobwebbed bronze eyes. Pinheaded madman with a knitting needle.

V. Fun For The Whole Family

Skinny/beautiful/insane boy moves his mad-eyed bride into his basement hideaway and looky here: her belly is swelling (and it's only been a week). Basement boy marches into the living room, right up to the shocked Upstairsians gathered before the TV, and says, Hi, I'm the semi-mythical ne'er-do-well and I really do exist and I'm going to be a daddy! They head quickly toward the front door but our hero says *No no no no NO* and corrals them (their mouths gape like those of belching cows) toward the door of the basement.

The skinny daddy-to-be uses the family's credit cards to buy all sorts of goodies by phone. In a month's time, his bride's belly is bigger than a Thanksgiving turkey, and baby's room is as high-tech as that room they call Mission Control in old science-fiction movies.

Meanwhile, the Upstairsians have been trained and/or surgically altered to deliver the new baby safely and effectively. This they do: and they don't even mind when the wee toothy young'un starts munching on them (good help is out here: one only has to look). Afterward, the widdle bitty cutey spins a cocoon and settles down for a nap.

The fifth vignette is entitled:

Power of the Cyber-Coma

Observe Yvek, so lovely in his black leather raincoat—a pale, mannish boy with soft black eyes, limp black hair, and a black clove cigarette between his black lips. He nods and sighs as he chain-smokes his way through eternity. When he speaks, his curving black nails lazily slice the air.

Yvek is the only biped inhabitant of Phomom, a rainy sleepworld of mossy hills and black crystal cities (this crystal is imbedded with diodes and fine black wires). In the basements and subbasements of the buildings dwell soft ultra-grubs: man-sized creatures that drowse for centuries in their oversized manila envelopes. The fine black wires lead into their fat tummies.

Rusted boltheads stare out from the eye-sockets of pigeon skulls. Chanting spiders spin phlegmy webs in a metal tree. Laughter like the chattering of beaked maggots. Elderly men with pendulous guts filled with beetles. A dagger carved from a piss icicle. A wee voice moans, *What have I done?*

VI. The Shocking Conclusion

After the cocoon breaks open, basement daddy decides that his screenplay probably will never become a movie. Baby is always hungry and growing ever-so-BIG! Pretty soon, there won't be anyone left to produce, direct, star in or even care about neo-cyber-absurdist movies.

The sixth vignette is entitled:

Hour of the Necrotrauma

Countess Mygnathalia drapes her flabby arms with pewter and copper and lead bracelets. A long string of misshapen pearls is coiled seven times around her throat. Her delicate uranium lashes are screwed into the bloated flesh of her eyelids. From her tower window, she gazes down her long, gracefully hooked nose upon the Republic of Lower Vyphaeus: a royalworld ruled by the diseased members of an Evylle Arystocracy. These jaded jackanapes mince through basalt hallways to observe the twistings and drillings and delicate excruciations of incorrigible farm-workers, in dungeons lined with the stained hides of—What else? Other incorrigible farm-workers.

Gap-toothed, boneless chauffeurs tool about in black-scaled limousines. Orange fluid drips from under a cretin's nails. Mannequins with live coals for eyes drink wine brewed from honey and sperm. Shrieking, effeminate gargoyles piss tar on the villagers. Giggling lumps writhe in an amber decanter. Hare-lipped priests. Simpering boys with knees that bend backwards.

* * * *

So ends the screenplay. Ambitious, yes—but is it art?

Basement boy and mad, sad wifey have been devoured, along with everyone else. Except, of course, for the devourer.

Through the mindless void now floats a planet-sized lump of stone shaped like a throne. And on this throne sits a fabulous Titan of holy yet godless beauty. This creature says nothing, for there is no need for idle chatter. No trace of emotion disturbs the perfection of its preposterous face: cheeks formed from diseased makeup; a hooked nose; green teeth; limp black hair; acid-flecked lips; and those all-seeing bulbous doe eyes. How intently the Titan stares, like someone waiting for a show to begin.

NOTES CONCERNING THE DEATH AND/OR DECOMPOSITION OF REALITY

Michael Collins met Joseph Prescott at a mutual friend's Halloween party. Both came as characters from Poe: Collins as the Red Death, Prescott as the killer orangutan from *The Murders In The Rue Morgue*, complete with bloody razor. They spent much of the evening sprawled on their host's enormous paisley sofa, drinking dark beer, sweating under their heavy costumes, and discussing literature, movies and music.

Collins discovered that Prescott was the manager of a local video store, an unpublished poet, and a two-time loser in divorce court. Collins asked him if he had ever been to the Red Rhino, a yuppie nightspot known for its abundance of young lovelies. No? Then perhaps they should go together some night, he suggested...

Later that week, they went to the Red Rhino's Alternative Music Night. A woman in a green suede jacket was enthralled by the fact that Michael's hair was black while Joseph's was practically white; she invited them to come home with her but they declined, although Prescott did ask for her phone number.

Collins was pleased that his new acquaintance had become a friend with relative ease. They both enjoyed oddities and esoterica—and what's more, their conversation rose above the bland exchange of sports scores that Collins usually experienced with other men. Still, Prescott had his quirks: he let Michael take care of minor expenses, such as tips, parking meters, and cover charges (but then, the poor guy was paying double alimony). He hit on every attractive woman in sight, and would make a cutting remark if a woman happened to find the dark-haired man more attractive.

One afternoon, Prescott showed up at Collins' apartment with a bottle of Chablis and a dark blue notebook. Collins fetched a corkscrew and two glasses from the kitchen. "What's in the notebook?" he said. "Love letters? Dirty pictures?"

"A list." Prescott paused, pushing a lock of white hair out of his face. "Notes on a theory of mine you might find interesting."

"Heady stuff." Collins began to uncork the bottle. "Most of my friends show me their drawings and watercolors. 'Feast your eyes on real talent, Mr. Sell-Out Art Director!' Usually they add that they've never had a lesson in their life. To which I can only reply, 'no shit.' So, this theory..." His friend riffled through the notebook. "Here it is. I've made a list of things that decay."

Dark flecks floated in the wine; corkscrews became corkmanglers in Collins' hands. He handed Prescott a glass and examined the list:

- THE UNIVERSE IN GENERAL (entropy)
- MATTER (disintegration)
- MOTION (friction)
- LIVING ORGANISMS (age, disease, injury, etc.)
- SANITY (disease, stress, etc.)
- CIVILIZATION (decadence)
- DEAD ORGANIC MATTER (microorganisms, chemical breakdown)

"Your science is a little askew. Still, things rot. Crows eat roadkill. Sour cream just gets sourer. What's the point?"

Prescott finished his glass and helped himself to more. "Jesus, I'll be picking cork out of my teeth for a week. Now tell me: where would 'reality' fit on my list?"

Collins thought for a moment. "Each of us has our own reality. I suppose it would fall under 'sanity.'"

"Not bad. But let me throw a couple 'what-if's' your way. What if reality is a living organism? What happens to us when it grows old and dies?"

"What happens to the fleas when a dog dies? Either we'll all die, too, or we'll just find another dog. So to speak." Collins closed the notebook and noticed a title penciled onto the cover:

NOTES CONCERNING THE DEATH AND/ OR DECOMPOSITION OF REALITY

He opened the notebook again and realized that almost every page was crammed with his friend's rounded handwriting. "Can I read this some day?"

Prescott shrugged and took the notebook back. "Maybe. Here's my other 'what-if.' What if reality was a living organism that has been dead since the origins of man? What will we do when decay sets in—and reality starts to ripen?"

"Very deep. And very disgusting. I hope you don't bring up this delightful topic on dates."

"As a matter of fact," Prescott said, "I shared some of my thoughts with a sweet young thing a few nights ago—Tammi, from the Red Rhino. Anyway, I think you see what I mean. The possibility exists that reality can decompose." On the fire escape, a cat yowled. Collins went into the kitchen. "What's more," Prescott shouted after him, "I happen to know a place where rot has already set in."

Collins returned from the kitchen with a dish of milk. He opened the window and a huge, one-eyed tabby jumped onto the sill.

"You shouldn't do that," Prescott said, watching the cat lap furiously at the milk. "It'll just keep coming back."

"I know. I've been feeding it for six weeks."

"It would be interesting to see how an animal would react to decayed reality." Prescott came to the window and scratched the cat behind the ears. "Animals. They're the lucky ones. They can fuck and fight and kill whenever they please."

"What a charming philosophy. Have you ever thought of writing children's books?" Collins was starting to develop a headache from too much wine. "Where exactly is this rotten hidey-hole of yours?"

The white-haired man grinned. "In my basement."

* * * *

Prescott lived in a large brick house several miles outside of town. Collins drove out to the house that evening bringing a bottle of wine (burgundy this time) and the tabby. With any luck, Joseph would keep the cat. He wanted it himself but his landlord didn't allow pets. Prescott hadn't gone into detail about whatever dubious wonders his basement had to offer. 'Decayed reality'? Dry rot, more than likely.

"Nice place," Collins said as Prescott led him into the living room. He briefly checked his appearance in the mirror above the fireplace. "Hope Popeye doesn't tear it apart. I brought him along so you can get an animal's-eye view of your basement decay-athon. Maybe I should have brought a Rottweiler."

Prescott gave him a deadpan look. "Pease. Stop. My side hurts. My ribs split asunder with laughter." He took the cat from Collins' arm and carried it into the kitchen. "I've got a few sardines for the old vagrant.

Since when did you give him a name? Bring the wine in here and I'll show you how to open it the right way."

Collins looked over the notes stuck with magnets on the refrigerator as he waited for his friend to find the corkscrew. He was surprised to find a number of ads torn out of personal columns.

"The rent here is great," Prescott said, searching in yet another drawer. "The last tenant killed himself and they didn't find the body for weeks. You can still smell something on rainy days."

Collins skimmed over the ads: men, women, couples, all demanding discipline. He suddenly realized that nobody knew where he was this evening. He moved away from the refrigerator; at least Prescott hadn't seen him reading the ads.

"Here we go," Prescott found the tool and began to open the bottle. "Now watch. You twist the bottle, not the corkscrew."

Soon they returned to the living room, where Popeye was scratching at a stereo speaker. Prescott nudged the cat away with his shoe. "An old man with a big mouth lives about half a mile down the road," he said. "He told me that this house used to belong to some backwoods types about twenty years ago. Cousins married to cousins, six-fingered kids. Every few months, the old guy would have to buy a new dog. They kept disappearing on him."

Collins sipped his wine; he didn't want to drink too much. "Cheery little place you've got: incest, suicide...and what about the dogs? Vivisection in the parlor? Is all that what made this—" This what? Patch of space-mold? He felt like a gullible fool. "—this basement problem?"

"Not quite. That only readied the grounds. I brought about the phenomenon myself." Prescott set down his drink and scooped up the cat from an armchair. "Follow me, troops. Time to check out the warzone."

They walked down a short hall to a door that appeared to be so heavily lacquered, Collins could see their reflection as they approached. Something about the image seemed wrong; the varnish appeared to have ripples in it. He brushed his fingers against the door and they came away wet with slime.

"Is this what you were talking about?" he said, wiping his hand with his handkerchief. Prescott shook his head, opened the door and passed through.

Collins looked inside. The walls, ceiling and stairs were coated with glowing pink flesh. Its texture was coarse and pockmarked; clusters of pustules had erupted in spots. These glowed a dull yellowish-green.

"Good God. What is this? Some kind of fungus?" His stomach churned as he saw Prescott disappear around a corner. Then his friend poked his head back into view.

"Not exactly," he said. "Are you coming?"

Collins walked down the spongy steps to the landing where Prescott waited. The white-haired man handed him the cat, then pulled a jack-knife from his pocket. With this he cut deep into the swollen wall. Collins shielded his eyes, expecting a gush of fluid. Instead, the wall seeped a scarlet ooze that stank of corruption. Prescott cut free a small chunk and began to chew on it.

Collins turned away with a cry of disgust. "What kind of diseased fuck are you?"

Prescott wiped his mouth on his sleeve. "A diseased fuck? You've got that right. Too many games with all the wrong playmates. My bloodstream is a veritable cesspool. Fortunately, that is no longer a problem." So saying, he continued down the stairs.

Clutching the cat tighter to his chest, Collins turned toward the door—but the passage behind him had closed like a raw, toothless mouth. There was only one way to go.

As he descended, he noticed larger patches of decay on the walls. The stairs seemed to go on endlessly; soon he reached an area where the ceiling was covered with ragged strips of flesh, hanging down from wet, ulcerated sores.

At the base of the stairs, he found an enormous chamber lined with dead-white tissue. The floor was a plain of greasy, luminous gristle, carved over with strange symbols and littered with piles of human and animal bones.

In the center of the chamber, Prescott sat on a throne composed of long bones tied together with bloody strips of cloth. "Welcome to Hell," he said, "albeit a rather private Hell. By invitation only."

"This can't be real," Collins said. Popeye squirmed free of his grasp and ran behind one of the piles.

"You're right," the white-haired man said. "It isn't. In this contained pocket of space, reality is dead. Dead and decayed."

"That's insane. How can reality die?"

Prescott rose from the throne. Reaching into its framework of bones, he pulled forth a claw hammer. "A ritual. One of my own invention, carrying the tenets of sympathetic magic to the utmost degree." He advanced, swinging the hammer. "Many of my playmates have accompanied me here—some more willingly than others. With each death, the reality of this place dies as well; my Hell takes on the qualities of the sacrificial flesh. Once liberated from the shackles of reality, I shall become a being beyond all limitations. I thank you in advance, my friend, for your contribution to my efforts."

Prescott raised the hammer and lunged forward. Collins jumped to the side, almost too late; the hammer sloughed a strip of skin from the side of his head.

Crying out with pain, Collins stumbled across the chamber. He picked up a heavy bone and threw it at Prescott, striking him across the face. He then ran to another hill of bones, where he found Popeye hiding under a torn green suede jacket. As Prescott ran toward him, he picked up the cat and flung it in his attacker's face.

Prescott cried out as the cat's claws raked across his eyes. He dropped the hammer and fell to his knees. A spray of his blood splashed on the carven floor.

Collins was about to pick up the hammer when a low rumbling filled the chamber. The floor beside Prescott began to swell and crack. Shards of gristle flew through the air as a gigantic wormlike form erupted from below.

The small, piggish eyes of the monstrosity scanned the chamber. Prescott reached out for the hammer; the creature detected the motion, swooped down and seized him in its seething lamprey-mouth. With a high-pitched squeal, the creature dragged the white-haired man down through the chamber floor.

Collins understood the nature of the creature. A scavenger—a maggot, feasting in Prescott's dead realm. The white-haired man had expected a transformation; perhaps that was what he would have become. A mindless, ravenous parasite.

Collins felt Popeye rubbing against his ankles. In the moment that passed as Collins bent to pick up the cat, a transition occurred. The dimensions of the chamber shifted, returning to normal in a brief, dizzying blur. The basement walls hardened to grey concrete; the hole in the floor closed without a trace. But the bones of Prescott's victims remained, and the entire room was streaked with rank slime.

Collins carried Popeye upstairs to the living room. Everything here was the same as before. He caught a movement out of the corner of his eye—his reflection in the fireplace mirror.

He looked down at his hands. They were filthy, but still firm and healthy. Popeye's fur was wet and matted; other than that, the cat appeared to be fine. And yet when he looked back in the mirror, he saw a bloated, leprous ghoul holding a writhing carcass.

Which perception was real? Collins set the cat gently on the couch and began to search for a dark blue notebook.

THE EXCEEDINGLY PRAETERNATURAL & MORE THAN A LITTLE DISCONCERTING LIFE-GIVING PROPERTIES OF THE PAELESCU RAY

The Paelescu Ray brought things to life—gloriously virulent life—life gone wacky—superlife, ultralife—luxuriant slaphappy psooodolife.

I (the least confusing designation for now) should know, for I am Paelescu.

The source of the ray's power was calcium—seashells & old bones. I *DARE NOT* say more. The machine resembled a flamboyant combination of three futuristic vacuum cleaners & a laptop computer for someone with an exceptionally large lap. I invented it in a burst of creative splendour one Sunday afternoon, using all of the gizmos & thingys & whatnots of silicon shamanism (not to mention several major appliances) scattered about my warehouse/wonderland/workshop. This was to be my finest electro-goody yet: the instant-golden-brown-tan simulator. At no time did it ever bestow such a miraculous tan upon anyone or anything & in that regard I failed, but so what? It's not like I could have been fired—I was self-employed—or more to the point, I was living off of a truly hu*mong*ous oil-money inheritance.

I took off my washed-out old suede slippers & turned my ray-machine upon them. Three greener-than-green beams shot from the machine's directional spouts & converged upon the slippers. Sparks crackled—smoke swirled—the hands of my wall-clock spun backwards, fast-forwards, perhaps even a teeny bit sideways. The slippers trembled & shimmied & out-&-out pulsated—then they sprouted waspwings & *fluttered.* They lapped at my coffee with their thick fuzzy tongues. They dribbled foul dollops of shoe excrement upon all my precious notebooks. Finally the winged shoes flew side-by-side out an open window (their tentacle/shoe-laces grabbed a roast-beef sandwich off my lunch plate on the way). My surreal guinea pigs were gone & O they hadn't even looked back.

Next I fired upon a bucket of T-bones & clam shells. The calciferous contents merged into a cow-eyed multi-mouthed snapping absurdity.

The shell-thing squirmed out of the bucket & clambered toward me with malicious intent—vile grins played upon its many bivalved lips. A moment later, the bucket quivered to life (metal, I decided, must take a little longer) & bounced about in a puppyish frenzy.

The shellozoid crept closer & closer & closer still! O the horror! I was in danger of being mauled by a grotesque conglomerate of dinner scraps—but O the delicious *bliss!* I suddenly realized that this creature was in effect, my *child!* Not the fruit of my loins, but of my so-very-clever, so-cunningly-wrinkled brain (& really, isn't the brain the ultimate organ of regeneration?). True, it wasn't my first or even second child—I felt a sudden & poignant pang of parental loss for the naughty shoe-fly twins.

My ghastly shell-urchin squealed & leapt at me—as I pushed it (lovingly!) away, I slipped on a plop of shoe-guck & upset my life-giving miracle machine. It fell on its side, hitting the ON switch & three mega-green beams sizzzzzled forth. I scrambled to regain my bearings & my shoeless right foot kicked out, straight into the mini-thunderball of green fire created by the merging rays. The blast was unbearable—not so much because it was painful but because it was too too *titillating.*

The bouncing bucket then hopped within reach. I grabbed the jolly oddity & slapped it over its clam/bone sibling. I turned off the ray-machine & raced out of the workshop, slamming the door behind me. I hated to run from my precocious darlings, but what's a father to do when a wee thing turns ne'er-do-well? I listened to find out if the shell-daemon was in pursuit. The clapping of its clam-halves grew fainter, as did the banging of the bucket. The beasties were moving away from the door, toward—the *window* perhaps? I am *not* one to learn from my mistakes. I cracked open the door for a peek, just in time to watch the impossible pair bound over the sill.

Saddened, I hobbled to the bathroom to splash cold water on my zapped foot, which was as puffy & red as a sickly chain-smoker's infected gums. I raised my foot onto the edge of the sink to get a look at my poor toes—imagine my surprise when they lengthened & twisted 'round to *LOOK BACK.* Each was tipped with a cluster of black spider-eyes, as well as a gaping mouth filled with weensy crooked teeth.

I do so wish that at this point, I could say, "It was all a dream & then I woke up," but such is not the case. At the time, however, I did wonder if I was living out an oh-my-god-I-ate-something-gone-bad-&-now-my-guts-are-utterly-*liquescent* species of nightmare. I limped from the bathroom to my bedroom to rest for just a tiny moment. But when my head hit the pillow, I lapsed into a deep sleep which lasted for three days.

Upon awakening, I found that my condition was progressive in nature. I was more alive than any human had a right to be & at this point, my truly singular first-person account must take on a distinctly plural stance.

For I had become a *WE*. Each organ had developed into a unique entity—all connected & interdependent & yet each possessing a newly-innate sense of identity. We were a modern-day Argus, with not only myriad eyes, but also countless ears, mouths & noses. We were a cluster/swarm, communicating through a sort of primitive telepathy—for each organ had its own tiny but very astute & truly hyperactive brain.

We ordered tons of pizza, fried chicken & take-out foods from every restaurant that would deliver—we told them to leave the food outside the door as we slipped the money through the mail-slot. We were hairy/scaly/wrinkled/bloated/striped & more more *MORE*. We experimented a few times with the ray-machine (even now, an old lava lamp is flying in batwinged circles above me) before we dismantled it. We were afraid that someday, we might accidentally zap ourselves again & fragment our self-contained organic community even further into total cellular *chaos* (eek!).

That, O world, was the last unanimous decision ever reached by the Paelescu-swarm. We lived in peace for as long as the members of any community can live in peace—a precious short while.

Eventually we developed a problem & it started with a pizza. Our fingers felt that they deserved the best bits of sausage—they, after all, had pressed the buttons on the phone to make the order. But the tongues felt that they would best appreciate the pizza's choicest morsels—whereas our one & only penis decided that it should get the best yummies because, well, *IT WAS THE PENIS*—& so on & so forth & on & on & on.

We argued for sooooo long that the pizza grew cold—then we argued over whose fault *that* was. Finally we ate the cold pizza in psychic silence.

From that point on, we argued over everything—what to eat, what to drink, what sleeping position was most comfortable, & especially what projects should be developed. Our work was horribly unfocused—we started hundreds of projects & finished none. Just a few weeks ago, we were working on a liqui-quartz industrial lubricant when a beaker slipped from a hand & fell on a foot. The foot reared up to bite the hand—so of course, we all fell over.

Soon all of our many parts were clawing & tearing at each other. As we squirmed & fought on the workshop floor, a tension gathered in the belly—then a gash appeared & the inner organs, eager for a fight, came *bursting out*. Intestines loooped around the neck & limbs, squeezing like an anaconda. Ribs opened & closed like long jagged teeth on whatever body part came within chomping range. The stomach splashed digestive juice everywhere. The eyeballs turned coward, audibly popped out of their sockets & hid in the armpits. Some fingernails came loose, meandered for a bit, then embedded themselves in the scalp. Quite suddenly we all began to feel a bit—wooooozy. Wheeling-down-a-big-black-vortex *giddy*. There could be no doubt—this was that unmistakable sensation known as *DYING*.

To right this incredibly scary wrong, our organs instantly began to work together to save the Paelescu-swarm. Various body parts sucked/absorbed/scoooped up as much blood as possible from the floor—since so much fluid was lost, we used a few beakers of liqui-quartz to lubricate the workings. Some organs were split in two/three/four & others were bent/broken/horribly distended & we weren't able to put everything back where it was supposed to go, but (sigh) we did what we could.

* * * *

It is midnight & we cannot sleep. We do heal very fast, but our scars & mutilations have made us *daemoniacally* grotesque, even by our own extremely *liberal* standards (you who have sound bodies—cherish your symmetry!). We do not desire to work ever again & we have burned the notebooks containing the plans for the ray-machine. There is no reason for us to stay in this house—these once most-comfortable furnishings are now completely alien to this new & utterly *askew* physique.

Would a centipede live in a dollhouse? Noooo—it would find a burrow, deep & dark & yummy. We shall be leaving soon. Into the warm (& mercifully mirrorless) womb of the earth we shall go & who knows? We are most inventive—& humble clay, in truth, is rife with alchemic secrets. Perhaps we shall suffer a dirt-change, damp & strange.

O world, think of the Paelescu-swarm not as a worm or monster but rather as a magnificent *FETUS*, so full of life & *potential*. This pen is beginning to run dry, but no matter. There is certainly enough ink to write the word Goodbye.

THE TALE OF THE CAT-HEADED MAN, THE MAN-HEADED DOG, AND THE LADY WITH RATS FOR HANDS

I.

Oh, you think you know so much. You think you know how this story will end. No doubt you are saying to yourself, "It's really very obvious. Cats and dogs and rats have hated each other since the dawn of time, so The Cat-Headed Man and The Man-Headed Dog are probably going to get into a big fight with The Lady With Rats For Hands." Well, I am sorry to disappoint you, my friend, but you are wrong. The strange-headed creatures and verminous appendages in this story never fight.

In fact, they get along quite well.

My name is Aristotle O'Leary, and I am a very old man, though I don't look it. Older than you'd guess, that's for sure. I've been a lot of things to a lot of different people over the years. Confidant. Servant. Host. Employer. King? Perhaps. Pawn? Certainly. Maybe even a Rook: certainly I have been able to move along ranks or files across any number of unoccupied squares.

I was once was the owner of Professor O'Leary's Mystic Carnival Caravan Of Diversions & Living Rarities. The carnival caravan disbanded after it stopped being mystic. Nothing can be mystic—strange and well-and-truly *indecipherable*—forever. With time and its changes, strangeness becomes ordinary, and the indecipherable finally becomes obvious. The carnival caravan was mystic for quite a long time, but it became considerably more commonplace after that night, that unforgettable night...

But I'll get to that later.

I am half Greek and half Irish. I never knew my mother, since she was struck by lightning a few weeks after my birth. My father was the creator of the steam-powered manservant, a remarkable innovation—it could prepare meals, fold laundry, and dispense hot Turkish coffee from its nipple-spigots. Other options were available to more discerning customers. My father made an incredible fortune from his invention. Unfortunately, he died in a freak explosion while trying to build a steam-powered horse. At age twenty-two, I inherited his great wealth.

I decided to use a small portion of the fortune to travel the world. I left the family estate in Ireland and wandered around Europe for a bit, hurrying along all the way—after all, I had a whole world to see. In a small village in Belgium I met Mimi, The Furry Woman. She was not a popular member of her community, since she was poor and so extremely hirsute, but she was very graceful and had a lovely laugh so I asked her to join me on my travels. In Poland we met The Cat-Headed Man, whose name was Premm. Like Mimi, Premm had endured a life of great hardship—people can be so unkind to those who are different—so we invited him to come with us.

In that fashion, more unusual people and person-like creatures joined me on my whirlwind journey. After Europe we went to Africa, and in Tangiers we met Khu, The Upright Pig, and he was very happy to travel with us, since he was constantly afraid that someone might try to cook and eat him, even though he spoke seven languages and walked on his hind legs. In the Congo we encountered Mnuggug, The Giant Monkey-Spider—her body was thirty-three inches long, not counting the eight legs and prehensile tail. She was extremely intelligent and well-spoken—a welcome companion. The boats, wagons and other vehicles we employed during our travels had enclosed chambers, so the more unusual members of our group were able to avoid prying eyes. Others were able to hide their physical differences with hats, veils, and other cunning accessories.

In Russia we made a comrade of Petra, The Lady With Rats For Hands, and in China we added Wu, The Bird-Faced Man, to our fold. In Australia we encountered Bullobu, The Pouched Man—he proved to be handy to have around, since he had that built-in pocket. We stopped for only a very short while in Antarctica, since there's not much to see there, and the cold disagreed with many members of our growing family. But we did meet and welcome aboard a creature called Nub, The Talking Chunk Of Quartz, who came to this planet on an asteroid and had some fascinating stories to tell.

Our next stop was South America, and in the Brazilian rain-forest we had a nice chat with Qexulli, The Hooved Boy, and since he was all alone in the world—his parents had been eaten by giant snakes—we decided to adopt him. In the United States, in a region called Kansas, we made the acquaintance of Tim, The Man-Headed Dog. At first he didn't want to go with us. He didn't want to leave his beloved family, which was composed of totally normal people. But they insisted that he leave with us, since they feared for his safety. The people of his town thought he was an accursed creature, and they were quick to blame him whenever something bad happened.

Unfortunately, we encountered a similar problem when at last we all returned to my estate in Ireland. The people in the neighboring towns had always considered my father a bit of an eccentric (and he was), but they tolerated him, since he spend a lot of money in the local shops, buying supplies for his experiments. Sad to say, they did not welcome my guests with open arms. Some even threatened to roast The Upright Pig, and they made shocking, hurtful comments about The Furry Woman.

My companions had enjoyed their travels with me, and many began to ask when we might start travelling again. I myself wanted to see much more of Europe—hopefully at a leisurely pace. But my friends had such unusual appearances, and I didn't want them to always have to be encumbered by disguises...

It was Petra, The Lady With Rats For Hands, who ultimately came up with the perfect solution. We were sitting by the fireplace at the time, enjoying some cognac and chocolates. "When I was little," she said, "a traveling show would come to town, with caged animals and clowns and some freaks, too. Why don't we become such a show? We could each have our own nice wagon, and people would pay you to see the rest of us. But let us not be called freaks. We should think of a more dignified term."

Tim, The Man-Headed Dog, had wandered into the room during the discussion, so he had heard most of what we'd said. "How about Rarities?" he said. "Or better yet, Living Rarities, so people don't think we're just fossils or fake deformed babies in big pickle jars."

"Living Rarities! How delightful!" Petra said. "Come here, my friend, eat some of these chocolates before my hungry rat-hands finish them off."

The next day, we shared our thoughts with the others, and they agreed that it was an excellent plan. We decided to begin preparations immediately.

Fortunately, there were people in the area who did not mind my guests, and among their numbers I found some workmen who agreed to build wagons to my specifications. One side of each wagon would open up like double doors, so that the living quarters inside became a stage. The two corners across from the opening wall would be partitioned off, so that the occupant could have a private bathroom and a storage space for belongings. The workmen said it would take them about a month to build the wagons.

My friends and I then had some time to decide how we would decorate the wagons, since they were to be part of a great show. During our world travels, I had taught most of my friends how to play chess, so they wanted the wagons to be painted with artwork reflecting a chess motif. Mimi had never really mastered the game (too difficult for her, though she liked the pretty pieces), so I told her she could pick the color scheme. Without hesitation she chose black and gold, which did not surprise me, since she had black and gold striped fur.

"Chess! What an excellent idea!" Premm said to me while we were peeling potatoes for dinner one afternoon. He nodded his big split-lipped cat's-head. "People will read all sorts of meaning into that artwork. It will be very exotic. Yes, we must all be very mysterious and esoteric. Churches do it, and look how popular they are."

I submitted sketches to some painters and they turned the new wagons into masterpieces on wheels. The chess theme—or perhaps I should say scheme, taking Premm's comments into consideration—was truly a delight to behold.

Tim, The Man-Headed Dog, had plenty of room to wag his tail in the Golden King Wagon.

Premm, The Cat-Headed Man, took up residence in the Black King Wagon.

Petra, The Lady With Rats For Hands, made her home in the Golden Queen Wagon.

Mnuggug, The Giant Monkey-Spider, spun her web in the Black Queen Wagon.

Khu, The Upright Pig, snuggled into the Golden Bishop Wagon.

Wu, The Bird-Faced Man, nested in the Black Bishop Wagon.

Qexulli, The Hooved Boy, made a comfy bed of straw in the Golden Knight Wagon.

Bullobu, The Pouched Man, pocketed himself in the Black Knight Wagon.

Mimi, The Furry Woman, received the Golden Rook Wagon.

Nub, The Talking Chunk Of Quartz, required only a pillow and a polishing cloth in the Black Rook Wagon. Nub was perfectly capable of resting upon the pillow himself, and the rest of us took turns polishing him every few days.

As for me, my wagon was simply painted white. I was Management, and did not require embellishment.

I made some inquiries in Dublin and found some cooks, jugglers, musicians, and various other unemployed carnival workers. I then arranged for the purchase of many more less-costly wagons, as well as horses, food supplies, and other necessities. I had my lawyers arrange all the necessary licenses, as well as the travel paperwork. Soon Professor O'Leary's Mystic Carnival Caravan Of Diversions & Living Rarities was ready to roll.

And roll it did.

II.

Our tour began, of course, in Ireland—but not too close to any of the communities surrounding my home. As I've mentioned, familiarity with my guests had bred contempt in the hearts of some of my neighbors. I rather enjoyed my role as the carnival caravan's host, Professor O'Leary. Many of our customers would return every night, to gaze upon The Furry Woman's black and gold curves ... to hear The Bird-Faced Man warble a haunting tune ... to watch The Hooved Boy dance a whimsical jig ... to listen spellbound as The Talking Chunk Of Quartz told tales of outer space ... to witness all the delights and wonders our show had in store.

After some pleasant engagements in Ireland, we rolled into England, fine-tuning our various acts along the way. Soon it became clear that our singular troupe was working its magic well. We usually spent four or five days at every stop, and the people found us, in a word ... fascinating.

We became a very close-knit ensemble. But, there were those who seemed to spent more time together as their own little group. Tim, Premm, and Petra formed such a group. Mnuggug was probably the most intelligent of all my friends, but after her, the three in that smaller group were surely the brightest. Sometimes those three would perform little vignettes for their audiences—scenes from Shakespeare, or occasionally their own material.

France was next on our itinerary, and the French loved us.

One morning, Petra knocked at the door of my plain white wagon. I showed her in and asked her to sit at my table. Though it was early, I gave her a glass of white wine. I thought she looked nervous, and could use a little something to calm her down.

"Some of us have been receiving presents," she said.

"That shouldn't surprise you," I said. "People enjoy our show. You are excellent performers."

"But these gifts are very expensive," she said. "Packages of smoked meat. Bottles of wine. Gold rings. Bracelets. Necklaces."

"The French must be having a good year."

"You don't think these gifts are excessive? Extravagant?"

"Perhaps," I said, "but what of it? Why should it worry you? I wish some of those people would give me a gift. I am the host, after all. And I pay the bills."

"There is more," she said. "Some of the audience members yesterday were folks who had seen our show in England. I have a very good memory for faces. Especially those with moles, or crooked teeth, or especially striking eyes. I even spotted a couple folks who had attended our Ireland appearances."

I had to laugh. "The real problem is, you are too accustomed to being disliked. That may be why you remember faces so well: you file the information in your mind, in case that person ever does you harm. You are suspicious of everyone—even people who obviously like you! I hope you are not suspicious of me, or the others in the group!"

"Oh no!" she cried. "You are all very wonderful. You have been so kind. So understanding."

I poured her some more wine. "You must realize that our carnival caravan is developing a following of enthusiasts. That is good news. You should be happy."

Petra smiled. "As always, you are right. And really, I am happy. I love my wagon and all my friends. Though I do worry that someday, I will have to pick between Premm and Tim."

"Why should you have to pick?"

"Because that is the way of the world." She sighed wearily. Her long, pale face was quite lovely in its sadness, like the face of some long-dead beauty in a centuries-old oil painting.

"Listen to you! Since when has anyone associated with this enterprise done anyhting by the way of the world? Rules are for sheep! And there are no sheep among the Living Rarities, are there? Not a one. Just do whatever your feelings tell you to do."

"What is I make a mistake?"

I gave her shoulder a friendly squeeze. "You will carry on. That is all. Mistakes are a part of the grand design. After all, Nature made a few mistakes when you were born, but so what? The mistakes only made you more elaborate. More interesting. The end result was a wonderfully complex you."

III.

Weeks passed, and we continued through France, from town to town until we reached Germany.

After my conversation with Petra, I began to pay more attention to the growing crowds. We did get plenty of returning customers—more and more with the passage of time. The performers continued to receive marvelous gifts. Some evenings, while we were all having a late dinner together, my troupe members would compare the gifts they'd received that day.

Even The Talking Chunk of Quartz received presents. Mind you, it must be difficult to think up a good gift for a rock—it has no use for food, clothing, jewelry or wine. In fact, it really doesn't need anything. Not even air. People use gave it gems and small pieces of crystal—perhaps they thought that these were its long-lost relatives.

One night, while comparing gifts, Wu, The Bird-Faced Man, mentioned, "Do you ever hear the people whispering?"

Mimi nodded. "Yes. I assume they are whispering things like, 'Oh! Mimi's fur looks very shiny tonight!' or maybe 'That Mimi, what a sex goddess—if only she would fall in love with me!'"

"They whisper, yes," Mnuggug said. "All the time they whisper. But while my ears are very sensitive, but I cannot make out the words. But I do not suppose they are calling *me* a sex goddess!" Her brittle, tittering laugh rang out.

Mimi laughed, too. "Do not sell yourself short! The men love long legs, and you have eight of them!"

"I have heard whispering," Premm said. "I just assumed they were being polite. They did not want to interrupt any of the performances."

Khu, The Upright Pig, looked from face to face. "Oh! You do not know? I thought you did. Am I the only one to notice? I guess so!"

Tim began to wag his tail. "What? What have you noticed, Khu?"

"Well, I do get hungry," Khu said, "and sometimes, out on the grass, I'll see an apple or a piece of candy that someone has dropped. I do hate to see food wasted. So I go out to get it, if I am between performances. After I get the morsel, I will sometimes sneak up behind someone who is whispering, to hear what they are saying."

"And—?" Petra said.

A smile curled into shape under the snout of The Upright Pig. "They are praying to us."

"Praying?" I could not believe my ears. "Surely you are mistaken."

"I can believe it," said Mnuggug.

"It would explain the gifts," said Bullobu. He pulled a little doll out of his pouch. "Someon gave me this figure of me, made of cloth and wire.

In its pouch is a smaller doll of me. And it has a pouch, too, with an even smaller doll inside."

Petra turned to me. "Should this worry us, Ari?"

At this point, the other nine also turned to me. They wanted, needed to hear my assessment of the situation. I was indeed becoming very worried, but there would have been no point in alarming them.

"So long as they pay the admission," I said, "they can pray as much as they like! Cherish your popularity while you can. People are notoriously fickle. Tomorrow they may be praying to trees, or comets, or bumblebees."

"They *should* pray to us," Mnuggug said. "It is good. It is right."

It surprised me, to see the others nod in response to that comment.

IV.

More time passed.

More miles were traveled.

More gifts were given.

More prayers were whispered.

Our course through Europe meandered in a leisurely fashion. Sometimes we stayed a bit longer than usual in some communities. Eventually we wound up in sunny Italy. Premm, Petra and Tim were staging their own short satire of *Romeo And Juliet*. They called their performance, *Romeo And Juliet And The Bogeyman*. Petra played Juliet, Premm played Romeo, and Tim strapped on rubber-and-wire bat-wings to pay The Bogeyman. Why they thought that The Bogeyman should have such wings, I do not know.

One afternoon, I watched the performance along with the audience, to hear some of the whispered prayers. I had listening at other performances, and it turned out that people usually prayed for their wishes to come true—the real nature of all prayers. Some people wanted to find love. Others wanted wealth. Some wanted their enemies to die. The same old thing. Anyway, at the end of the play, an old woman turned to me and said, "I did not know that The Bogeyman had bat-wings. I have learned something this day."

"It's just a costume," I said. "They were probably just being fanciful. Amusing."

"Blasphemer!" the old woman cried, slapping me across the face. Before I knew it, others in the audience were punching and kicking me. "your filthy mouth is crammed with lies!" one man said.

Suddenly, the attacks stopped as quickly as they had started. I saw then that Khu had climbed off his wagon and was rushing toward me.

"Leave him alone!" The Upright Pig shouted. "He is a good man! He is like a father to us!"

Dozens of gasps rose up from the crowd. "The father!" I heard people say. "The father of the gods!"

"I am so sorry!" the old woman wailed. "We thought you were only their servant! We didn't know!"

"We didn't know!" The cry spread through the crowd. "We didn't know!" "How *could* we know?"

Khu led me away, to a grassy spot under a shade tree behind his wagon. A few of the other members of our troupe joined us, and they tended to my injuries. Premm, Tim and Petra were among those assisting, and I realized with a start that Petra's belly protruded a bit. Was she pregnant?

Suddenly I heard metallic click. I looked around, and saw a man standing in the shadows a few yards away, putting a camera back into its carrying case. He then began writing in a large notepad.

"You there!" I shouted. "What are you doing? Who are you?"

He stepped forward, into the sunlight. He was middle-aged, and wore a dark-blue suit that had seen better days. "I am a reporter for the *London Eye*." That was the leading newspaper in England at the time.

"Are you writing a story about us?" Premm said.

"My story is about your churches, so yes, I suppose it is about you."

"What churches?" I said, astonished.

He nodded slowly. "Ah. I wondered if you knew or not. It makes sense, really—you have never returned to any of the towns you've visited."

"Tell us about these churches," said Tim.

The reporter pointed toward Khu's wagon. "They look like these carriages of yours, except they are bigger, and made of metal and stone. Inside are statues of chess pieces and the carnival caravan's performers."

"How could these things have sprung up so quickly?" I said. "We've only been traveling for ... for ..."

"For decades," the reporter said. "Forty years at least."

"What? Has it been that long?" I looked at all the faces of the friends who had been tending to my wounds. "That can't be. None of us look any different. I saw my face in the mirror while I was shaving this morning. No wrinkles. No grey hair."

"That," the reporter said, "is probably one of the many reasons why they worship you folks." He pointed toward me. "Oh, but they don't really worship you. Sorry. You're just a sort of ... liaison agent. I gather, then, that none of you know about any of the miracles? The miracles that take place in your churches?"

"No," I said, "and right now, I don't think we want to know."

"Ari is right," Petra said. "We have more shows to do today. We can't be distracted with all this talk of miracles."

"I see. You are too busy being gods to worry about the results." The reporter tipped his hat to us. "Interesting. Perhaps even commendable! Good day to you." He then walked off, back into the shadows.

V.

As I gave the reporter's words more thought, it dawned on me that yes, more time had passed than I had realized. Seasons had whirled by. A veritable army of workers, jugglers, musicians and other employees had worked for the carnival caravan. Certainly technology had progressed, though I had turned a blind eye to its advances, deciding instead to keep doing things the old way.

But Petra's pregnancy—that was a development that I could not ignore. I did not ask her—did not *want* to ask her—the name of the father. Surely she would tell me in her own good time.

More reporters began to appear. Perhaps that too was a sign of the times: people desperately needed to know everyone else's business. No doubt the reporters were drawn by Petra's news. Their curiosity dismayed and enraged me. They did not want to know more out of concern. They were probably drooling to know which of the others had sired the child, and what sort of freak she would spawn. I hired extra security personnel to keep the reporters at bay, far away from Petra.

As her belly grew larger, I noticed that she seemed to be spending more time talking with Mnuggug. That was good. Mnuggug was very wise. She had learned much in the jungles of Africa. Premm and Tim both waited on the mother-to-be attentively.

One night, I was sitting on the steps outside my wagon, looking at the stars, when Mnuggug came creeping up to me.

"Petra will have her baby soon," she said. "I think tonight."

"We haven't consulted any physicians," I said. "If there is a difficulty, what will we do?"

Mnuggug simply laughed. "So you do not always have all the answers!" She crept closer. "There will be no difficulty. You know much, but I see there is still room for more knowledge in your head."

I picked her up and sat her on my lap. "Do you have this all figured out?"

"I creep on the ground. I swing from high branches. I see every situation from every angle," she said. "Something glorious and eternal dwells within the labyrinth."

Her words sent a chill up my spine—perhaps because I knew a great truth was about to be told. A truth I didn't know, but perhaps suspected. "Go on."

"You have created a grand labyrinth," The Monkey-Spider said. "That is the nature of the carnival caravan. It is also the nature of any mythology. Strange creatures following twisting paths through time and space. A pantheon of travelers. Soon we will find what lurks at the center of *your* labyrinth."

Suddenly a cry echoed through the night. A cry of pain from Petra. "It is time," Mnuggug said.

I carried Mnuggug to the wagon of the Golden Queen, The Lady with Rats for Hands. The doors of the wagon had been thrown open, and Petra was resting on stacks of pillows on her bed, which had been moved out of the private corner, into the stage area.

Tim was sitting on the bed to one side of Petra, and Premm was seated on the other side. I studied their eyes, but saw no jealousy or rivalry there. Only concern, and of course love.

The other members of the troupe were gathered in front of the open wagon, like an audience.

Suddenly I heard a light crunch of footsteps. I looked around and was just in time to see a man with a camera as he dodged behind another wagon.

"One of those damned reports," I said, "looking for a story."

"His own story shall soon come to a quick end," Mnuggug said, springing from my arms and disappearing into the shadows.

Petra cried out again. I moved closer to the stage. I wanted to do something, but there was nothing for me to do. I could not help Petra to give forth life, and I could not prevent Mnuggug from taking a life.

Suddenly I was blinded by a burst of light. I then heard a cry that was high and piercing. It was human and animal, and something else, too. Something that suddenly made me feel very small.

I felt something against my leg. I reached down and felt Mnuggug's coarse hide, so I sat on the ground beside her, still washed in that blinding, unending light.

But then Mnuggug left my side.

A moment later, I could see. The doors of Petra's wagon had been pulled shut from the inside. I could not see any of the troupe's members, so I figured that had to be inside the wagon with the baby. Light poured from out of its windows and around its doors. I walked up to the wagon of the Golden Queen. Once the way is clear, a queen can move in any direction as far as she pleases.

A moment later, Tim and Premm came out.

"Do you want to come inside?" Tim said.

"Am I welcome?" I said. "I'm not like the rest of you. I'm not different."

"Yes you are. You have always been one of us." Premm tapped me on the forehead. "In there."

The inside of the wagon had become an endless shining abyss. Mnuggug explained to me that Petra had given birth to the new Messiah, a creature that glowed with the holy light of pure love. Premm and Tim had both fathered the child. A certain book had chronicled how once a virgin had given birth—so if it is not impossible for a child to have less than two parents, why then could it not have more? An abundance of true love had liberated the beast at the center of the labyrinth.

Since then, the power of that all-encompassing love has done something truly wonderful. It has *expanded* the labyrinth. I realized that the moment I came out of the wagon and looked around.

That is why now, my friends, the sky is a glorious night-black and noonday-gold chessboard, and the Earth is a chessboard, too, of rich black soil and golden sand. That is why all the plants and animals, even down to the insects, are fabulous hybrid creatures, and why I now have the head of a beautiful black and gold giraffe. That is why the world has become an endless carnival, ruled by a glowing beast-god and its pantheon-family of loving gods and goddesses. I am no longer the host of the show. Rather, I am the now the Messenger, and forever more, it will be my duty to explain ... to guide ... to instruct.

So do not be frightened. You've probably noticed that things have been different lately. I trust my story has explained the changes to your satisfaction...?

But that is why my carnival caravan has become commonplace. The diversions are now everyday happenings, and the rarities are anything but rare.

And you know what?

I wouldn't have it any other way.

ABOUT THE AUTHOR

Mark McLaughlin's fiction, nonfiction, and poetry have appeared in almost one-thousand magazines, newspapers, websites, and anthologies, including *Black Gate, Galaxy, Fangoria, Writer's Digest, Cemetery Dance, Midnight Premiere, Dark Arts*, and two volumes each of *The Best Of The Rest, The Best Of HorrorFind*, and *The Year's Best Horror Stories* (DAW Books).

Collections of McLaughlin's fiction include *Motivational Shrieker, Slime After Slime,* and *Pickman's Motel* from Delirium Books; *At The Foothills Of Frenzy* (with coauthors Shane Ryan Staley and Brian Knight) from Solitude Publications; and *Raising Demons For Fun And Profit* from Sam's Dot Publishing.

HorrorGarage.com features his online column, *Four-Letter Word Beginning With 'F'* (the word in question is Fear). An expert on B-movies, he was recently interviewed by an AOL columnist about Gamera's place in cinematic history. GravesideTales.com features his horror-movie history column, *Time Machine Of Terror!*

Also, McLaughlin is the coauthor, with Rain Graves and David Niall Wilson, of *The Gossamer Eye*, which won the 2002 Bram Stoker Award for Superior Achievement in Poetry.

With regular collaborator Michael McCarty, he has written *Monster Behind The Wheel* (Corrosion Press, with a new edition forthcoming from Medallion Press); *All Things Dark & Hideous* (Rainfall Books, England); *Professor LaGungo's Delirious Download Of Digital Deviltry & Doom* (Darkside Digital); *Professor LaGungo's Classroom Of Horrors* (Bucket o' Guts Press); *Partners In Slime* (Damnation Books), and more.

He is also a successful marketing and public relations executive who regularly writes articles for business journals, newspapers, trade publications and websites.

To find out more about his work, visit www.BMovieMonster.com and www.Facebook.com/MarkMcLaughlinMedia

www.ingramcontent.com/pod-product-compliance
Lightning Source LLC
Chambersburg PA
CBHW020757250626
47155CB00003B/1116